THE
ENGAGEMENT
PARTY

ALSO BY DARBY KANE

The Last Invitation
The Replacement Wife
Pretty Little Wife

THE
ENGAGEMENT
PARTY

A Novel

DARBY KANE

WM

WILLIAM MORROW
An Imprint of HarperCollinsPublishers

THE ENGAGEMENT PARTY. Copyright © 2023 by HelenKay Dimon. All rights reserved. Printed in the United States of America. No part of this book may be used or reproduced in any manner whatsoever without written permission except in the case of brief quotations embodied in critical articles and reviews. For information, address HarperCollins Publishers, 195 Broadway, New York, NY 10007.

HarperCollins books may be purchased for educational, business, or sales promotional use. For information, please email the Special Markets Department at SPsales@harpercollins.com.

FIRST EDITION

Designed by Diahann Sturge

Library of Congress Cataloging-in-Publication Data has been applied for.

ISBN 978-0-06-322562-6 (trade paperback)
ISBN 978-0-06-322564-0 (international edition)
ISBN 978-0-06-334507-2 (hardcover library edition)

23 24 25 26 27 LBC 5 4 3 2 1

For all those who learned the hard way that unexpected and terrible things can happen in beautiful places

Sometimes victimhood seemed inevitable. And sometimes it seemed like the best thing that could happen to a girl. Once you were dead, you could be loved forever. Once you were dead, no one asked if you had fought back hard enough, if you hadn't really wanted it after all.

—Sarah Marshall, "The End of Evil," *The Believer*

THE
ENGAGEMENT
PARTY

CHAPTER ONE

BOOK NOTES: LOST AND FOUND

Emily Hunt disappeared on the Saturday of graduation week-end. No one noticed until Sunday afternoon.

A blonde with big brown eyes and a deep, soulful laugh that lit up her face wasn't the type to blend in. The recent college grad dreamed of becoming an investigative reporter, of breaking big stories, getting awards, and doing splashy interviews. Even ignoring her questionable talent, she lacked the patience and drive it would take to survive years of mind-numbing, day-to-day plodding, stockpiles of phone calls and messages, and notoriously unreliable pay. Now, none of that mattered.

Local police and college officials rushed to grab microphones at the press conference and blame alcohol for Emily's disappearance. Men decked out in business suits and uniforms shook their heads as they lectured the public about the dangerous mix of binge drinking and too much partying on college campuses.

In the span of a few hours, Emily morphed from *a young woman with promise* to a cautionary tale. The quick pivot to "this is why we don't allow fraternities and sororities on campus" by the college's president ignored the fact neither institution played a role in her being missing.

By not showing up at her parents' planned celebration lunch, Emily had forfeited the presumption of innocence in her own disappearance. *Did you see her dress the other night? She seemed out of control at the party. I tried to warn her, but she wouldn't listen.* The whispers carried more than a hint of reprimand. But a simple continuum between a fixed point where Emily made smart choices and one in which she invited tragedy didn't exist no matter how determined people were to bend and twist her story to make it fit.

The rumored explanations for her failure to sleep in her own bed that weekend overlooked the obvious details. Her car hadn't moved from the school parking lot. Her upended purse sat at the bottom of the steps of the campus's Museum of Art. Her abandoned cell phone with the newly cracked screen rested a few feet away.

As the hours rolled on, pontificating gave way to panic. Before sunset on Monday night, they formed a search party. The "they" included the official cadre who'd engaged in enraged finger-wagging about Emily's partying and the supposed "friends" who barely knew her yet spilled half-truths disguised as secrets in exchange for less than five minutes of fame and attention. Within hours, a couple in their sixties who happened to be boating in the area found Emily's body. There she was, four miles from campus, partially clothed and tangled in weeds in the New Meadows River.

She'd been twenty-two for nineteen days and a college graduate for one afternoon.

The water cleansed her crisis-manufactured guilt. Her role shifted again, this time from *the cause of her own demise* to beloved victim, forever enshrined as young and beautiful. Her personality locked in place, waiting for the passage of time to polish and mute every flaw into oblivion.

Her death turned out to be a horrible beginning to a winding and tragic tale rather than an ending. Not an accident. Not a result of alcohol. A murder.

The saddest part? None of this would have happened if she'd gotten into Amherst as she'd dreamed.

CHAPTER TWO

SIERRA

Sierra Prescott groaned when she stepped in her office and saw the unshuffled stacks of bids, bills, and invoices swamping her desk. If she squinted she could almost make out the glass that held down the important scraps of paper, like her computer password.

Screw privacy issues. Her business partner, Mitch Andersen, insisted on swapping out intricate strings of numbers, letters, random capitals, and nonsense symbols every month. He was a safety guy. Thirty-five going on *living in a bunker.* He worried about everything. He could find a tiny hint of potential trouble in every bit of fantastic news. Then again, with his background being skeptical wasn't a surprise. It was a survival mechanism.

She'd been out in the field, on a landscaping job for the new boutique hotel in Rockport, for nine days. It would take another five for the ache in her knees to subside. So, she switched to desk work. Clearly not a great decision.

"Mitch?" She shouted his name into the empty office suite.

Because it was Sunday, rational people remained at home, playing with their kids and puppies, and enjoying this thing called a weekend. Not that she or Mitch had any needy creatures in their care. Both were single. Both lived alone. Both worked too much. Neither of them bothered to file a piece of paper until the threat of being buried alive in a pile of overdue bills overcame them.

"Hey." Mitch appeared in the docrway. As usual, he wrapped up his entire greeting with that one word.

He wore jeans and a zip-up sweater to fight the cooling September winds. His brown hair had that ruffled, don't-own-a-mirror look. He was a handsome-without-trying type. A mix of *boy next door* and *hot single dad on the playground*. His lazy smile kicked up on one side without any emotion or lightness behind it. Not that he was a psychopath, but he'd been raised by one and had learned early how to navigate a series of emotional land mines.

Sierra picked up the crumpled postcard by her foot and held it in the air. "Is this garbage or part of some basketball game you were playing, using the trash can?"

"Garbage."

His tone actually said *problem*. Intrigued, she unrolled the paper to find an invitation addressed to Mitchell Andersen with a handwritten note on the side.

We expect you to be here. —W

She didn't have to ask who W was. Though she'd only talked to him on the phone, she knew all about Will Mayer. Mitch's college friend, or one of them. Part of a supposedly unbreakable group of friends that shattered one spring, twelve years ago. A topic Mitch rarely discussed.

"Will's getting married," she said, as if Mitch hadn't read the card before junking it. "To someone named Ruthie Simmons."

"Uh-huh."

"I wonder if her parents actually named her Ruthie or Ruth." Mitch didn't say a word, so Sierra kept talking. "Weirdly, it's a printed invite to an informal get-together happening in three weeks. A call would have made more sense, but the event is clearly low-key." She pointed at the card. "Says so right here."

"I don't know Ruthie."

"You're a few seconds behind here, and I'm guessing that's on purpose." The more painful the conversation became, the more determined she was to push through it. Not for any reason other than getting together with old friends should matter to Mitch even though he was trying mighty hard to prove it didn't.

He leaned against the doorframe. "I can't go."

"Right." She glanced around, taking in the paperwork carnage. "I know the office looks like we got hit by a cyclone, but it's manageable. I can—"

"I don't *want* to go."

There it was. *Finally.* Only took him a bunch of cryptic sentences to get there. "That's a different answer."

He shrugged but didn't leave the room.

"You haven't been back to Maine since . . ." *Well, shit.* She'd meant to avoid this topic. "Uh . . . college graduation."

His smile looked genuine this time. "Subtle."

"Sorry." She'd intended to sidestep the two subjects guaranteed to make Mitch's mood dive and his sarcasm spike, but she'd managed to crash right into one. Biting humor was his go-to avoidance move. She'd taken exactly one online psychology class, so she knew these things.

"It's fine," he said. "Don't worry about it."

"Okay, but this event isn't about what happened back then. It's an engagement party." She tried to make the occasion sound fun but was pretty sure she'd failed. "Maybe it would be good to replace a terrible memory with a good one."

"Have you ever found revisiting the past to be a positive thing?"

"Well, no, but . . . Okay, no. But it's possible you might need to go back?" She winced as she said the words.

"You think I haven't moved on."

Hell, no. He hadn't moved an inch. He didn't date, kept most people on the acquaintance and easy-to-drop superficial level, and restricted his deep friendship circle to exactly one—her.

He liked and trusted her. She was in love with him. End of sad story.

Romance or not, she wanted more for him. If not with her, fine. She'd muddle through, but he'd been dealt a really shitty hand in life. The kind of personal history that would break most people, and she feared he was moving closer to broken-and-unfixable as the years ticked by.

"You can see your friends. Remember the good times." He looked less convinced the longer she droned on, but that's what she did. When she wanted to win him over she tended to clobber him with arguments until he either let her win or he walked away in a grumbling haze of profanity. She had no idea which way this time would go. "Go celebrate Will and this Ruthie person then report back on what she's like because I'm nosy. I'm betting she's a blonde and wealthy. Have you seen photos? Is she?"

"I don't want to remember anything about that time of my life."

She sighed at him. "You can't ignore four years of your life because of . . ."

His eyebrow lifted. "A murder?"

Well, shit. She'd done it again. She'd taken that damn psych class thinking she could support him. She wanted her money back. "Okay. Yeah, I can't imagine what that was like for you or what it's still like. I also can't imagine college since I didn't go, but the party feels monumental. Adult. Like, you need to reconnect with these people who shaped so much of who you are so you *can* move on."

He exhaled long and loud in a you're-never-going-to-shut-up-about-this-otherwise way. "Come with me. The invitation says it's for two. If I'm going, I'm not going alone."

She flipped the card around a few times before she saw the additional handwriting at the bottom about a guest. "Huh. I missed that part."

"And I vowed never to step foot in Maine again, so we're even."

Right. That. The impact of the moment hit her. Her rah-rah support ignored his distress and ran right over his trauma, and she never meant to do either.

"You know what? Ignore me. I wasn't thinking about . . ." The right words abandoned her. She didn't want to mention *murder* or *police,* so she just stopped talking.

He shrugged again. "We're going. Pack a sweater and whatever weapon makes you feel safe at night. My experience is you'll need both."

CHAPTER THREE

ALEX

The same invitation Alex threw out two days ago either crawled out of the garbage can and leapt back onto the kitchen counter or, worse, his wife had found it. Seeing their names, Alexander and Cassandra Greene, on it made him twitchy.

He held up the postcard, catching her attention across the granite-topped kitchen island. "I dumped this in the garbage for a reason."

"And I fished it back out."

He exhaled, hoping to find the necessary patience to get through this conversation. "Attending this party would be a huge mistake, which—see my previous comment—explains why I tossed out the invite."

"Your concern is noted. I noted it yesterday morning when you made the same argument."

Cassie meant before they left for the law office around eight. The same office suite they shared in a refurbished bank in downtown Providence. It housed their newly formed eighteen-person firm. Bound together in life and in business . . . and by a more-than-decade-old secret that ruined everything.

He stepped around the island and grabbed her arm. "Please listen to me."

She shrugged him off, almost dropping the pan of stir-fried vegetables she held. "Hey!"

"Sorry, but I'm not joking about this."

He loved her. That was his burden because most days he also hated her.

The physical attraction, once all-encompassing, had leveled off to more of a simmer with occasional flare-ups of madness. Love watered down by time and secrets that proved heavier to carry each year.

She was still stunning. Put-together, tall and lean, with a short brunette bob. She walked into a room and owned it because she led with confidence. She'd grown up poor, hungry, and scared and fought for a different life. Mapped out every milestone well in advance and ruthlessly stuck to her schedule out of a fear that any deviation could send her back to the trailer park and an up-bringing she despised.

Their daughter, Zara, arrived four years after they graduated from law school, exactly on the timeline Cassie had set out for their lives before they even left undergrad. Marriage. One pregnancy. No time off from the legal ladder climb.

Cassie had vowed to set them up in their own firm, be their own bosses, before Zara started kindergarten. Their daughter was a few months shy of four, which meant Cassie had hit every life goal target on time or early, as if she held complete control over the entire universe.

Their daughter was one of the reasons Alex wanted to move forward and never look back. She needed them, so he tried to reason with Cassie again. "You know that going to Maine can only end badly."

"That's not a very romantic way to talk about the place where we met."

Bowdoin College. It had been his dream school until graduation weekend, when it became a nightmare.

"We got out and we need to stay away." They'd escaped. Not everyone in their group had been that lucky. "Smart people avoid situations that can blow up and fuck them over."

"Did you read that in a book?"

Her personality shifted to cold and detached whenever he had the nerve to disagree with her or say anything that threatened to tangle up her well-laid plans.

"How can you be so calm about this?" he asked, needing to understand.

Some of the tension ran out of her shoulders and her voice grew softer, more coaxing. "It's a small get-together with some of our oldest and dearest friends."

Flirting. It was her fallback move. Smile at him the right way. Walk toward him, leaving no doubt what his reward would be if he was a very good boy.

He wished he didn't love her—or fear her—as much as he did.

"Honey, it's only a problem if you make it one." Cassie stopped in front of him and wound her arms around his neck. "Aren't you even a little interested in meeting Ruthie in person and hearing about this whirlwind romance? When we saw Will a year ago for dinner he was with a different woman he claimed to love."

Alex wanted to push her away and stay focused, but his hands landed on her waist. He gave into temptation and pulled her close. "Counting this woman, Will has been engaged four times in the twelve years since we graduated. None of those relationships actually ended in marriage. Why get attached to this woman?"

Cassie kissed the underside of his chin then trailed her mouth down the side of his neck. "That's not fair. You know Will has commitment issues."

"Not that knowing someone for years guarantees happiness either," Alex muttered.

Her body stiffened as she pulled back. "Excuse me?"

"I'm tired of pretending, Cas. It's going to take all of my energy not to mess up or say the wrong thing during this trip."

Her hands fell as she stepped out of his loose hold. "It's one weekend, counselor. You can handle it."

"Daddy!" The high-pitched little girl voice floated into the room from a play area twenty feet away.

Zara . . . the reason he stayed. Well, one of them. The other reason was much darker.

He started to leave then stopped. "This conversation isn't over."

Cassie shrugged. "What do you want me to say, Alex? How about the truth? *Not* going is more dangerous. We can't control the conversation if we're not there."

She might be right, and he hated that.

"Daddy!"

Cassie nodded in the general direction of Zara's voice. "Go be superdad and let me handle the travel arrangements. We'll contain any damage."

Alex admired her confidence because he worried they were about to lose everything.

CHAPTER FOUR

SIERRA

For the first time in her life, Sierra seriously considered throwing herself out of a moving vehicle. Mitch's college friends had that effect on her. Alex and Cassie possessed a *we're in-sync* outer shell that clashed with their actual vibe. Everything about them screamed *we fought on the way to pick you up*. Silences stretched between them until they became barbed.

The couple drove in from Rhode Island and spent a night in Boston before Sierra and Mitch joined them for the rest of the drive. They all piled into the SUV Alex had rented for the excursion and started on the hours-long merry ride to the engagement party that everyone but Sierra seemed to dread.

Good times.

One benefit of the togetherness was that she now knew what *smart casual* meant in terms of a dress code because these two embodied it. No jeans and T-shirts for them. But the current running under the *right* clothes and big sunglasses for her and a fancy sports watch for him skimmed along a toxic edge. They smiled and said the right things until they looked at each other. Then their wide grins fell and silence crept in.

Mitch had filled her in on the basics. Hyper-focused and

determined Cassie met superjock Alex during freshman year at Bowdoin College. They dated through college then law school before getting married. They excelled at overachieving. Neither came from money but they had stacks of it now.

Alex practiced maritime law. Sierra wanted to make a joke about pirates but wasn't convinced either of the two people in the front seat had a sense of humor. Cassie's corporate law career sounded less convoluted. Boring and technical, but comprehensible. But how two desk-job, stockpile-money types with every hair in place and not a wrinkle in either of their starched cotton shirts were friends with always-outdoors, never-on-time Mitch made little sense.

Alex smiled at Mitch via the rearview mirror. "Happy you lowered your standards and joined us."

Cassie turned in the leather seat and looked at Mitch. "Years ago, we agreed to meet up once a year, but we've never managed that. Until this weekend, Mitch has graced us with his presence exactly twice in twelve years, and one of those times was for our wedding."

"He was in it. He didn't have a choice," Alex said as he eased the car from one lane to another despite the lack of traffic.

Mitch ignored the pressure tactics from the front of the car and looked at Sierra. "Cassie threatened to come pick me up, force me into the car, then sing to me during the entire ride to the church. You haven't heard her sing." He whistled. "No one could survive that."

Cassie snorted. "The tactic worked, didn't it?"

For the next stretch, the talking stopped. The only noise came from the radio and the thump of the wheels as Alex drove over a section of road the state's construction crews had forgot. Cassie continued to sneak peeks into the back seat. Her gaze slid over Mitch in the same way she might look at her young daughter. Protective. Caring.

Sierra decided to ease up on the judgment and give these two a chance. They might suck at hiding a spousal argument, but they clearly cared about Mitch, alternatively dragging him out of his sulky state into conversation and smiling at him.

Cassie let out a small huff as if she'd given herself some sort of pep talk. "Okay, spill. Have either of you met Ruthie? They've only dated for a few months."

"The newest possible Mrs. Will Mayer?" Alex laughed at his own joke. "*Possible* being the most important word in that question."

"A guy buys engagement rings in bulk and right away his friends question his ability to get the deed done." Mitch mumbled the joke as he looked out the window. When the round of supportive laughter died down, he spoke again. "Sometimes I think Will's determined not to be happy."

Alex shot Mitch another look via the rearview mirror. "So, you recognize that sort of thing in others just not in yourself?"

Mitch answered with an eye roll. "Does that dad-glare trick work on Zara?"

"Yes." Cassie laughed. "But so do crackers. The nanny is likely using that trick right now to keep her quiet."

Nanny. Sierra had grown up in a whirl of day care, school, afterschool programs, and sports teams that kept her occupied until her parents picked her up. She didn't have a choice because *no complaining* had been her father's motto.

Silence descended again but this time it carried a note of comfort. Sierra watched the world whiz by outside the window. A perfect display of fall foliage loomed. The bright orange and red leaves hinted at the full explosion to come.

Never one to be confined, she lowered the window and smiled as the cool air brushed over her skin. She'd grown up outside of Boston and spent her entire life there. Her view of the world consisted of the limited destinations she'd traveled in her family's minivan. Never far and never fancy because her parents always had just enough money to cover the bills. Venturing north now allowed her to experience a different view, one less crowded, where buildings peppered the landscape while paying homage to it.

Mesmerized by the way the setting sun broke through the towering trees and bounced off the leaves in shades of gold and pink, she'd missed that they'd turned down a narrow lane and now eased out of the safe cocoon of branches. Blue water stretched out in front of them.

They all sat up straighter in their seats as the vehicle rolled to a stop in a makeshift gravel parking lot in the middle of nowhere. No buildings or people. Just a boat launch and gas pump, a few parking spaces under a carport, a car that likely belonged to Will and Ruthie, and what looked like two locked sheds, one big enough to house an office. The other the size for boating gear and little else. Two out-of-place golf carts sat on the right side, locked to a pole with heavy chains.

"This is the right place," Alex said.

Cassie studied the map on her cell phone. "The email Will sent said we park the car here, get into one of those golf carts, and drive across the causeway."

"It's why we skipped lunch." Alex pointed near the golf carts then to the car's GPS screen, which showed only blue. "Will said the carts only go fifteen miles per hour and we had to get across in time."

"In time for what?" Mitch asked, fully engaged now.

Sierra didn't understand why only Mitch showed a glimpse of the anxiety she had to beat back to keep it from spilling over into wild, panicked screaming. Alex and Cassie talked as if *drive into the ocean but do it fast or you'll drown at high tide* was a welcoming way to introduce them to this part of Maine.

Every low-budget horror movie started this way.

Sierra inhaled through her nose and forced her muscles to relax. That meant ignoring the spray from the water lapping up onto the dark rocks only a few feet away. She'd hoped the causeway would be an obvious paved road, but no. It amounted to an extra-wide makeshift sidewalk, rising maybe five feet above the waterline, buffered on both sides by jutting boulders. She assumed their job was to hold back the water at low tide but that was asking a lot from a bunch of rocks.

The lane stretched out for what looked like the distance of more than two football fields then curved toward an island and a structure she couldn't quite make out in the fading sun but assumed was a dock. More rocks gave way to grass and trees and a few buildings. She spied the outline of the side of a three-story house.

The whole scene probably held a quaint charm for some. Not her. Too isolated.

"How did you guys pick this place?" Mitch asked, sounding as skeptical as Sierra felt.

Cassie waved a hand in the air and her massive diamond caught the light. "Not us. Ruthie. Her family owns it."

Mitch frowned. "They actually own an island?"

"A lot of people do," Cassie added.

"Uh, no." Sierra felt like she'd gotten into the wrong car. "What people?"

Mitch leaned forward. "Who the hell are you guys hanging out with these days?"

"You two ask more questions than our four-year-old." Alex finished his comment by closing everyone's windows and getting out of the car. He stopped to grab his cell. "Let's get the luggage and get going before we get trapped."

"There are so many things wrong with that sentence," Mitch whispered.

Cassie got out then poked her head back inside the SUV. "What happened to your sense of adventure?"

Mitch scoffed. "It died when I was fifteen."

Sierra didn't appreciate the use of the word *died* right then.

"Hey, this is Ruthie and Will's thing. Let's play along." Alex thumped his hand against the roof of the car before walking away. "The road is going to wash out if we don't move."

Sierra hated everything about this. "Why does he keep saying that?"

Cassie shut the door behind her and walked over to the chained golf carts and started talking Alex through unwinding one from the other. They used a key Will must have sent them to unlock the vehicles.

Sierra was in the middle of giving herself a this-will-be-fine pep talk when Mitch looked at her. The flat line of his mouth spoke to his lack of excitement for this venture.

"I told you we shouldn't have come."

CHAPTER FIVE

BOOK NOTES: WHO WAS EMILY?

Emily grew up in Darien, Connecticut, one of the richest towns in what was probably the most affluent county in America. Hers was an idyllic and pampered existence that she neither downplayed nor oversold. She took the ability to do or try whatever she pleased for granted as later generations of wealth tended to do. Buffered by comfort, privilege, and overindulgent parents who preened and praised while pushing and molding from behind the scenes.

Not many people told Emily no. Her family name gave her a reserved seat at the popular table. The expectation was that she'd act in a way that kept her there because rumors ran rampant in her town and memories of slights could produce years of infighting and survive generations.

The family lived in a sprawling waterfront estate, complete with every gadget and every big toy with an engine. Emily was the oldest with twin brothers almost four years younger, an overly enmeshed mother who ached to relive her homecoming queen days, and a supportive but emotionally unavailable father. They served cocktails with every meal except breakfast, which came with a side helping of medications to survive the day.

In her youth, Emily hosted bake sales and book drives to support communities in neighborhoods with fewer resources. Whatever act sent the right message and allowed for praise for her ingenuity while performing it, Emily did it. She loved to bike and to boss her brothers around. She shied away from sports until her father told her being on a team would look good for college admissions, then she tried out for soccer. She made the team because she usually accomplished whatever goal she set. Except one.

Her dream had been to attend Amherst like her best friend from high school. A goal her father already viewed as beneath her, as if settling for anything other than Ivy League or, specifically, his beloved Princeton, destroyed her chance for future success. In a rare but crushing blow Emily didn't get into Amherst. That failure led to many family dinners filled with lectures about doing her best and talk of tutors and transferring to a more preferable collegiate choice sophomore year.

Emily picked an equally impressive alternate school, Bowdoin College, and surprised everyone by falling in love with it. Probably because at Bowdoin she maintained her top-of-the-heap status. She collected friends, enjoyed a good party, and made it her life's mission not to disappoint her parents again.

Ignoring that academic blip, she was a dream daughter. She looked right—pretty and dressed as if a camera crew followed her nonstop. She said the right things. At home she obeyed curfew. She obtained birth control to avoid what her father viewed as the ultimate dream killer for any teenage hopeful—pregnancy. That sort of thing didn't go over well at the country club or on company hiring committees.

Emily was also a dream friend . . . except when she wasn't.

Despite what the fawning magazine articles and true crime specials would later put forward, Emily was very human. Flawed and imperfect. At times, self-important and devious. At others, charming, caring, and considerate. After years of wading through privilege and money, getting what she wanted right when she wanted, she possessed an overblown sense of her abilities and a shallow understanding of her needs. It's not that she lacked genuine emotion or genuine feeling. It was more that she'd been programmed every day of her life and no longer recognized *genuine*.

Rather than grapple with growing pains and the tangle of insecurities involved with figuring out who she was, she borrowed large pieces of her personality from the people around her. Their dreams became her dreams. She assumed their needs, their rage, their beliefs, and their desires. Her friend wanted to go to a specific school, so Emily had to go there. The friend picked journalism as a major, so Emily picked it. The friend had a boyfriend, then she wanted that boyfriend.

She never had to develop a sense of self or work for what she believed in because both were commodities she could pick and choose from others. She didn't recognize how much of her life mirrored those around her, of course, or that she was always looking for shortcuts and the life equivalent of extra credit to avoid putting in the actual work. The idea of defying the odds and working to attain goals remained elusive concepts up to her premature end.

If asked to describe herself she would say she was a great friend who listened and tried to help. That assessment was both right and wrong. Under the perfect smile and the right words, the confident walk and enviable manners, lurked a different

Emily. Still friendly and funny but she liked to play games. The kind of games she insisted were harmless, generally victimless, even though they were born out of her need to push boundaries. The kind of games that might invite anger and disappointment. Might accidentally let an enemy get too close.

Games that likely led to her murder.

CHAPTER SIX

RUTHIE

The party was a mistake. Ruthie realized that truth the second after she'd dropped the invitations in the mail. Who mailed things these days? She only did because she couldn't count on Will to remember to email his friends. But once the invites left her fingers dread swamped her. The idea of opening the locked door to the past set off a whirlwind of anxiety inside her. She hadn't felt this nervous, this unsure, since she arranged to *accidentally* meet Will ten weeks ago.

They ran into each other at a wine and cheese party at the Garren Studio, an art gallery she helped manage in Beacon, New York. She showed and sold artwork. Held receptions. Met with buyers and artists.

Except, she really didn't.

Her friend owned and managed the gallery and let Ruthie use the building as a staging area to meet Will. That night, Ruthie had cradled a glass of champagne, engaged in her best rounds of subtle flirting, and joked about how strange it was he'd received an invitation to the private reception when she had *no idea* who he was.

She'd played the game, thinking they'd go out on a few dates.

She'd build trust and get him to talk. But he pushed their dating into hyperdrive before she had what she needed and now the possibility of explosion loomed. A fake job led to a fake meeting and a ridiculously rushed fake engagement. Fake on her part, not his.

When Will stunned her by proposing, she'd stumbled and said yes to keep the ruse going for a little bit longer. The party was her way of trying to push her agenda and set a deadline before she skipped out on the wedding planning and Will forever. Because what kind of guy proposed after six weeks of *okay but not life-changing* dating?

In reality, she'd known everything about Will before they ever met. She'd studied him. Stalked him. Collected every scrap of information she could find about him.

His parents: an American businessman met the Japanese up-and-coming airline executive who would become his wife while living in Yokohama. Will's parents had been married and divorced twice—to each other—and both also had been married to others, divorced, and remarried again. They'd produced a litter of step- and half-siblings for Will and burdened him with a profound need for stability that he spent the rest of his life chasing, all while they shipped him off to boarding school then college and forgot about him.

Ruthie used all of that stockpiled hurt and hidden pain, the years of confusion about unconditional love, and his string of failed relationships, against him. Tapped into every insecurity and need. Moved in and talked about forever love. Dazzled him by being brilliant and fiery, sexy and driven. Proud of who she was. Proud of her mixed French and Trinidadian ancestry. Proud of being a self-made successful Black woman who didn't depend on Daddy's money for clout. Someone accustomed to a certain lifestyle but determined to earn it on her own.

Will's arms wrapped around her from behind and his hands settled on her stomach. "They're finally here."

She looked out the front window of the house's great room. A golf cart came to a stop next to the house and people piled out. The punch of panic hit as she counted. "There are four of them."

"Right."

No, wrong. There should be three. He *told* her three. She'd planned for three. The three she'd studied.

Will pressed his cheek against hers and provided a quick rundown of their guests. "The two who look like they stepped out of a clothing ad are Alex and Cassie. The one who's contemplating taking his chances and swimming back to the mainland is Mitch. The cute brunette with the sunglasses on top of her head and the confused frown must be Sierra. I wrote a note on your invitation and told him to bring a guest this weekend. I'm surprised he did."

Ruthie forced her runaway breathing to calm down again. "Sierra. That's the woman you all think Mitch needs to open his eyes and marry?"

"Or at least date her." Will made a humming sound. "He didn't bother to tell me she was coming until yesterday. Sorry. I thought I'd passed that on."

Typical and no. Ruthie had heard so much about Mitch and his background. All sordid and painful. His hesitant gait reflected the way he moved through the world—carefully. His blank expression didn't give away his thoughts. He lifted a duffle bag and small suitcase out of the back of the cart, taking peeks at Sierra as she surveyed the island. "He keeps track of her. Watches when he thinks she's not looking."

"He's got it bad." Will stepped back. An eagerness to head for the door and welcome his friends thrummed off him. "He's not great about keeping in touch, but when he does there's a lot of *Sierra this* and *Sierra that*."

Four of them. With Will, five. Ruthie didn't like feeling outmaneuvered or outnumbered.

Will's smile faded. "What's wrong? You're not nervous, are you?"

Wary. Cautious but optimistic. She pushed all hints of those feelings out of her voice. "Never."

"They're going to love you." He winked at her. "We'll enjoy a few days on the water. I'll reconnect with old friends. We'll make new memories. Then we'll go home and deal with unrelenting rounds of exhausting wedding stuff."

Little did he know that wasn't the plan. Not even close.

He held out his hand. "Ready to meet everyone?"

She slipped her fingers through his. "Definitely."

Time to get started. After all, she'd been planning this showdown for almost six months.

CHAPTER SEVEN

SIERRA

More than an hour after arriving on the unexpectedly secluded island, Sierra struggled to understand the group dynamic unfolding in front of her. Mitch's friends were the *stand around the kitchen island drinking wine* types even though a perfectly comfortable-looking sectional sofa sat ten steps away in the open great room.

They'd all found their phone chargers and plugged in their cells immediately after splitting up to pick bedrooms and unpack. She'd almost balked at the idea of sleeping in the same room with Mitch until she realized the choice was that or sleeping alone in this place.

Up close, the house had that trying-to-look-rustic feel. The overstuffed furniture and open living room with the two-story soaring ceiling said *wealthy upgrade*. The whitewashed bookshelf and perfectly broken in throw pillows and frayed accent rug cried *vintage*. The entire mix of decked-out-in-oatmeal-and-other-soothing-colors vibe and curated pieces made Sierra worry about spilling something.

Cassie made a quick call to say hello to her daughter and had to walk around the room to find a signal that held the call for more than two minutes. She'd giggled with the girl in a way that sounded sweet and loving but then got off the phone and complained nonstop about the spotty service until five minutes ago.

The couples milling around Sierra matched in apparent economic status. They looked like they walked right out of a casting call for a television show. The engineer and the art gallery manager. The successful lawyer duo. All attractive but pretending looks didn't matter. Put-together, laughing at all the right jokes. Skipping over the difficult parts of their collective past, settling on safe talk about homes, work, and the upcoming wedding instead.

Mitch joined Sierra where she leaned against the sink, slightly away from the group but facing everyone as they talked. She sensed she needed to be ready . . . but for what?

"She's not a blonde." Mitch whispered the phrase against her ear.

Sierra studied Ruthie over of the rim of her water glass. She'd taken off her cardigan and now wore a sleeveless shirtdress that showed off her fit arms. Pretty with big brown eyes, a genuine smile, and black hair that fell in layered spirals just past her shoulders. Unexpected in some ways, but not in others. This was a Ruthie type who sent out written invitations to a casual weekend instead of picking up the phone or sending an email. That choice still fascinated Sierra.

"I admit I made some assumptions," Sierra said. "But you didn't correct me."

"Going by historical data, your guess at Will's new partner being the blond WASPy country club type seemed accurate. He's always gone for a certain look and been relentless in pursuing it."

Ruthie picked that moment to break away from the group and join Mitch and Sierra. "What are you two whispering about?"

Sierra couldn't exactly say *you*, so she lied. "Did you grow up here?"

"What?" Ruthie's glass bobbled a little in her hand, but she managed not to spill any of the precious wine on her light blue dress.

"On the island." Mitch nodded in the direction of the rest of the group. "Cassie said your family owned the place . . . or maybe it was Alex."

Likely trained by years of fatherhood, Alex picked his name out of the mumble of conversation and answered. "Will told me and I told Cassie."

All other conversation came to a screeching halt.

"I did?" Will asked.

Ruthie waved away the confusion with a flick of her hand. "Actually, a friend's family owns the place. We're borrowing it for a few days."

"It's a hell of a landscaping job. I want to take a closer look at the rock retaining wall later." Mitch nodded as he left the sink and wandered closer to Cassie and Alex. Cassie immediately wrapped an arm around him, pulling him in for a hug.

Sierra tried to focus on something other than Mitch's back. Ruthie's big round diamond seemed like a good place. "Your ring is gorgeous."

"It belonged to Will's grandmother."

Since he'd been down the engagement road many times Sierra wondered if that meant the ring had had several temporary owners or that Will had more grandmothers than the average person.

Sierra forced herself not to ask. She went with a nonsense re-sponse instead. "Nice."

Ruthie's fingers wrapped around the wineglass. She held it in a tight clench. "I'm happy you came."

Was she, though? Her body seemed rigid. Her smile didn't quite reach her eyes and there was . . . something. Sierra couldn't put her finger on it. An underlying nervousness. The jittery way Ruthie moved around the kitchen, filling glasses and putting out snacks. She likely wanted to impress her soon-to-be-husband's oldest friends, but it came off as more than that.

"Sierra worried I wouldn't behave myself, so I dragged her with me," Mitch said as he wandered back to join them and grabbed a water bottle out of the refrigerator.

Alex snorted. "We all worry about your bad behavior."

The comment earned a middle finger from Mitch.

Cassie studied the living space and staircase that led to an open landing and a series of second-floor-bedroom doors above. "When did you two get here?"

"Yesterday afternoon." Will refilled his wineglass. "I needed to figure out the tide schedule, so I didn't accidentally drown all of you."

And silence.

The words wandered a bit too close to the collective horror they all pretended to forget. Sierra ached for them but knowing she wasn't the only one who stumbled into these verbal potholes provided some relief.

"Okay, let's get this out of the way." Alex held up his glass in a toast. "To Emily, who we loved and lost, and to Jake, who walked away, and we still miss him."

"Does anyone see Jake these days?" Ruthie asked. "I was trying to find him for the wedding invitation list."

A sudden tension choked the room. Labored chatter morphed into suffocating awkwardness.

Alex stared into his glass. "No."

"We can talk about that later," Will said.

"Jake prefers not to be in touch, which can be hurtful." Cassie grabbed a handful of chips. "Maybe a new topic?"

Sierra really wanted to leave. Like, leave the island. She didn't want to be here, trapped and surrounded by rising water, stuck with a group of people determined not to talk about the tragedy that bound them to the past.

Ruthie squeezed closer to Sierra, dropping her voice to a whisper. "Whoops."

"Not your fault. I made the same mistake several times when talking with Mitch about this weekend. Jake apparently drifted away years ago because being with the group reminds him of what they lost."

"They've all known each other for years but they still tiptoe around talking about Emily." Ruthie shrugged. "She deserves more than that."

Sierra silently agreed. If the saying was true about someone not being truly gone until the last person who knew them stopped talking about them, then Emily was coming dangerously close to complete extinction.

"They were young and foolish. They were celebrating and drinking that weekend, and she just disappeared." Ruthie took a long sip of wine. "What does Mitch say about—"

Sierra watched Ruthie's brown eyes widen as her voice cut off.

"The garage." Ruthie set her glass down with a loud clink.

Talk about a conversation curveball. Sierra wondered if she'd blanked out for a second and missed a topic shift. "Are we saying random words? If so, I pick *coffeemaker.*"

"No. I mean the garage door is open. It was closed." Ruthie turned around to the rest of the group. "Did one of you go in there?"

Mitch frowned. "Isn't the bigger question something like, Why is there a garage on an island?"

"They wouldn't have been able to get into it, hon. Remember? It's locked," Will said as he moved closer to the window and had a turn looking outside.

Ruthie took over the explanation. "When we first got here, we walked around the island. There's a bunch of outbuildings, like a shed and a boathouse. Another place for storage. We were given keys. I tried to open the garage lock but couldn't."

Okay, weird. Sierra didn't like weirdness because she couldn't control it.

"Yeah, no key for the garage or the shed." Will acted unconcerned, as opposed to the rest of the room.

"Is there a caretaker on the premises?" That sounded a bit more Scooby-Doo than Sierra wanted, so she tried again. "Like, a property management person?"

"I picked up the keys before we left New York. We're supposed to be here alone, but then who opened the garage?" Ruthie asked.

After a few seconds, Cassie's wary expression morphed into a smile. "This is some sort of puzzle or joke, right? A mystery weekend type of thing."

Ruthie shook her head. "No."

"Hold it." Cassie set her glass down. "Before our imaginations run wild, let's think of a reasonable explanation. Maybe the lock fell off."

"That's not how locks work," Mitch said as he took a step back from the crowd at the window.

The men started talking over each other while Sierra scanned the yard and the greenhouse, over to the small toolshed and the area surrounding the lap pool, now covered in preparation for winter. Her gaze bounced along the grass and through the trees. Skimmed past the piles of falling vibrant leaves, past the empty gazebo.

One question screamed in her head, so she said it out loud. "If someone else is on the island . . . where are they? Why would they hide?"

CHAPTER EIGHT

ALEX

There's a reasonable explanation." Alex made the comment more to ease the panic inching its way up his throat than to convince anyone else. Garage door locks didn't fly open on their own, but he was determined to pretend they could.

"Clearly it's a gardener or someone like that. Go out there and check." The warning in Cassie's keep-your-shit-together expression suggested he do it now.

"Come on. This must be a joke of some kind. I'll go with you," Will said.

"Actually, you can help me." Cassie issued orders and rallied the troops in her usual no-nonsense style. "You and Ruthie have been around the property. You know the floor plans and general layout."

Will snorted. "We've only been here a day."

"Still." Cassie put an arm around Ruthie and the other around Will as she corralled them and guided them in the direction she wanted them to go, which seemed to be toward the staircase to the second floor. "Those three will check the garage while you two fill me in on the rest of the property in case we need to break into groups and do a bigger search."

Mitch made a strange noise. "Do I get a vote about going to the garage?"

"I was wondering the same thing." Sierra shifted closer to Mitch until barely a whiff of air separated them. "Honestly, I'm not sure we should split up. This could be dangerous."

Cassie refused to ruffle. "Or it's perfectly innocent and no big deal."

Sierra frowned. "Then why didn't the person who opened the lock knock on the door and explain why they're here?"

It sounded like a fair question to Alex.

"Okay, look." Cassie exhaled before untangling her arms and holding up both hands. "Let's stay calm and not make this into a thing."

Alex could count on Cassie to be Cassie in any situation. Nothing shook her. She handled things. She took command and cleaned up messes. Skills she'd been forced to learn because her mother's untreated depression shoved the responsibility onto Cassie.

He supported Cassie's stubborn refusal to see a potential problem here because it would cut down on the fighting later. "We're all a little tense. Blame being surrounded by water. Cassie's right. We'll handle this situation then we can concentrate on dinner."

No one said a word. Sierra and Mitch looked at each other, communicating in silence before she marched over and grabbed the fireplace poker.

Alex admired her self-preservation instincts. "That's badass."

"And smart," Ruthie said. "Now I want to go with Sierra."

Will winked at his fiancée. "I'll protect you."

"Yeah, you're a hero." Cassie nodded for Alex to head outside. "We'll figure this out then feel ridiculous for ever worrying."

Alex didn't buy his wife's *no big deal* attitude. The firmness of her voice pointed toward trouble. The tougher she sounded, the bigger the worry lurking underneath. But delaying wouldn't make the situation better, so he rushed to follow Cassie's division of labor before any member of the group balked at her orders.

The cool wind enveloped him as he opened the side door off the kitchen, almost pulling him onto the small porch and down to the grass. With each step he tried to trick his brain into believing there was an obvious explanation. All the lame self-lectures fizzled out by the time Alex stood in front of the open garage door and discovered something new to worry about.

A car, smashed up and abandoned, sat inside. On an island.

"The engine is running." He said the obvious because nothing else fit.

"Why? I mean . . . *Why?* How?" Sierra sounded stunned. "We would have noticed this when we walked up to the house, which means someone started the car and opened the door while we were inside."

Alex hated that she'd voiced exactly what he was thinking. "Okay, so where the hell is the driver?"

Anxiety roared through him as he studied the nondescript but damaged sedan. The driver's side door stood open. A dent that bordered on a cave-in ran along the back passenger door toward the fender. The trunk looked uneven as if jimmied and mangled then propped up but not quite open on one side.

Sierra took careful steps toward the driver's side with the poker lifted high, ready to strike. A second later, she lowered her arm until the tip of the weapon knocked against the ground. "I don't get it."

Alex moved to the opposite side of the car and peeked inside. "Nobody's here."

She scanned the front and back seats. "No wallet or bag. The key fob is on the seat. The outside of the car is a mess. None of which makes any sense."

They'd confirmed the most confusing part—no driver, which meant the person could be roaming around anywhere. But why park the car in the garage? And how did anyone get this wreck of a vehicle across the water and onto the island?

Worse . . . why hide?

Alex's thoughts went to Cassie and a warning light flickered to life in his brain. He reached for his cell then remembered he'd left it on the table in the house. "Maybe we should find the others."

"The trunk." Mitch stood behind the car and had stayed quiet until then. He touched the puckered metal before sliding his hand into the damaged trunk opening.

"Careful." Sierra tightened her grip on the poker as she joined him. Her voice sounded breathy, as if she'd been running and could barely get the word out.

A loud screeching noise echoed around them as Mitch pulled and shimmied the lid. He got the trunk open then his hand froze in midair. The color drained from Sierra's face as she looked at the darkened interior. Her mouth moved but no words came out.

"What is wrong with you two?" Alex walked over to Mitch, anxious to see whatever had them mesmerized. "What's going—" Air punched out of his lungs on a harsh breath as he took a reflexive step back. "Damn."

It took a few seconds for Alex to process what he was seeing but nothing prepared him for the sprawled, unmoving body. The blood. That face.

The familiar tattoo.

Alex fought the panicked yelling rising inside him.

"Is this a joke?" Mitch reached into the trunk as if to shake the body awake.

"Stop." Sierra grabbed his hand. "You could contaminate the evidence."

"I don't understand." The rush of blood into Alex's head made it difficult to hear his own voice. He fought through the banging crescendo of white noise and the whispered but rabid denials fighting for space in his head. "He shouldn't be here."

The words seemed to shake Sierra out of her shock. "Wait, who?"

"This can't be happening." Mitch repeated the phrase as he stepped back from the car. His hand went to his mouth then his hair. Anguish showed in every muscle. The frenzied energy emanating from him. The jerky movements. Distress so thick and painful that it traveled and bounced off everything and everyone around him.

Two words seared and burned a path in Alex's scrambled mind: *not again*.

"Hey." Sierra put a hand on Mitch's arm as she flipped from confusion and horror to caretaker mode. "It's okay."

"It's not." Alex wasn't sure if he said the words or if Mitch did.

A rumbling sound blared across the quiet, so out of place and shocking it pulled Alex's attention away from the body. The noise vibrated through him. A motor. A boat. The blue flashing lights.

The police.

CHAPTER NINE

SIERRA

A dead body in a car. Sierra once had a nightmare that started this way. Her dreams had merged with reality in the worst possible way. She wanted to unsee all of it, to rewind her life and make smarter decisions. The steep decline had started with that damn invitation. She should have thrown it in the trash and continued with her daily workload, fueled by an unrequited love she couldn't kick.

It's okay. It's okay. It's okay.

No, it wasn't. She'd regretted tagging along on this vacation and really regretted not grabbing her phone before coming out to the garage. Now she wanted to run, get into the police boat, and take Mitch away from here and his old friends and the stench of death that seemed to cling to them.

The officer shouted but the words sounded muffled. She was about to yell back and beg for help when Alex grabbed her arm. "You can't tell him."

The manhandling jackass. She jerked out of his hold. "What's wrong with you?"

"He's dead." Mitch's hollow words barely sounded above a whisper.

Right. Mitch. She needed to get him out of here. "Reasonable people report dead bodies. I'm not listening to—"

"Be quiet," Alex said in a harsh whisper.

The controlling lawyer bullshit didn't impress her. "Find another tone, asshole."

"I'm sorry, but we can't tell the police." Alex visibly reined in his frustration, but the corners of his mouth remained taut. "Not yet."

All of her *he's not so bad* thoughts about Alex vanished. "What are you talking about?"

She remembered exactly one thing from her peek in the trunk—blood-caked hair. The memory flashed nonstop in her head until bile rushed up her throat.

"This." Alex reached into the trunk before shutting it. "The note."

Nausea battled with a catastrophic level of *what the hell* she'd never experienced before. "You took that off the body? Have you ever watched a true crime show?"

Alex showed the paper to Mitch. A voice in Sierra's head warned her not to look, not to get sucked any deeper into this mess, but in keeping with her suddenly poor decision-making skills she did.

TIME TO TELL THE TRUTH

The unspecific yet terrifying threat sent a new wave of dizziness spinning through her. It was like battling the worst case of motion sickness while still being thrown around on a lurching boat. "Truth about what?"

Mitch frowned. "Alex?"

"Don't make it sound like I know." Alex shook his head. "I drove to Maine *with* you. I was inside the house with the rest of you."

That didn't answer any of the thousand questions pinging around in Sierra's mind. The most obvious one demanded attention. "But you two know who the dead guy is?"

Neither man responded.

Damn it, Mitch.

This part of the island angled down a steep embankment toward the open water and a floating dock. Near the causeway around the other side of the house where they first entered the island was the main dock, set on pilings, but the policeman guided his boat here. After a few quick moves with ropes, he tied the boat in place and headed toward them.

"Stay calm," Alex said. "Let me do the talking."

Screw that. "I've known you about an hour. I'm not going to jail for you."

"Sierra, please." He managed to make the request sound more like an order.

They spoke in hushed tones. Words rushed together as they shot comments back and forth.

She didn't want to get any closer to this screwed-up friends group. "You have ten seconds to explain before I start screaming."

Alex's jaw tightened. "We can't—"

"Nine."

He looked at Mitch. "Do something."

She refused to let Alex pull Mitch into whatever this floating horror show was. Not when Mitch stood there, looking so lost. So ready to drop over.

"Don't act like Mitch controls what I do." They had a nice life. Boring, maybe. Not as exciting or together as a couple as she wanted, but one without any criminal investigations, and she planned to keep it that way. "Seven, and I'd hurry. This police guy is a fast walker."

The officer wore a uniform and carried a gun, and both comforted her right now. He might be in his early thirties. His hair touched the top of his collar, which was a bit longer than she was used to on police back home, but his frown looked like his go-to expression. What stuck out was his badge. It flashed in the fading sunlight as he moved closer.

"How did he know to come now?" Alex asked.

"Maybe we got lucky." Even though Sierra felt anything but at the moment.

Alex plastered on a fake smile and waved to the officer. "Doesn't matter. I'll explain after he leaves."

There's no way she was agreeing to a scenario where the bloody body stayed locked in with them on an island while the trained guy with the gun left. The officer reached them and nodded hello, but Sierra didn't respond. Not yet. Once the words started tumbling out they might not stop.

"Good afternoon, folks." The officer's gaze wandered over the back end of the wrecked car. Without a word, he stalked in a slow circle around it in the garage, studying every dent and bit of crumpled metal. He stopped his slow surveillance by standing in front of them again. "What's going on here?"

"We had an accident," Alex said, sounding fine. Too fine for the circumstances.

"Apparently." The officer looked ready to say something else then stopped. "Ma'am, are you okay?"

She didn't have the energy to lie. "No."

"She's shaken up because of the car." Alex shifted until his body partially blocked hers. "Is that why you're here?"

"Just out on a routine check of the area. Some of the houses on these private islands remain empty for most of the year and that can lead to trouble." The officer nodded again. "Speaking of which, how exactly did you get the car across the water?"

They didn't. No one could . . . and that *no one* was hiding somewhere on the island right now. Not spewing any of that information stole all of her control.

"The tide looked low enough. I thought I could see sand, so I raced over that pseudo bridge of sorts, thinking we'd be fine, but the rock banks on the sides made the drive impossible." Alex's smooth voice carried the right mix of *can you believe it* wonder and deference. He sold the wild tale, never giving her or Mitch a chance to contest the facts. "Totally my fault. I smashed up the car and I'm going to have to pay to have it removed. I'll also reimburse the island's owners for any damage to the island and path in."

Why is he lying? Sierra couldn't figure out if that or the fact he was so good at it scared her more.

The officer put a hand on the partially jimmied trunk. "Do you want me to look—"

"We're good." Alex waved the policeman off. Didn't miss a beat.

Slippery. The word played over and over in Sierra's head. Mitch's friend lied like he charmed—with ease. He might have perfected the skills in law school, but she guessed years of practice, both personally and professionally, before and after, explained the level of expertise.

"Look, I'm not going to write a ticket because I figure you have enough trouble ahead of you paying for the removal of the wreck. We're at high tide. You have about twenty hours before you can move this thing, but don't delay. There's an early fall storm rolling in. Expect fog and rain."

Storm? "Can we leave the island with you now?" She'd been shifting her weight from foot to foot, ready to launch the question.

The officer looked at Alex then Mitch before returning his focus to her again. "Why don't the two of us step over here and have a talk first?"

Yes. That. She nodded, intending to spill, then . . .

Mitch's fingers tangled with hers and he whispered low enough that only she could hear. "Don't."

His desperate plea sounded like a death rattle.

Mitch, why?

The rumbling in her chest exploded. Panic crept up her throat and tingled in her hands. They were a package deal. If she left, he left. That meant the horrifying opposite was also true. She couldn't leave him here even though staying was the worst decision possible.

Swallowing a lump of fear and every ounce of common sense that screamed at her to run and not look back, she forced a smile in response to the officer's concerned expression. "We're fine."

"You sure?" The officer frowned at her until she nodded. "Take this." He reached into his shirt pocket and pulled out a card. "If you need anything, call me. But contact marine transport and make the necessary arrangements about the removal. Pack up tonight and be ready to go."

She saw the name Dylan before tucking it in her pants pocket. One glance and she'd lost the last of her nerve. The trust she'd developed with Mitch, never tenuous, still had limits. She'd spent so much energy treading water through turbulent emotional times over the last few years, keeping them both afloat, but she would not let him drag her under. He needed to start talking and fast.

The officer's gaze lingered on the car's trunk for a few minutes before he walked away without opening it. Long strides took him down the small hill. With every step, Sierra felt her last layer of protection being stripped away and discarded.

Loving Mitch might actually kill her this time.

"Tell me why I shouldn't call for him to return," she said without dragging her gaze away from the officer's retreating back.

"It's complicated," Alex said.

She was *so* done. "Wrong answer."

Mitch squeezed her fingers. "It's my fault."

She didn't know what that meant. "What is?"

Mitch's glassy-eyed stare didn't change. "The man in the trunk is dead because of me."

CHAPTER TEN

RUTHIE

Ruthie followed Cassie and Will around the second floor of the house as Cassie asked questions about the property on their time-wasting search for evidence relating to the open garage door. The garage was outside, not in . . . though that suggested being inside might be safer.

She stopped before they got to the third floor when she heard a revving noise and bolted down the stairs, followed by Cassie and Will, reaching the garage in time to see a boat's wake as it left the island. She turned to ask the gathered group what happened . . . then she saw Sierra's face.

Shattered. That was the only word Ruthie could think of. Mitch, Alex, and Sierra all wore the expression. A milky-pale combination of shock and disbelief. None of them moved. Only Sierra bothered to look around. Her gaze traveled from Alex to Mitch and back again, growing in fury with each pass.

Something had happened. Something bad. The kind of horrible, unexpected thing that caused the air to go still and the trees to shake and bend as they telegraphed impending disaster.

Ruthie took a deep breath and dove in, silently hoping all of her plans hadn't blown up while she'd tried to pull out of

Cassie's confining orbit upstairs. "We saw a boat. Are you guys okay?"

Sierra ignored Ruthie and the fact they were all together again. Her entire focus centered on Mitch. "Who is it?"

"On the boat?" Ruthie asked.

"We need more information here. Fill us in." Will adopted his serious work voice. The one Ruthie had heard him use on online conference calls to settle differences between team members.

"Don't make me call the police back here." Sierra reached into her pocket and pulled out what looked like a business card. She shook it in Alex's general direction. "He gave me his number and I will use it."

Will frowned. "Police?"

"Wait a second." Cassie clapped, as if trying to referee the debate rather than ease the anger thrumming off Sierra. "Did the person who opened the garage leave on the boat?"

"That was a police officer." Sierra's hold on the business card tightened.

"Why were the police here? And what—" Cassie stopped talking when Alex handed her a slip of paper.

Ruthie dreaded any note that made Cassie shut up. "What is that?"

Sierra stared at Mitch. "Answer me."

So many things were happening at once. The paper Ruthie still hadn't seen and a business card. Someone on a boat. She'd planned every second, every conversation, of this weekend. She'd sketched out every single epiphany she needed to witness, but she hadn't planned for this chaos. She still didn't understand the police's role here. "What's happening?"

"This." Sierra reached over and yanked the trunk open. The

metal squeaked and crunched before she stepped away to give them all a better look inside.

The sight of a bloody body, so unexpected, so horrifying, had them all groaning and looking away. Ruthie gulped in fresh air as she took a giant step back and knocked into Cassie, who seemed frozen in place. Ruthie's mind called out commonsense directions. *Run. Get out. Never look back.* Her brain sputtered even as it begged her to look away. But she couldn't. Now she understood the reason for Sierra's unblinking stare.

"Who is that?" Ruthie asked but no one answered. Just like no one had answered Sierra.

Ruthie instinctively reached for Will. He just stood there, not saying a word. Just like the rest of them. Not running for cover. Only frozen.

The same question kept spinning in Ruthie's mind. *What kind of hell have I unleashed?*

Sierra finally continued. "They all know who the dead man is. Look at their faces. The note says it's time to tell the truth, so do it. One of you. I don't care who."

Time to tell the truth? Ruthie shook her head as the words sunk in. She'd started a chain of events that, once again, landed this group in the middle of a blood-soaked nightmare.

Struggling to make sense of this turn, Ruthie kept talking. She needed to buy some time to think this through. "With the blood it's hard to—"

"The tattoo." All of the air seemed to rush out of Mitch as he forced out the two words. His shoulders slumped and his body curled in on itself. "We recognize the tattoo."

A scream raced up Ruthie's throat, knocking and clawing to

get out. What kind of animals saw a dead body and studied it for details? Who didn't turn away in horror?

Mitch visibly swallowed twice before talking again. "A name in fancy scroll. Esme."

A strangled sound, maybe a gasp, escaped Sierra. "That's your mother's name."

"I've spent over twenty years wanting him dead." Mitch didn't look anywhere but at Sierra. "And now he is."

CHAPTER ELEVEN

BOOK NOTES: THE GAME

Emily liked to play a game. She viewed it as innocuous, victimless. A gift, really.

She'd pick a boy she viewed as beneath her. Not as popular or attractive. Usually someone from a different socioeconomic background, sometimes not, but always a guy for whom she would be considered a long shot, a fantasy. Way out of their league.

Once she acquired a target, she'd shower him with attention and affection. Build his confidence. Clean him up and show him off. Let him take her places and bask in her self-perceived worthiness. She laid it out in her diary . . .

Target acquired: Patrick O'Keefe. Tall and gangly in that hot, subversive kind of way. He actually comes from old Rhode Island money but hides it in an unironic wrapping that says, "Don't look at me." But I'm looking. I like when they glance away when I throw them some attention. He might be a fun midterm diversion . . . and I bet he can help me with this required science class.

Emily justified the move by saying she *lifted* those boys to her social status. She shaped them and made them relevant. Gifted them with popularity they'd never experienced before. She denied the ego boost, the adrenaline high, she got in return and insisted it was all about giving.

She tested the game in high school but failed because almost every boy at her private school came from the same social strata. There was no one to play with who she could later point to and claim as her finished project. Not words she would say out loud, of course, but the diary found after her death—the one her parents insisted never existed—laid out her grand social experiment in excruciating and vicious detail, from the sex to the unequaled thrill the game gave her. Her version of walking on the wild side.

Pick the guy, the loner, the quiet one no one else noticed, and shine a bright light on him. Gift him clothes or whatever he needed to look how she thought he should look. Then reel him in. Get him to do her bidding. The public outings, the rounds of alcohol-fueled sex, the molding and bending—she viewed it all as a benefit to the boys.

Friends thought she had an odd taste in the social misfit type. Most chalked up her need for sex and desire to be in control to her upbringing, like a silent shot against her parents' wealth and expectations. Not mean, exactly, but not birthed from a genuine place either. A manipulative practice that she craved like an addict's hit, but others chalked up to a rebellious phase that would pass.

Cassie will not stop. She keeps pushing Will on me. As if I'd be interested in Will. I do have someone in mind. Someone close to me who needs an upgrade but it's risky. One mistake and all our friends would be forced to choose sides. I couldn't do that to him . . . I think.

Anyone looking from the outside saw a harmless yearning, an unexpected aspect of her personality, but not one that would cause any harm. The boys seemed happy. Their social credibility rose. She gave them what they needed but hid what they gave her in return and how they fueled her need for power.

No harm. No questions.

Until she picked the guy no one expected. The young man who everyone believed murdered her.

CHAPTER TWELVE

SIERRA

Esme. Sierra had blocked the name, tried to tuck it back in a dark corner of her mind and never think of it. She always feared using it, saying it in any context, would make it more likely she'd accidentally launch the name into the middle of a conversation with Mitch and shut him down forever.

She never asked him for more information about his mother and what happened. Sierra didn't have to when there were thousands of online links, videos, and true crime podcasts that spelled out every painful detail. But, standing there now, Sierra couldn't manufacture a logical connection between the woman's name and that body. Not one that made sense . . . or maybe she didn't want to let her brain make the obvious leap.

She stared at the man who occupied so much of her thoughts and tried to find a verbal path forward. "Your mother's name—"

"That tattoo belongs to Tyler Edwards," Mitch said.

She knew that name, too. It haunted Mitch and anyone who loved him, and she stood at the head of that line. "That doesn't make sense."

"Have you seen the tattoo before?" Ruthie asked Will.

He nodded. "In a video."

"What does all of this mean?" The stiff way Ruthie held her body signaled her frustration. "Could someone . . . you guys all seem to—"

"We should go inside," Cassie said. "I feel exposed out here."

Ruthie let out an exasperated huff. "What are you talking about?"

Cassie gestured toward the house. "We'll go in and—"

"No." Sierra's thoughts jumbled and crashed together. She had questions and ached to clear the confusion, but Cassie's serious lawyer voice had ticked Sierra right off. "There's a dead man in a car. We're not going anywhere but off this island. Now. We can swim for all I care."

Alex frowned. "Then what?"

"Sierra, you know what finding him here, with me, means. Even without that note, I'm screwed." The flat affect lingered in Mitch's voice, and his face, usually tan due to his hours in the sun, stayed a chalky gray color.

Ruthie raised her hand. "Explain it to me."

Sierra talked right over her. Every word directed at Mitch, begging him to listen and leave. "I've been with you the whole time since we left Boston. We drove here with Cassie and Alex. You have an alibi." Sierra looked to Alex for an assist. "Tell him."

Instead, he shrugged. "It's all pretty convenient. The circumstances look suspicious."

More lawyer bullshit. Sierra never had an anti-attorney thing until right this second. "How can you say that?"

"That doesn't mean he thinks Mitch did anything. He's being realistic," Cassie insisted.

"Stop!" Ruthie's yell echoed across the calm water. "Could

one of you please explain why Mitch knows the dead guy in the trunk?"

Will reached for her. "Hon, come here."

She shrunk back from him. "Don't call me cute names. Don't ask me to be calm. This is horrifying. There's blood and a body, and you're all acting like this is something we should workshop and study all the angles of before reporting it."

"No one is doing that," Alex said.

Sierra understood the wild, trapped-in-hell look in Ruthie's eyes and the pleading in her voice. The conversation started rolling and sounding packaged as it inched further from the point.

"Tyler and I were best friends growing up. We lived on the same street, almost since birth, and did everything together. Running around. Bikes. He was always at our house because his mom was a nurse and worked these long shifts, so he'd stay over." Mitch took in a huge gulp of air. "My mother was his eighth-grade teacher."

Sierra wanted to stop him, help him, figure out a way to heal him. She hadn't succeeded in doing any of that during the six years they'd known each other. Today, in this moment, she was as far from reaching those goals as she'd ever been.

He continued in a voice devoid of any emotion, any life. "I didn't know, but . . . she was . . . She groomed him. Flirted with him. Slept with him. We were fifteen when it all blew up."

Sierra regretted ever wishing for him to open up.

"That's awful," Ruthie whispered. "I'm so sorry."

But it was worse. So much worse, and Sierra braced for the punch line.

Mitch nodded. "Then my mother and Tyler—the guy in the trunk—killed my dad."

CHAPTER THIRTEEN

ALEX

Alex took advantage of the stunned expressions and unusual silence and ushered everyone back to the house. Cassie was right. That note . . . *what the hell!*

One possible explanation rocked him. Maybe someone had discovered *his* secret and this was just a warning shot about things to come.

Standing out there, in the open, made them all targets. The adrenaline racing through him told him to move, so he bolted and dragged them with him. He aimed for calm and reasonable as he stepped onto the house's side porch. They all crowded there, huddled around the two lounge chairs and a small table as anxiety pinged off them, cutting through their heavy breathing and panicked mumbling.

Alex used the opportunity to mentally rally the troops. Unleashed fear would paralyze them, and they needed to be able to work this out with as little collateral damage as possible. "We can't go anywhere tonight. It's high tide. We're losing light. Let's get inside and calmly talk this through."

Sierra stared out at the water. "How deep can it be?"

"Good question." Ruthie inched closer to Sierra's side as she talked. "A car drove through it."

"Okay, stop." Cassie let out a long, labored exhale that suggested her nerves had reached the snapping point. "That's enough."

"You know what, Cassie?" Sierra's shoulders fell as she looked away from the water and back to the group. "I get that you're used to being in charge, but we don't work for you. I barely know you, so stop issuing orders."

Will snorted. "You might as well tell her to stop breathing."

Alex thought the same thing but was smart enough not to say it.

"When did this mess become about me?" Cassie reached for the door, likely wanting to escape the pile-on.

"It's not. It's about me. My messed-up family." Mitch touched Cassie's arm and she stopped trying to wiggle away. An unspoken conversation, a feeling, something passed between them because Cassie nodded and moved back. She balanced against the railing as Mitch shifted to stand in front of them all.

Sierra's pinched expression didn't ease. "Mitch. You don't need to—"

"Ruthie has a right to know." He hesitated but eventually pushed the words out. "My mother lied to Tyler and said Dad was abusive. Won Tyler over with sex, affection, and promises of a future." Mitch stopped again but started before anyone could say a word. "They then hatched a plan to kill Dad. They shot him in the driveway one night when he came home from work."

"I really am sorry," Ruthie said in a strained whisper.

"My mother told the police someone followed Dad. That it was a road rage incident turned lethal. Something similar had happened in the area months before and been all over the news. I guess she patterned her excuse on that."

Alex knew the story because it had garnered a huge amount of attention in the years after the murder as Mitch's mom went to trial. Before Alex got on campus, before he ever knew Mitch, Alex had been sucked in by the spectacle. He'd laughed and made jokes with friends about their hot teachers as every horrible fact, every intimate detail, hit the internet and got repackaged and replayed on late night talk shows and comedy specials.

Then, years later, whispers had raced around campus. *The kid with that crazy sex-starved mom got accepted on some scholarship.* Alex could admit he'd been intrigued but the amusement ended freshman year when he sat next to Mitch in a required history class. Mitch had taken a couple years off before college, so he was older but didn't seem like it. He was tough on the outside but vulnerable. He kept to himself, using the quiet as a shield.

Journalists tracked Mitch down on campus and approached him about a true crime documentary. A few anything-for-a-buck types tried to take Mitch's photo for a where-are-they-now retrospective. The boy who testified against his mother. Alex saw the toll being involuntarily famous took on Mitch five years after his dad's murder. The need to protect kicked in during that class and never wavered.

But Alex didn't see how making Mitch regurgitate the worst moments of his life answered any questions today. "That's enough. Sierra's right. You don't have to relive this."

"He kind of does." Will rushed to fix his mess after Ruthie smacked his arm. "What? I'm not saying he killed Tyler. None of us is."

"Of course he didn't." Sierra's voice shook as she launched the comment like a warning shot, daring anyone to disagree.

Alex had only eased up on his protector status when Sierra came into Mitch's life and took over the role. She and Mitch met on a hotel landscaping job when they both worked for other people. Mitch once let it slip that he heard Sierra laugh and was stunned by how free it sounded. After that, he tried to work near her so he could hear it again, all while pretending to ignore her. Lucky for him, Sierra saw the awkwardness as the cry for attention it was. Quietly and without debate, but very effectively, she created a shield around him and gave him a safe place to be himself.

"I want to explain." Mitch's voice evened out. The pain that so often crept into it was absent. He talked like he was spelling out the dry facts of someone else's life. Another person's heartbreaking trauma. "I thought about killing Tyler every day for years. That continues until now . . . or did. Not daily though more often than you might think, I'd mentally walk through how I'd make him beg and cry. But I promise you my revenge fantasies never looked like this."

"Okay." Ruthie exhaled as if she'd mentally downshifted into a less scary emotional place. "That all explains *who* the victim is. My question is about why he's here now, dead, and how that relates to the note . . . and us."

Alex assumed from Ruthie's sudden calm that Mitch's screwed-up family news wasn't a total surprise to her. Will must have told her some of it. Will sucked at communicating and tended to take his girlfriends for granted, like an obligation he could check off and ignore in favor of work, which likely explained why he had so many exes, but no way would he bring

Ruthie on this vacation without some warning about the string of deaths in their pasts. Even Will couldn't be that clueless.

"You clearly aren't friends now. Seeing Tyler is a huge surprise, right?" Ruthie continued after Mitch nodded. "Then where has he been and why would he show up here?"

"He testified against my mother back then after . . . everything. In exchange, he got a deal for conspiracy, not murder, and went to a juvenile center. He got out at twenty-one."

Ruthie frowned. "What kind of sentence is that for murder?"

Cassie straightened. "Is today the first time you've seen him since the trial? You were, what? Sixteen or seventeen when the trial happened. You're thirty-five now. It's weird for him to show up after such a long delay."

Alex could see his wife's attorney brain kick into gear. She was searching for the holes she could tear open, for the information Mitch was trying hard *not* to say.

"He would randomly call but stopped . . ." Mitch looked around, making eye contact with each of them. Almost weighing what he thought their responses might be to his news. "Until a few weeks ago."

Alex stared up at the porch ceiling. Counted each plank to keep from yelling.

"Damn it, Mitch." Sierra sat down hard on the end of the chair. "Are you kidding?"

"He left messages on my work cell about needing to talk to me because something bad was about to happen. That he saw something or someone. I don't know." When everyone started asking questions, Mitch talked over them. "It's not as if I have another dad he could kill, so I ignored him."

The comment landed with a thud. Alex knew Mitch was trying to cut through the tension with acerbic comments to cover up his emotional scar tissue. He failed.

"Yeah, the calls clearly didn't bother you," Cassie said, loading her words with sarcasm.

"You didn't tell me." Sierra, so practical and clear. The one who built a wall around Mitch and bit and clawed at anyone who tried to fight their way in.

Something in her tone or in the way she sat there, almost shriveling before their eyes, got to Mitch. His voice softened and the pain he so carefully banked flashed in his eyes. "I should have. I'm sorry."

No one said anything for a few seconds. Finding the right words proved impossible, so Alex didn't try. He earned his living negotiating and convincing but every sentence that popped into his head rang hollow.

Mitch turned to Ruthie. She hadn't lived through the horrible first time he told them this story in college, unguarded as they lounged on the grass at Will's parents' house during fall break.

"My mother is in prison and always will be." Mitch shrugged. "She writes. I give the letters to Sierra, unopened. That's it. No contact on my part for about a decade."

Cassie shook her head. "We're missing something. Let's go inside."

No one said a word as they opened the door and stepped into the kitchen. Cassie hit the switches and bathed the downstairs in white light.

A second note was right there on the kitchen counter.

YOU HAVE 24 HOURS TO CONFESS

Alex read it and reread it. He wanted to touch it, turn it over, rip it up. His legal training taught him not to do any of those things, and he blocked the rest of them from trying. Any of them could have dropped it when going in and out of the house, but he didn't see a hint of betrayal in their expressions.

Cassie moved in closer, studying every word. "Where are these notes coming from?"

"Who's doing this?" Will asked.

"That's it. I'm calling that policeman." Sierra pulled the card out of her pocket and headed for the living room. She stopped a few seconds later. Her hands shook. "What . . . I don't . . ."

Mitch frowned as he watched her. "What's wrong?"

"The cell phone doesn't work. I can't even dial 911."

Trapped without any means of communication. The threatening notes. Someone wanted them to pay, but for what exactly?

CHAPTER FOURTEEN

RUTHIE

This couldn't be happening.

Uneasy. Uncomfortable. Freaking terrified. All of those described Ruthie's mood. She'd gathered them here for a reason, for *her* plan, which relied on the element of surprise. But as the minutes ticked by one thing became clear. Someone else had a bigger splash in mind for this island getaway.

Seven people. One dead. That still left a lot of potential suspects, all of whom stood within ten feet of her.

She tried to stop this runaway train one more time, desperate and hoping this was all part of some misguided, *what is wrong with you* joke. The kind of asinine shit people who've known each other for a long time laugh off as they gossip about some remembered stunt from years ago. "If you're doing some kind of *scare the new girl* thing or a grown-up form of sorority rush week, I'm out. This isn't funny."

But no one listened to her. Her voice barely rose above the din of uncomfortable shuffling and mumbling. Everyone focused on a task, none of which inched them any closer to an answer. Cassie and Sierra looked at the phones and checked the charging cords. Alex and Will talked to Mitch in hushed tones, insisting all would be fine when no rational person could believe he'd killed Tyler.

"Unlock these." Cassie passed out the cells. "The service was iffy when I called Zara earlier but not like this. Something happened. Anyone have a signal or any type of access?"

Everyone milled around, held up their phones. Anything to catch a signal.

An uncontrollable shaking started inside Ruthie—a wild bucking and rolling—then it moved to her hands. She flexed her fingers, trying to throw off the panic. She forced her mind to stay in the moment, on task. She unlocked her phone, turned it off, and then on again. Nothing worked.

Will stopped walking around. "What would do this? Some sort of signal jammer?"

Alex stood by the side door but didn't look up from his screen. "They're illegal."

"I'm sure the person who killed Tyler will be horrified to hear they violated some sort of FCC regulation."

Everyone stopped fidgeting and stared at Mitch. Will had warned Ruthie about Mitch's odd sense of humor but was now the time for that?

After a few seconds of strained silence Cassie answered. "If it's a jammer it has to be close."

"How would you know that?" Ruthie's crafted façade cracked. She needed to play the role of a woman in need of guidance. Fluff up their egos and let them think they led the conversation, all while she undermined them. But the idea of being with these people—these potential killers—until tomorrow morning put a snap in her tone and, worse, made her less careful.

Cassie took the case off her phone and turned the cell around, as if looking for an easy way into it. "You learn a lot of useless information as an attorney."

"Believable?" Sierra whispered the question.

Ruthie didn't realize the two of them now stood alone in the kitchen until that moment. "I'm not sure," she answered in a voice barely above a breath.

Cassie controlled her world with an iron fist. She didn't show fear or worry. Ruthie couldn't read her at all.

"How close would this device have to be?" Will asked.

Cassie shrugged. "Depends on the device. A small one, probably thirty feet. Within the house. The type law enforcement use are more powerful. A device like that could be anywhere on the island. Maybe even back at the car."

The woman spewed facts like she'd researched them. At least that's how the response struck Ruthie. Cassie also protected Mitch. Most of them did, but Ruthie could see Cassie taking it too far. "You seem to know an awful lot about how to strand people without phones."

"And you're the one who brought us here," Cassie shot back.

Interesting. Also, uncomfortable, but Ruthie had found a crack. Questioning Cassie set her off. If they survived the next few hours that information might be helpful.

Alex exhaled as he glared his wife into glancing in his direction. "Okay, let's calm down."

"No, she wants answers. Well, so do I." Cassie dropped her useless cell on the table and looked into the kitchen. "Anything you need to tell us, Ruthie?"

Ruthie hadn't expected that.

"Hey." Will moved in on Cassie. "Knock it off."

But Cassie wasn't the type to back down. If anything, trying to tamp down on her control fired her up. "We don't know her."

Ruthie almost laughed at how true that snide comment was.

Cassie just kept rolling, ignoring every attempt to derail her. "You plant yourself in our lives, convince us to come out here, send out your invitations, and now someone is dead."

"What's wrong with you?" Sierra asked.

Ruthie appreciated the support, but she didn't need it. She had this. She'd been ready for the surface sheen of friendliness to melt away. For every question she asked to be greeted with a *how dare you?* attack. An immediate rush to anger and practiced victimhood.

She'd been dealing with overly confident blowhards her entire life. Fake friendliness, demeaning comments disguised as compliments about how articulate she was. She had to play this to perfection, which was exactly what she planned to do.

She slipped back into the role she'd created. Back before the death and the games. "I wanted to meet you all before the wedding because you matter to Will. The idea was to celebrate." It wasn't but she still needed them to think it was.

"Right. The wedding." Cassie snapped her fingers. "The superfast, not-at-all-suspect wedding. You'd been dating, what, six weeks or so before the proposal?"

Alex groaned. "Cas, stop."

"I didn't know this Tyler person. Other than Will I've never met any of you before today." If they wanted fire, Ruthie vowed to light the damn match. "For all I know Tyler was innocent."

Will swore under his breath. "Jesus, Ruthie."

Ruthie saw Sierra studying her and rushed to steady her one

potential ally in this room. "I'm not blaming Mitch. I'm saying maybe someone out there *thinks* Tyler got a bad deal and blames Mitch for that."

Sierra didn't break eye contact. "Who?"

Ruthie turned back to Mitch. "Why did he really want to talk with you?"

"I swear I didn't wait around to find out."

"*Wait around?*" Sierra's voice sounded deadly cold. "Did he get a message to you, or did you actually see him?"

Mitch sighed. "He visited that converted copper refinery site twice. Security kicked him out without me seeing him the first time. They just told me an old friend stopped by and gave me Tyler's name."

Ruthie wanted to look away from the intimate, painful implosion happening between Mitch and Sierra. Sierra's shoulders slouched. Her expression, flatlined and strained, reflected the pain slashing through her.

"You said earlier you hadn't *seen* him, and made it sound like you got a random message." Sierra's voice didn't contain an ounce of whatever emotion had to be flowing through her.

"I can't relive this, Sierra. He's my nightmare."

Ruthie wanted to chalk up the verbal bouncing to a rough childhood, but Mitch was a grown man. A businessman. Letting the truth leak out in tiny drops didn't help his case.

"But you made it sound like it happened twice." Cassie waved off the stress tearing the two people in front of her apart. "What about the second time you saw Tyler?"

"He said I needed to be careful and not trust anyone. I was being followed. Watched. Then Security dragged him away." Mitch shook his head. "That's it."

Cassie frowned. "Are you telling us the whole truth this time?"

"Cas, shut up," Alex said.

She turned on her husband as if she did it every day, like a habit. "Don't talk to me like that."

"We need to stay focused on the dead man in the trunk." Ruthie no longer cared what they thought about her because she already thought very little of them. "What would Tyler's killer think you need to confess to, Mitch?"

"Technically, we don't know the notes and the killing are tied," Alex said.

Ruthie pushed on, ignoring the audience and targeting Mitch. "Were you ever accused of collaborating with Tyler and your mom?"

Mitch didn't immediately answer. After a lot of uncomfortable staring, he gave in. "Yes, but I didn't kill my dad."

CHAPTER FIFTEEN

ALEX

Cut off on an island. Bad weather looming. A hidden dead body. Phones useless. No way to call for help. The combination played on repeat in Alex's head. He took the pieces apart and put them together again and still the journey from his regular life to now didn't line up. He worked. He made dinner. Read to Zara. Took out the trash. All normal. This convoluted mess of old secrets and new death? Almost too unbelievable to be real.

He had to find a way through this for Zara. Being her dad grounded him. Gave him purpose. One look at that little scrunched up, ticked off face when she was born, and he fell. He hadn't known it was possible to love that much. He'd give up anything for her. People threw that kind of language around, but he lived it by slowly surrendering who he was and what he wanted from life to ensure her security.

He needed off this island and waiting for low tide so they could use the causeway would take too long. That meant finding a boat or a working phone or staying awake and taking the risk of swimming away at first light. With morning still hours away, he focused on what he could accomplish right now. "We need to search the house."

"We're all going to go hunt down a killer who has a vendetta against Mitch?" Will asked.

Mitch leaned against the back of the sectional and stared at everyone huddled in the kitchen. "Thanks, man."

Alex fought for patience. Losing it now would send the room into a tailspin and they didn't have time for that sort of emotional baggage unloading. "We're looking for the jamming device. Find it and destroy it. That's the plan."

"Three of you already searched the house," Sierra said.

"Not for any sort of device." Will tapped on his phone then froze before dumping the useless thing on the counter. "Since I can't exactly look it up, what would this jamming thing look like?"

"Some are handheld and sort of look like a phone or a walkie-talkie." Cassie used her hands to show the size as she talked. "Some are bigger, like a box with a bunch of antennas sticking out of them. Just look for anything suspicious or out of the ordinary."

Alex saw the skeptical expressions and tried to head off further discussion by keeping them all moving. "We'll split up and meet back here in a half hour. Call out if you find anything or have trouble."

Sierra frowned. "This is how people in horror movies die."

"Sitting around doing nothing is how they die," Mitch said.

Ruthie let out a groan. "Could we stop using the word *die*?"

That sounded like good advice, so Alex jumped over all the tension and anxiety and stuck to issuing orders. "There are three floors. Each couple takes one. No one is alone. Okay?"

"I'm not going upstairs and risk getting trapped up there." Ruthie grabbed Will's hand and pulled him closer to the kitchen sink as she made that pronouncement.

Alex decided not to argue. "Fine. We'll take the bedrooms and do a loop around the immediate outside of the house. Not the island, just a ring around it to check windows and such. Everyone be careful and quick."

Cassie's natural tendency was to handle this sort of thing—to manipulate and mold everything just how she wanted it—but she wasn't operating at full speed right now. The mini show-down with Ruthie had resulted in uncharacteristic silence. Quiet meant plotting and Alex planned to ask her about that when they were alone.

Mitch looked at Sierra as he gestured toward the stairs. "I guess we get the third floor."

Five minutes later they'd spread out to their assigned search areas. Cassie didn't say a word as she checked the desk and area around it on the second-floor landing. She opened drawers and got on the floor to look at the underside of the furniture, shifting and moving without taking breath.

She stepped into the first bedroom and flicked on the overhead light to reveal an untouched space. Alex stared at the queen-sized bed and Shaker furniture and wondered if they were wasting time.

"I hate this." Cassie didn't break stride as she looked behind the photos of Nantucket hanging on the wall. "I want to go home. I actually miss taking Zara to tumbling class."

Finally. They'd been together a long time. Long enough for Alex to know his wife needed a few minutes to think through every angle of a problem before she could talk, and he'd been waiting.

Alex shut the door with a soft click. "What the hell is going on?"

She tossed the throw pillows off the bed and started stripping down the sheets. "How would I know? I've never met this Tyler guy."

Tension, panic—something—had her wound tight. Did she really think whatever was happening on this island related only to Mitch and not to graduation weekend? "Cas, come on."

Her arms fell to her sides. She looked as if all the energy had drained out of her. "Don't."

He didn't have to spell it out. The shake in her voice signaled that she knew what had him worried. "It's too much of a coincidence, Cas. What if someone figured out what really happened? What we did back then?"

"*We?*"

Neither of them moved for a few seconds. He was about to reach for her when she turned to him with that determined expression that warned him of the fight to come.

"Listen to me." She sounded stern and half pissed off, but fully back in control. "Do not go looking for trouble. This, whatever the hell is happening here, isn't about us."

She could not wish or order this away. No matter how angry she got they had to talk this out. "The players in this twisted game—"

"No." She put her hand up as she always did to let him know his job was to back down. "The body, the notes. They're about Mitch and his horrible mother. We don't have anything to do with any of that. We did what we had to do back then and now . . . we're fine."

The bobble in her voice as she talked meant trouble. He waded through her words and all that feigned self-confidence to her panic. It pulsed off her, blanketing the room with claustrophobic levels of tension.

"Okay." He stepped carefully because he hadn't seen this combination of conflicting emotions battle inside her in years. College graduation weekend and then years later when she started bleeding while pregnant with Zara. And now.

"Good." She exhaled. "Conversation closed."

But it wasn't that simple. The darkness always lingered, just out of reach, waiting for one wrong word, one exhausted moment when the wall between them bent to the point of breaking.

"I knew we shouldn't have come this weekend." He forced the *I told you so* bitterness from his voice because they couldn't afford to turn on each other.

She ignored the comment. "The only way to get through this is to stay focused on Mitch's family."

Family. Not Cassie's favorite topic. She viewed her upbringing as a burden. Instead of celebrating how far she'd come and understanding the limits and pain her mother tried to fight through, Cassie ruthlessly hid her past and maneuvered around any question about it. She didn't want praise or admiration. She despised stories about people outdoing expectations. Any talk of childhood smacked of oversharing, and she shut it down.

He knew pieces of her history, all carefully curated and shared under duress. After waking up screaming one night, she told him about being left alone as a little girl to watch over her baby sister and fighting off a shitty landlord. She'd shared tales of stealing other kids' lunches because her mom forgot to buy food, or pay the bills, or do any of the grown-up things required of her. Cassie hated all of it and used her scholarship to Bowdoin to escape it and never look back.

The lack of everything. The instability and fear. The sister who, even as a teen, bounced from man to man, picking the worst and having babies but no resources to care for them. Cassie was very judgmental on this point, holding poverty and a lack of ambition in equal low esteem, refusing to hear any argument about them being very different things. She planned every aspect of her life to avoid what she referred to without any empathy as her childhood "pitfalls," a term stretched to cover and dismiss even her mother's mental health issues.

Like so many people, he'd gone to college focused only on those four years and maybe having fun, and drinking too much beer, and playing soccer. He met Cassie and got swept up in *her* drive and *her* focus and, eventually, sucked into her big plans not to be like her mother, going from boyfriend to presumed husband in a blink.

But they both needed to stay in the present. "Mitch's mother wouldn't have waited this long to seek revenge. I mean, how would she know Mitch is even on this island?"

Something sparked inside Cassie. A renewed energy that had her standing straighter and wearing that smug expression that warned of impending destruction. "I think one person knows all the answers to your questions."

Uh, okay. "Who?"

"The person who arranged all of this." Cassie smiled. "Ruthie."

CHAPTER SIXTEEN

SIERRA

Sierra stomped up one flight of stairs then started on the next one. She'd hoped the pounding would drown out the fear that held her in a stranglehold. It battled with the gnawing sense of betrayal that Mitch had kept one more part of his life from her.

Savior complex. That's what her very practical mom had called the intrinsic need to shelter the underdog and rescue people who never asked for help. A need Mom warned could lead to heartbreak and disappointment. She hadn't been wrong.

Sierra tried to hum. To tune it all out, but her mind clogged with unspent shouts of anger and a bone-shaking anxiety that came with being hunted and not understanding why.

That damn invitation.

"I know you're furious." Mitch made the comment from one step below her. He'd followed, wisely not saying a word until right then.

At least he recognized emotions in others. She guessed that was some sort of progress. "I want to get out of here and never see your friends again."

"That won't resolve the problem of Tyler and the car."

"*Problem*? That word is too tame." Even for him and all the pain he'd suffered, that was too flippant. She missed a step and almost splatted on the hardwood. Mitch's hand on her ass balanced her. Any other time, she would have savored the sensation. "He's dead, Mitch. He's not out somewhere, driving around. He wasn't in an accident, no matter what nonsense Alex told the police."

"I'm aware."

His touch mixed with the chaos threatening to overtake them and she quickened her step, skipping two stairs at a time. "But you're not upset."

"Stunned. Sort of empty, like my mind won't go there. But don't ask me to mourn for Tyler. The way he died and maybe the reason for it, if I knew what that was, might suck. But I can't grieve. Not after what he did to my dad."

She got it but still hated every word of that explanation. Arguing that he continued to let his mom's and Tyler's terrible actions define him would have to wait. She didn't have the bandwidth to keep her mind clear enough to tackle his issues right now.

"Sierra . . . would you . . ." His fingers trailed over her back. "Please stop."

Face it. The words echoed through her. Holding on to her anger only depleted the energy she needed to get through whatever lethal darkness lurked ahead. She stopped and turned to look at him. "What?"

"I didn't tell you about Tyler coming to see me because I knew you'd worry."

"You make me sound like a grandmother."

He leaned against the wall with the handrail digging into his back. "You're the one person I don't want to disappoint yet I continually do it."

She sucked at being pissed off. After a lifetime of listening to her practical parents talk about the things they wanted to do once they retired only to have those dreams derailed by her father's colon cancer then her mother's losing fight with the same, she'd vowed to appreciate the moments and the people who mattered. To be a caretaker, despite the potential downside, and a voice of reason. Mitch was the recipient of all that.

She sat down two steps from the third-floor landing. "Stop being a martyr. You're not that bad."

"And right on cue you're defending me." He shook his head. "I don't deserve it, you know. Even I know I do things that rightly piss you off."

"Amen to that." If only she could hold on to the frustration for an extended period of time. "Did you know Tyler would be here?"

Mitch sat down next to her, squishing their bodies together on the narrow step. "I didn't kill him."

"I know that, you jackass." Not having anywhere to hide or any room to shift and put some space between them, she balanced her head against the wall. "I'm trying to figure out if this Tyler guy has been following you around or if someone killed him and deposited him here for you to be blamed. Even though, scary enough, both of those things could be true."

"He hasn't called or tried to see me, that I know of, since that time at the copper refinery. I'm sorry I was an ass—"

"You were." He always apologized. She wished he would stop inflicting the pain that required the groveling in the first place.

"—and hid that from you." He knocked his leg against hers in the playful way he did things. "I really was trying to protect you . . . and maybe protect myself, too."

There. "Was that so hard to admit?"

"Actually, yes." He stared at his hands as he turned them over and back, rubbed them together. "I've spent years trying to forget and failing. Existing, eking out the smallest degree of stability. So, when Tyler tracked me down at work, my one place of peace . . ." He sighed. "I don't know. The thought of opening the door and inviting him back into my life threw me. I've wanted to kill him for so long, and feared I would, but I swear someone beat me to it."

Living with hate. The idea was so far off her radar she had trouble imagining it, but from his stark expression she could tell it cost him something to admit it.

She tried a joke even though this moment, this weekend, called for the opposite of amusement. "Let's not lead with that last part when we talk to the police."

"Forgiven?"

"Always." Which she now believed would be her downfall.

He stood up and reached a hand down to her. "Onward and upward into the creepy attic."

She accepted the help up, relishing the last few seconds before reality intruded. Her drumming heartbeat had nothing to do with love and everything to do with dread for the night ahead. "We're calling this the third floor because attics are terrifying, and I've hit my maximum in the terror department today."

"Fair enough."

They got to the top and stepped into an open section. There

was a makeshift sitting space at one end of what likely once was little more than a storage area that had been built out with drywall. The other end of the gabled room had two twin beds and a rocking chair. Practical rather than cozy and welcoming.

An overflow space with questionable ventilation and white walls . . . and hundreds of photos pinned and pasted on those walls and hanging from the ceiling.

Mitch's smile collapsed. "What the hell?"

Sierra's eyes refused to focus. All she could see was a sea of pictures. Most looked like copies or prints, not originals. Sierra picked out the same face of a woman in every single photo. Sometimes by herself and pensive but most times not. Some of her as a teen. Some from later years. Many of her laughing.

Mitch unpinned one photo. This one showed a teenage girl in a soccer uniform and included a caption about a regional award.

"Oh, shit." He doubled over with his hands balanced on his knees. "I don't . . . what is this?"

No, no, no. Nothing else. No more. Not one more horror. The words rose above the shock and slammed into Sierra.

She wanted to close her eyes and disappear. A scream begged to get out, but she swallowed it. Falling apart would put them in more danger. Then she looked at Mitch and saw the way his knees kept buckling as gulping breaths shook through him.

"This doesn't make sense. I can't . . ." He inhaled a few times before standing up.

Sierra brushed a soothing hand over his back. She wanted to tell him everything was going to be okay, but she couldn't form the lie.

"Emily." Mitch turned the paper over, studied it, then looked around the room. "They're all photos of Emily."

Another dead person from his past. More trauma he hadn't processed. A new unwanted nightmare for her to share.

"Why would they be here? How are Emily and Tyler even connected?" Sierra had so many questions but those rose to the top.

"Me." Mitch exhaled. "The only connection is me."

CHAPTER SEVENTEEN

BOOK NOTES: WHO KILLED EMILY?

When a woman goes missing suspicion first falls on those closest to the victim. Family. A boyfriend or former boyfriend, a teacher, or a neighbor. Someone from her inner circle. That boy she turned down for a date who might have been unstable and furious and wanted revenge.

Emily, a college student full of energy and life, didn't have any obvious enemies. That meant everyone, from known predators in the area to loved ones, fell under suspicion. Everyone who knew her and many who didn't demanded answers. They craved a simple, easily packaged explanation that provided quick closure. One that confirmed this murder was about Emily *only* and they were safe in their homes and on their streets. A solution that allowed them to treat the violence as an aberration and sink back into their lives after shedding a few tears for the loss of a young life.

A group of uncomfortable bedfellows, consisting of law enforcement, concerned citizens, and online true crime warriors, dissected the lives of every man who had known or come in contact with Emily. Her father, Phillip, didn't escape scrutiny.

Each hour away from the family home, including those unaccounted for during graduation weekend, came under suspicion. His usual schedule consisted of day trips to New York City and longer trips to other cities "for work."

Clocking all those business hours backfired on him. Phillip's much-touted work ethic boomeranged into a haunting misdirection of *Did her dad kill her?* and *What happened behind those closed doors?* until a zealous podcaster overstepped and physically followed Phillip. This podcaster found Phillip's mistress and their secret two-year-old daughter in the Upper West Side brownstone he owned in the city. The second family and additional property Emily's mother never knew about.

Phillip's reputation disintegrated into a sinkhole of name-calling after that. Online sleuths launched wild accusations and shifted his life to center stage on every gossip site. His marriage imploded into a fiery wreck of a divorce that raged on for years after Emily's death.

Emily never knew about her father's fall from grace but every mention of her parents both in the news and in whispers around town to this day start with a reference to the couple's murdered daughter.

While that fiasco raged, the police quickly ruled out Emily's younger brothers, who were out of school and seen all over the hotel and town of Brunswick with their mother during the weekend Emily vanished. Law enforcement then turned to interrogating friends and former boyfriends. Not a quick undertaking because Emily's friend circle turned out to be wide. It included people who thought they were friends and *actual* friends. High school friends, many of whom she abandoned for college friends, as well as obligatory through-other-old-money-families friends.

Emily dated but not with an intensity that ever suggested she'd found *the one* or even fell in love. Her taste in young men others might find odd intrigued law enforcement. Television analysts obsessed with archaic diligence about what they viewed as Emily's overactive sex life. How she dated but never found a *real* boyfriend or potential husband, as if that were the only reason a woman would go to college.

The pundits and self-proclaimed experts debated for hours about how, without her, some of her partners might be considered incels—part of an online subculture of misogynists who are unable find a romantic partner or are "involuntarily celibate" and sometimes violent.

These talking heads all ignored the reality that the young men she dated, even after the inevitable breakups, didn't hate her. They stumbled over themselves to go into graphic detail about the sex and how much she loved to "do it" in public places, mere feet away from anyone who might notice. She *made* them popular just by being seen with them.

One guy stuck out. A loner with a tragic past reminiscent of great literature. Once the police learned about him they dug in.

CHAPTER EIGHTEEN

RUTHIE

Ruthie jammed her finger against the number keypad of her cell, trying to make something happen. When that didn't work, she scanned her apps. "There has to be a way to get a signal out."

Kitchen cabinet doors banged around her as Will rummaged through the shelves in his usual half-assed fashion when doing a task he didn't want to do. He'd barely looked around inside, then *thud*. "We find the jammer then we can make the calls."

She heard his voice. Normal. Watching him now, she saw the engineer at work. Methodical. Logical. No panic.

Depleted and terrified, sure someone with a knife or some other equally lethal weapon spied on them as they moved around the main floor, Ruthie didn't understand his sense of calm. She balanced her hip against the counter. "You're not shaken or confused."

He switched to staring at the lower cabinets. "I'm trying to find this—"

"There's a dead man in a car fifty feet away from us." Screw the jammer and his friends and her ridiculous plan of coming to an isolated island for this weekend.

Will crouched down and balanced on the balls of his feet as he opened another set of cabinet doors and performed a cursory inspection. "It's farther than that."

Talk about missing the point. Unless the nonsense was on purpose. "Tell me what's going on in that supposedly beautiful mind of yours. You know none of what's happening makes any sense, right?"

He stood up and stared at her. Didn't make a move or try to quiet her pulsing nerves. She wanted to write his flat reaction off as some sort of defense mechanism, but this was who he was. He viewed himself as stable and dependable. To her, he came off as unemotional and indifferent.

A dead body should produce a reaction. Maybe not screaming but a noise of some sort. "Well?"

"Mitch wouldn't kill anyone."

Not what she expected but she did have a response for that one. "Wrong. You heard him say he wanted the dead guy dead."

She hadn't dreamed that part. The sound of Mitch's voice played over and over in her head. He didn't doubt his ability to take another life, and neither did she. Chalk it up to a dysfunctional upbringing, a hideous monster of a mother, or a general lack of affection. The end result was the same. Mitch was odd. As far as she could tell the best thing about him was Sierra, and he failed to recognize what he had there or how she evened him out.

"That wasn't . . ." Will made a strangled sound. "I don't have an explanation for the car, but Mitch wouldn't lure Tyler here and put us all at risk."

She secretly hoped some stellar, unassailable argument would pop out of Will's mouth next, but he didn't continue until she glared at him.

"Even if Mitch did plan ahead once he knew the address for our party and put the wrecked car on the island, he couldn't go out to the garage and kill a guy without us knowing."

Not nearly as stellar as she'd hoped. Engaging in timeline subterfuge didn't convince her at all. "Very rational."

"I mean, sure, we split up to get settled in our rooms and that sort of thing, but Sierra was with him. You can't believe she's in on this." Will's voice became more animated. "Right? Why would she?"

Ruthie welcomed the reaction. Any reaction. "He could have killed this Tyler guy earlier then dumped the car here for the big unveiling today."

Will rolled his eyes. Stared at the ceiling. Generally, pulled out every male frustration gesture guaranteed to piss her off.

He delivered one last sigh. "Listen to what you're saying, hon."

"The name is Ruthie."

He ignored her and trampled right over the reminder about her hatred for pet names. "If he wanted to kill Tyler, then why not do it back at home and bury the body? Mitch is on construction sites all the time and could hide any number of crimes. Putting a body where someone would find it, where he's temporarily staying, points the finger right at him."

A little too dismissive but not wrong, so she rolled with it. "Who would want to frame Mitch? Could all of this, the notes specifically, have something to do with Emily?"

"What?" Will shifted his feet. Took small steps without going anywhere. Not pacing, exactly, but only because there wasn't a lot of room between the kitchen island and the stove to move. "Why would you ask that?"

Nervous. That was new. He usually pivoted away from conversations that required him to feel something. This time he let the anxiety creep in and overtake him.

Her plan for this weekend had been all but obliterated by the need to survive it, but she hadn't forgotten her original goals. "Think about those notes. They suggest someone in this house is hiding something very big."

"They don't mention Emily."

He'd switched to denial. Not the first time he'd done that since they'd known each other. Every time she'd broached the topic of Emily, he threw up an emotional stop sign. She hadn't made one inch of progress on that front.

Now wasn't the best time but this fake engagement would never progress to an unwanted marriage, so she had to take her shots when she could. "I know you don't like talking about her, but—"

Any thought of diving into the subject vanished at the sound of the side door opening. Cassie and Alex came in from their outside search. A second later heavy footsteps pounded on the stairs. Sierra jogged down with Mitch lumbering behind her.

"Photos." Sierra sounded out of breath. Her eyes were huge and haunted. "Maybe a hundred of them. They were plastered all over the third floor."

Sierra dropped at least a dozen pictures on the kitchen island. Spread them out to investigate further. They all gathered around, but Ruthie didn't need to lean in close. She knew what the photos were, or more accurately, who was in them. Emily. Young Emily. Emily closer to the time of her death. All Emily.

Will's head shot up and he pinned Ruthie with his gaze. "How did you know all of this was about Emily?"

Not all but some. "I didn't."

But Ruthie could tell he didn't believe her.

Maybe he really was as smart as people said.

CHAPTER NINETEEN

BOOK NOTES: EMILY'S DIARY

It's not often you get to hear from the victim once she's dead. Emily's diary provided that insight. Her parents fought to get the writings back. To bury them. Made every argument about privacy and irrelevancy and, when those failed, insisted to the public the diary didn't exist.

The contents were leaked to the press within four days of her death. The murder of a pretty college graduate in a place where that sort of thing rarely happened, where she should have been safe with her parents right there in the same town, proved too explosive to contain.

The pages of handwritten scrawl expressed a yearning for a change she doesn't define or explain and has no idea how to make happen. Emily seesawed between wanting her parents' approval and judging every belief they held. Not really an uncommon occurrence in a young twenty-something. The age called for wonder and exploration, for bucking against trends and the binds of upbringing. For believing you knew so much when you had experienced so little.

In many ways, the diary highlighted how similar Emily was to her peers. She had friends and the usual squabbles. She gossiped and got angry. She daydreamed and hoped for bigger things. None of that helped the investigation. The lack of flowery language or pages about nasty relationship breakups or bad dates left the police floundering . . . until they focused in on what the diary did say.

She mentioned many young men. Those she targeted for her *Emily upgrade*. They were categorized and described, as if she'd performed surveillance on them. Covert sightings. Ratings. Pro and con lists about choosing one over another. Rumors and histories about each. When she did pick one, pages outlining what they did together in excruciating detail, both sexually and otherwise, followed by plans on how to end each informal relationship on a positive note and move on to a new target.

The game she played made the grown men investigating her death squirm. Male college students engaged in this sort of behavior all the time, keeping scorecards about the women they had sex with and passing the information around for laughs. Doing so might be considered boorish or even disgusting, depending on how secretive the information stayed, but forgivable in a *boys will be boys* way. Stumbling over a young woman maneuvering the same path horrified every adult who knew.

Despite the moral judgments, all of Emily's collected intel satisfied law enforcement's need for a suspect pool. They couldn't believe she'd played the game so well, with such finesse and experience beyond her years. She picked her playthings with insight, but the police decided she must have failed one time, and that person killed her.

The theory sounded good. It sure played well among internet sleuths. The more prurient the story, whether true or not, the more people talked about Emily. They reasoned that, maybe, she did deserve it. After all, she wouldn't be the first woman to act in such a way that the public concluded she'd invited her own murder. White upper-class college students usually didn't fall into that category, but their logic assumed she could possess a hidden diabolical side. A rancid, rotten core that *asked for it*.

Problem was, just as Emily didn't fit the stereotype, neither did the young men in her diary. Most frustrating, they all could account for their whereabouts and produce witnesses to verify. Two had alibis for each other—Mitch Andersen and Jake Parker, two of Emily's closest friends. Two from her most personal circle. Two with backgrounds that called out for a second look.

Both had suffered childhood trauma. Both fit the loner personality Emily was drawn to. Both had earned special attention in Emily's diary. If Emily ever had a genuine crush, it might have been on one or both of these two. And they were with Emily on her final day.

Mitch and Jake became the lead suspects. Then the real investigative work began.

CHAPTER TWENTY

SIERRA

They'd stumbled over photos of Emily in a state where none of them lived, in a house they'd never been to. But *stumbled* didn't really fit. The photos hadn't been hidden. They'd been strewn around, specifically laid out for them to find. Taunting them until every question they meant to ask became jumbled up in a growing mass of fear and paralyzing stillness that kept them from creating a feasible escape plan.

After rounds of shrieking and shouting about the photos, they all hovered around the great room's coffee table on the U-shaped sectional. Sitting when they should be swimming or at least running. Instead, they pawed through the pictures and ignored the danger lurking all around them. So methodical. So . . . practiced.

The rumbling inside Sierra blocked out any rational thought. She tried to make logical connections using the pieces she knew, but her brain kept blanking out. Every nerve ending fired until she was little more than a bundle of unspent energy. She had to hold a throw pillow in front of her and hug it to keep from bolting for the door . . . but to where?

Six of them trapped on an island. One of them a killer. A sick twisted piece of garbage who thought killing and forcing them to look at a dead girl's image was somehow justifiable.

The silence picked and poked until Sierra broke through it. She looked at Ruthie, the only other person in the room not touching the photos. "Were these on the third floor when you and Will got here yesterday?"

Will answered. "Of course not."

Ruthie's focus was on Cassie. "Don't look at Alex like that. Will is telling the truth."

Cassie stopped spreading out the photos and arranging them in a pattern only she could see. "You expect us to believe you walked the grounds and looked through the house yet somehow missed a running car in the garage and a third floor filled with photos?"

Sierra had the same questions but hearing them come out of Cassie's mouth twisted them. She had a way of speaking that sounded more like condemning.

Sierra tried to ease the tension because Cassie and Ruthie taking verbal swings at each other would only add more drama to this adrenaline-fueled fire. "Hey, counselor. Ease up."

Alex finally dropped the photos and leaned back against the sofa cushions. "Okay, but Cas's question is a fair one."

"We didn't go to the third floor yesterday. We were on the second floor and realized how stuffy the house felt and went downstairs to turn on the air." With each word, Ruthie seemed to crowd closer to Will on their part of the sectional. "I forgot we skipped that floor until Mitch and Sierra came down with all of these photos."

Cassie shook her head. "Convenient. So was your comment when we first got here."

"What are you talking about?" Will asked.

"Your fiancée told us that all the bedrooms were on the second floor. We had to pick from there. She specifically apologized to Sierra and Mitch for making them share a room." Cassie lifted both hands. "Interesting, no?"

Alex hummed in response.

Not one to back down, Ruthie came out firing. "Maybe instead of you two sitting there, lobbing veiled accusations, you should just say whatever you have to say. What do you think I did?"

"I don't trust you." Cassie folded her arms in front of her. "How's that?"

Ruthie snorted. "Right back at ya."

Will groaned. "Both of you stop it."

"That's how you defend me?" Ruthie asked.

Will shrugged. "You're the one who mentioned Emily earlier."

That comment had Cassie sliding to the front of the couch cushion again. "What?"

"Why?" Alex asked in a less volatile tone but only slightly.

The mood, already tenuous, disintegrated. They'd tipped from careful and assessing to blame-throwing, and Sierra feared if emotions continued to tick off in mini explosions none of them would make it to morning. One of them likely was a killer. She really didn't want to piss that person off more than they already were.

She tried to ease them back to a less stressful route. "Ruthie, could you just explain what you knew and when?"

But Ruthie's attention stayed on Will. "I didn't know about the photos. You have to believe that."

"I'm trying . . . but I . . ."

Alex whistled. "Yeah, you two are ready for marriage."

"And you all wonder why I don't come to these things," Mitch said.

Sierra tried one more time. "Let's talk about what we do know. The car wasn't running in the garage yesterday when Will and Ruthie got here."

Cassie frowned. "How do *we* know that?"

"It's how cars work," Mitch said. "They run out of gas if you leave them turned on for a day."

"Exactly." Sierra appreciated the support. Having Mitch chime in seemed to ratchet down the smothering tension. "And Ruthie and Will didn't notice the garage door being open earlier, right?"

Will nodded. "Right."

"So, the car may have been in there but turning on the engine and opening the door likely happened once we were all here, picking rooms and getting unpacked." For a bunch of college-educated smart people they seemed to need to be baby-stepped through this, so Sierra kept going. "Cassie, you took Will and Ruthie earlier to look around while we were at the garage. Did you go to the third floor then?"

"Nope." Cassie looked far too satisfied. "Ruthie stopped us."

Will scoffed. "Come on. That's not true."

"I ran downstairs because I heard an engine, which turned out to be the boat," Ruthie explained.

Cassie shook her head. "Again, convenient."

Sierra had reached her limit. Ran headfirst into it and ceded the floor. "Okay, counselor. Tell us what you think is happening here."

"I have no idea." Cassie gestured toward Ruthie. "This is her show."

Ruthie looked at Will. "Still nothing?"

"Damn, man." Mitch shook his head. "I'm starting to see why your engagements don't stick."

"At least I can get women," Will shot back.

Sierra found Will really unimpressive. She didn't exactly like Cassie and Alex either, but at least they talked. They made their positions clear. They acted like grown-ups. Will sat there without saying a word then spouted off passive-aggressive garbage.

"*Get?* You're not in college anymore. All of you, grow up." Sierra shot Mitch a look after the last comment. This was not the time for his sarcasm either. "We don't know if these photos were on the third floor before today, but it probably doesn't matter. The point is someone who knows you or, sorry to say, *is* one of you, has been on the island and in the house causing trouble. The cell jammer, the car, the messages, and now the photos. Someone killed Tyler. Someone clearly wants your attention."

"Why?" Alex asked.

Well, since he asked . . . "You're the ones who knew Emily. You tell me."

CHAPTER TWENTY-ONE

ALEX

As far as summations went, Alex thought Sierra had done a good job. Impressive arguing from a woman who spent her days outside with her hands in the dirt. But all those pieces and all that talking didn't get them one inch closer to an answer. And with the photos of Emily, he knew he had to step in and control the conversation before it veered even deeper into dangerous territory.

"Emily has been dead for twelve years," he said. "She's irrelevant to this engagement party."

That's what he needed them all to conclude. Talking about Emily, being dragged willingly or unwillingly into the past, invited trouble. They had enough of that right now. They didn't need to go looking for more.

Cassie didn't look convinced. "Is that true, Ruthie?"

Ruthie sighed. "Last I checked, Sierra and I are the only two in this room who weren't around when Emily was killed."

That was exactly the type of logical jumps Alex needed them to avoid. He couldn't exactly call a time-out or drag Cassie away for a consultation, so he pressed his thigh against hers. Any other time she'd recognize that as a signal to back down. Not this time. Not with Ruthie. They seemed locked in a wrestling match for control of the room, each refusing to give an inch as they launched verbal bombs at one another.

"What are you saying?" Cassie asked without breaking eye contact with Ruthie.

Mitch groaned. "Stop acting like every sentence is an accusation. Things are strained enough."

"Emily was killed on graduation weekend. She was with all of you celebrating . . . until she suddenly wasn't." Ruthie pointed around the circle. She skipped Sierra but everyone else fell under her scrutiny. "All of you and Jake Parker, the mysterious *missing* friend."

The way she said it, as if she knew more than she was telling, pricked at Alex. "Jake's not missing. He's just not here this weekend."

The sound Ruthie made carried a hint of *gotcha* in it. "Maybe we should ask why."

"Now who's throwing around accusations," Mitch said.

Ruthie shrugged. "I made a simple comment."

Will went from sneaking questioning peeks at his fiancée and remaining mostly silent to wide awake. He leaned forward with his elbows balanced on his knees. "What would Jake have to do with Mitch's mother and the dead guy?"

"His name is Tyler," Mitch said. "And literally nothing."

"Do we know Tyler really is dead?" Sierra asked.

Shit. Alex hadn't expected that.

"I didn't touch him. When Mitch tried, I stopped him." She didn't blink as she stared at Alex. "You didn't either, right?"

"Are you kidding?" Cassie asked. "It's been hours. He would have made a sound or come into the house."

"Only if he could move or was conscious. No, Sierra is right." Ruthie nodded. "We need to check."

The last thing they should do was run around outside. Alex couldn't believe he had to explain that. "Absolutely not."

Sierra ignored him. "We all go out. We stay together."

"Right. It's getting dark." Ruthie stood up. "Let's just go."

Alex dreaded the idea of Ruthie and Sierra teaming up. The combination sounded formidable and problematic, especially with Cassie knocked off her game. She sat there not saying a word. But he knew he'd lost the battle when she stood up and joined the other women.

Before he could come up with a good reason not to go, they all piled onto the side porch again. The sun had gone down, bathing the sky in deep blue. The wind whistled through the trees and whipped up fallen leaves. The temperature had dropped at least ten degrees.

Alex switched on the outside lights. The white glow revealed the trail straight to the garage and plunged the rest of the island in shadows.

The chill coming off the water mixed with the smell of evergreen. They walked in a huddle to the garage. No one strayed or ran ahead. They took careful steps, keeping to the pebbled path. They hadn't closed the garage door. Alex tested the small building's interior lights, but they didn't come on. The trail lights allowed for a cursory inspection but not much more.

Alex started with the obvious. "The car's not running."

"Didn't you turn it off?" Cassie asked.

"No, we were all too stunned to do much other than fight to keep from throwing up." Sierra took a step closer to the vehicle.

Mitch pulled her back. "Maybe it finally ran out of gas."

Alex opened the trunk and winced at the now-familiar me-tallic crunching sound as it lifted. He was about to reach in and check for a pulse when Sierra stopped him.

"Wait." Her fingers tightened on his arm. "Someone moved him."

"That's ridiculous." Cassie motioned for him to shut the trunk. "We were all upset when we saw him before. There's no way you—"

"Look at his hands," Sierra said. "Before, his left hand was over his right so you could see the *Esme* tattoo. Now the right is on top and you can't see it."

Alex swore under his breath. "That probably happened when—"

"No." Mitch shook his head. "I see that damn tattoo in my nightmares. Sierra's right. That's not how his hands were posi-tioned before."

"Not possible because we've all been together." Cassie sounded so sincere as she said the words.

"Not really. We split up. We took separate floors to look for the signal jammer. I went to the bathroom. You and Alex went outside." Sierra looked like she wanted to say something else, but the sudden sound of rain stopped her.

"We need to get in the house before this turns into a down-pour," Will said.

Sierra didn't move. "Aren't you forgetting something? Is some-one going to check for a pulse or are we going to miss that step again?"

Cassie did the deed. She touched Tyler's wrist and neck then shook her head.

Standing out there, in the open, not knowing who or what

watched them made Alex twitchy. "There. We have our answer. Let's go."

Sierra nodded. "Fine, but once we're inside we need to have an honest talk about why someone would move Tyler's body and why this Jake guy is so upset with all of you."

A biting wind blew over them as the rain picked up. They didn't debate or argue about Sierra's comment as they all took off for the house.

Alex caught Cassie's arm right before she broke into a run. "We messed up."

"Not now." She struggled out of his hold and raced toward the side porch.

But the conversation couldn't wait for long because Alex knew exactly who'd touched the body while no one was looking—Cassie.

CHAPTER TWENTY-TWO

SIERRA

They all hesitated on the side porch as Ruthie struggled to turn the knob with wet hands. Will finally took over but before Sierra could follow the group into the house, Mitch stopped her. He motioned for her to stay back until the rest of them filed inside. That left her alone with him as the rain coated the steps behind them and a fine mist sprayed over the exposed part of the space.

The last of the fading light disappeared as dark clouds rolled through the sky. She could no longer see the faraway parking lot. A distant outline was all that tethered her to the coastline.

"Don't go anywhere on this island or in the house without me," he said in a harsh whisper.

The sound of crashing waves. The smell of rain. She usually loved both as much as she loved him. Not today.

She shifted her weight from foot to foot to keep the blood pumping. She couldn't afford *not* to be ready. "Are you worried they'll blame you if something else happens?"

He stepped in closer, blocking the entry light behind him and her path to the door. "I'm worried because the best way to get to me is through you."

She put aside the sensation of a trap snapping shut and pinning her inside and focused on his face. She could barely make out his features, but the grim line of his mouth stuck out. So did the concern in his voice. "Mitch . . ."

"I can't deal with you being hurt or—"

"Hey." She rubbed her hands up and down his arms. "I'm fine." That wasn't true in any sense but asking him to take on her fear on top of his escalating panic was too much.

He scanned the area around the house, never fully relaxing or stepping off informal watch duty. "Whatever's happening here is more than a warning. It's been planned and more of us are going to get hurt. I can feel it."

She wanted him to be wrong. She *really* wanted to chalk the warning up to his general paranoia and ongoing belief that bad luck followed him around in a cloud, enveloping and infecting the people he cared about. She'd become an expert at brushing off his warnings, but she couldn't laugh this one away.

She swallowed a sigh and shoved aside every lesson she'd learned over the years about how to tiptoe through the emotional land mines of his past. "Tell me."

He frowned. "What do you mean?"

"Whatever secret you're keeping. Whatever piece of you, or thing you did that haunts you or makes you feel dirty and won't let go. It's time to let it out."

"Sierra, I—"

"It's just us talking, but you need to share so I can be prepared. So we can formulate a plan to get out of here without more bloodshed. I won't judge you." She stumbled over the last part. The most honest version: she'd try not to judge. She hoped that would be possible.

"I told you the worst. I would have killed Tyler for what he did to my dad. Not just years ago if I'd run into him. Hell, I probably would have done the unspeakable if no one had been around on that copper refinery job a few weeks ago. I wish I could tell you my humanity, or my father's voice in my head, or even thoughts of you would have stopped me but that's not how hate works. It sits there, waiting for an opportunity to kick back to the surface."

She ached for him because she believed him. She knew him as a good man. Hardworking, careful, practical, devoted to their business and to her. The idea of him blowing the trust of his uncle—the man who'd rescued Mitch from years of bouncing around foster care—in return for a fleeting moment of satisfaction both didn't make any sense and did.

Every horror, every death and detail, shaped Mitch. With her, he acted differently. Lighter and more generous. Open to trying some new things and willing to share the workload. She'd twisted that around to believe she meant something to him and fed off every emotional crumb he dropped for her over the years.

But in this moment, on this island, she felt hollowed out and starved of hope. She desperately needed him to care enough about her not to lie to her.

"Please." She could hear the begging in her whisper. "If you know anything else, please tell me right now."

"I don't."

He stared at her without blinking or looking away. That either made him an exceptional liar, a psychopath like his mom, or the unluckiest person she'd ever met.

She tried again. "Maybe a joke went wrong or there was an accident."

"None of that happened." He lowered his head, bringing

his mouth close to hers. "I've fucked up a lot in my life. After Dad . . ." He shook his head. "In addition to my uncle and aunt taking me in, what saved me was that scholarship to Bowdoin funded by my dad's old office. I ignored the opportunity for two years while I pretended to *find myself,* which really meant drinking until I couldn't feel anything, but my uncle convinced me that was a shitty way to honor my dad."

She adored Uncle Bud and knew he'd done his best in a terrible situation. He was a practical man who loved fishing and ATVing and Mitch but didn't trust doctors of any type. Desperate to make up for the sins of his baby sister, Uncle Bud didn't make Mitch go to therapy. It was his one big mistake because Mitch's trauma festered and grew and instead of combatting it, he pushed it into a dark corner and suffered when it whipped out without warning.

"I didn't blow that chance, Sierra. I didn't run around college in a murderous rage."

"That's not—"

"I put the bottle down and enrolled, older than most of the students in my year, but I went. Even experienced being normal for a few years . . . and then that was taken away, too," Mitch said.

"You are normal." *What did that even mean and who got to decide?* "You should be a mess and unable to function with your history, but you're not."

"You're confusing being able to go to work every morning with being okay." He exhaled. "We both know I'm not like other people."

The desire to dive deeper into what made Mitch be Mitch lost out to needing to know more about what could save their lives today. "We have these disparate pieces. You, Tyler, Emily, possibly Jake, and those threatening notes. What ties them all together?"

"I don't—"

Adrenaline coursed through her. "You *do* know. Buried in there, under that blanket of horrors you've taught yourself to shove aside and ignore, you have an idea."

He held up both hands in mock surrender.

No, no, no. "I can't trust anyone in that house but you, so I need you to think, Mitch. What are we missing? What part of the puzzle do we need before we can work this out?"

"I'm out of ideas."

"You've never offered an idea. Do it now." She wanted to shake him into action. Make him drop all those defenses. Get him fired up and thinking. "I'll be the bad guy and ask the nasty, intrusive questions of your friends but you have to give me some direction. Some theory you have, or maybe something *you* question or need to know."

The confusion cleared from his expression. The dark world closed in around them and the waves grew louder, but she experienced the first spark of hope since they'd come across that damn causeway.

"Who." A new confidence filled his voice.

They were close to finding a way in. She could feel the energy revving up around him as he spoke. He'd figured something out. Now he needed to spill it in a way she could understand. "What does that mean?"

"The missing piece could be a *who*."

Not any clearer. "Okay."

"Brendan Clarke."

CHAPTER TWENTY-THREE

BOOK NOTES: NEW SUSPECT ACQUIRED

Law enforcement's focus on Mitch and Jake took a sudden turn. After days of questioning and digging into their respective pasts, the attention quieted. Not online. The keyboard warriors made sure Mitch and Jake remained the main targets of accusations there, with every painful detail about their tragic histories posted and dissected with morbid glee. But the police had moved on.

Law enforcement interviewed fellow student Brendan Clarke six days after finding Emily's body. He was a year behind her at Bowdoin. A computer science major who took classes like Optimization and Uncertainty while Emily wrote a thesis on the role of unlikable female characters in literature for her honors project. Brendan and Emily didn't have a single class in common. They didn't live near each other. They didn't share the same hobbies, interests, or friends.

One text connected them, and it colored the whole trajectory of Emily's homicide case.

You'll regret this

Brendan texted the message to Emily two weeks before her murder. He had her number, and his name was in her contacts. They never dated, though he did fit her let-me-remake-you type of temporary boyfriend. Her friends knew of Brendan mostly because the campus was not that big, but they didn't remember ever meeting him or hearing Emily mention his name.

Brendan's text led to a review of phone records, which led to interviews with people on campus and in the town of Brunswick. One person who worked at a gelato place on Main Street knew Brendan and remembered seeing him with Emily more than once, though he couldn't say for sure when or if the two looked like they were on dates.

A few logic leaps later, the police declared Brendan the spurned former friend, possibly boyfriend. And their top suspect.

Brendan grew up in farm country, Lancaster County, Pennsylvania. The only child of two high school teachers. People described them as good parents who maybe coddled Brendan too much. He came later in their lives after years of yearning for children, only to have every hope end in miscarriage. They considered him a precious miracle and were devoted to making him happy.

They never forced him to join teams or even play outside. They accepted their son as someone who preferred to be alone and get lost in the stories in his head. From the time he could hold a pencil, Brendan designed and wrote his own comic strips. His love for computers eventually edged out his other interests. Dreams of art school turned into plans for a career that merged his love for graphics and computers.

Though the press would later describe him as a loner and paint him with an outcast veneer reminiscent of so many high school shooters, Brendan was well-liked. Shy, but he had friends in the computer science department at Bowdoin. None of them ever saw Emily with Brendan or heard him talk about her. All were surprised they'd exchanged phone numbers. No one could pinpoint when or how that happened.

Brendan had the same roommate for his freshman and sophomore year. That roommate called Brendan a "nice guy" but quiet. He stayed in his room gaming and talking online. His closest friend happened to be a cousin by marriage who went to school in New York. They relied on their shared passion for computers to stay in touch. The friend was adamant that Brendan didn't have feelings, unrequited or otherwise, for Emily.

The police had hoped to unbury a hidden treasure trove of emails and text messages between Emily and Brendan, but only that one existed. Brendan didn't even make an appearance in Emily's secret diary.

Whispers shifted to finger-pointing. Despite the lack of credible evidence tying them together, people decided Brendan and Emily had clashed, culminating in a horrifying escalation that ended with her death.

Brendan and Emily's lives become inextricably merged. No one referenced one without referencing the other. At twenty, and without any proof other than one text, Brendan became *the boy who probably killed that girl.*

The drumbeat of accusations grew louder each day as the press and true crime addicts physically and virtually hounded Brendan. He denied any involvement. Insisted that life-defining text was a misunderstanding about a school project. A dramatic text on his part because he tended to be intense when he explained things, but innocuous.

The public and police didn't believe him. His beloved computer—his sanctuary and his safe space—became a battlefield. Comment sections berated him. People called him a killer. There were calls to investigate whether other women were missing in the area.

An answer had been declared and people told him to confess. He had a crush. He threatened her. He killed her. Solved.

The whirlwind of bad press whipped up from speculation to frothing demands for his arrest. His parents hired a lawyer. All the adults in Brendan's life told him things would be fine and vowed retribution against the unknown person who leaked his name to the press.

None of those calls to action ended with Brendan hauled away in handcuffs. Two weeks after a forensic team fished Emily's body out of the New Meadows River a truck driver spied Brendan's body on the rocks under the Frank J. Wood Bridge.

The untimely deaths bound the college students' stories together forever.

CHAPTER TWENTY-FOUR

ALEX

Numb and wet from the start of the downpour, they shuffled into the great room. They grabbed blankets and towels from the downstairs linen closet and sat bundled in groups of two on the sectional sofa again. For a few minutes no one spoke. The only sound came from the fierce winds rattling the walls of the house and the driving rain pinging against the windows as the bellowing storm raged.

Alex knew he had to take control of the conversation and fast. The truth about what they did—what really happened—had been trampled on and hidden for so long. Letting it slip out now, by accident or out of panic, would make the sacrifices of the last twelve years meaningless. He had too much to lose, including his family. Zara depended on them. Admitting the pieces they knew would condemn them all and destroy her.

"It was graduation night." He wanted to stop the second after he started. Not talking about this, pretending the pain happened to different people in a different time, had been the fallback position for so long. Now he understood why Cas fought every whisper and every mention of that horrible night and the weeks that followed. Opening this door stole a piece of him. "The ceremony was in the afternoon. We had this big celebration with relatives and friends after the formal program ended."

"We?" Ruthie asked without judgment.

Alex assumed she was trying to understand the players and ran with that to prevent a renewed battle between Ruthie and Cassie over a misplaced word or manufactured slight. "Mitch and Emily. Cas and me. Will and Jake, plus some assorted friends, but mostly the six of us."

Cassie nodded. "We had a meal and agreed to meet back up to toast graduation, which meant party and get hammered."

Sierra frowned at Mitch but didn't say anything.

Alcohol, the easy answer to every horror that unfolded that night. In those moments when he fell deep into brooding and the guilt swamped him, Alex knew better. "We started at the apartment Will and I shared but the party spilled into the street. We visited other parties. Plowed those drinks. Stumbled and laughed. Bickered about stupid shit."

Cassie squeezed his hand before taking over. "We piled into cars, which we shouldn't have done, but that was the least of the sins committed that night. A bunch of us, our group and other friends, went to Smith Boathouse, on the river where . . ."

"Where they found Emily days later," Mitch finished.

They'd already talked longer about this than Alex wanted to. He tried to drag them to the finish line with as few details as possible. Too much information would derail them, possibly rip apart every ragged tear they'd sewn together that night. "After a few hours of partying, the crowd died down. Mitch drove this small pickup truck. We piled into the back, including Emily. There's a museum on campus. Mitch dropped us there."

"And that's the last we saw her." Will shrugged. "On the museum steps."

"No one left campus with her or walked her home?" Sierra asked.

Alex could hear the *if only*s and *what if*s in Sierra's voice. The same unspoken blame he'd pummeled himself with for years. "We were all sort of wandering around at that point, trying to sober up and either meet up with relatives or get enough sleep to look presentable for a brunch Emily's parents were throwing for us the next morning."

"Wait." Ruthie held up a hand to stop the swirl of conversation. "So, you all went off in different directions and left Emily on the steps?"

"It's not as if we left her in an abandoned parking lot," Cassie explained. "It was graduation weekend. People walked around and sang and . . . Look, she was not alone."

"I don't remember how I got home." Alex said the lie without thinking. It slipped out as if lying had become his full-time fucking job. He hated so much about his life starting with that night, but his ability to compartmentalize and justify was what scared the hell out of him. "Cassie and I probably did what dating drunk college grads do on graduation night."

She rolled her eyes. "Yes, we did. The next morning, we woke up a mess and stumbling around with headaches and had to shower and get dressed up and go. We got to the brunch but Emily wasn't there."

Alex nodded. Saying anything else, letting even a sliver of light into the darkness they'd all plunged their memories into, could unravel it all.

"What about you?" Ruthie said, looking at Mitch. "Do you remember details or is it hazy for you, too?"

"I offered to take everyone home, but they wanted to stop on campus and then walk to their respective places. All but Jake, so we left."

Ruthie frowned. "And?"

"That's it. We got some food and went home." Mitch leaned back into the couch cushions with his leg pressed tight against Sierra's.

Cassie squeezed Alex's hand again. The small move eased some of the tension spilling through him. They'd provided a stark outline of what happened that night long ago. Not that different from what they'd told the police, but none of it explained being hunted this weekend.

"So, no one heard from Emily again?" Ruthie looked around the room, studying every one of their faces, even Sierra's. "You all scurried off and Emily was alone and vulnerable."

Cassie let out one of her I'm-done-with-this exhales. "Don't judge us."

Ruthie shrugged. "I'm trying to understand."

"Hope you have better luck because we've been trying for twelve years."

Ruthie's eyes narrowed at Mitch's comment. "The police thought you killed her."

"Ruthie. What the fuck?" Will tugged at Ruthie's arm, trying to get her to sit back or shut up.

Alex hoped she'd take the hint.

"No, she's right to ask. I would want to know if I were her." Mitch waved off all concern. "I was questioned. Emily kept a diary and for some reason Jake and I were mentioned in it, so we both got called in and interrogated for hours."

"Back then the security video system on and around campus wasn't as extensive as it is now, but the police saw Mitch's truck near the museum for the drop-off. That plus the diary reference led them straight to him," Will said.

Mitch made an odd sound. "Having a killer for a mother probably didn't help my case."

"What did the diary say about you?" Sierra almost whispered the question.

Whether to keep her calm or forge a connection, Mitch put his hand on her leg. "The police insinuated stuff, asked if I had a crush on her. It's a blur."

Ruthie frowned at him. "Come on. Really?"

"Yeah, you'd think my second time as a murder suspect would have been easier." He stared at Ruthie for a few beats before continuing. "A photographer snapped a picture of me coming out of the police station early in the morning and that reignited all the online shit about my mother."

Alex jumped in because he didn't want Mitch to get mentally thrown back in time. Protecting Mitch, shielding him from loads of paralyzing crap, turned out to be a hard habit to break. "The police were checking phone records and camera footage when the focus on Mitch and Jake stopped and that text from Brendan Clarke leaked. He'd threatened Emily."

"He jumped off a bridge after being questioned," Cassie explained in a flat voice. "He landed on the rocks. Most people thought the suicide proved his guilt."

Alex was done. Time to shut the whole thing down. "That's

all we know. The investigation stopped. Whatever evidence the police collected clearly showed Brendan killed Emily. It was awful and abrupt, but none of it explains why Tyler is dead now."

"Of course it does." Ruthie snorted. "One of you thinks Mitch killed Emily and is pushing him to confess."

CHAPTER TWENTY-FIVE

RUTHIE

Everyone froze.

"You don't know when to stop." Cassie's cool voice chilled the room.

Ruthie was not in the mood for Cassie now or ever. "I didn't say I believed Mitch did anything wrong. I'm saying one of you does. That's the only way Tyler's murder makes sense."

She'd looked at this terrifying mess from every angle. Pulled apart what she knew and focused on what she didn't. If one of these supposed friends thought Mitch killed Emily and got away with it, framing him for Tyler's death would be a good way to turn Mitch's world upside down and shake the truth loose. Drag him out of his comfort zone and ramp up the tension. Take away any tools he had to control his anxiety then destroy what little control he thought he possessed.

After all, that last part described her exact plan for all of them this weekend. It wouldn't surprise her if someone else created the same playbook.

Mitch nodded. "My mother is a killer, so I must be a killer. Is that it?"

His deadly quiet voice vibrated through the room. Ruthie

vowed not to let his sad backstory and that attractive face derail her. He knew more than he was telling. She could hear it in each carefully worded sentence he spoke.

"I've said this ten times already. I wasn't with you all back then. I'm trying to figure out which one of you arranged this nightmare before one of us, metaphorically or actually, joins Tyler in the back of that car."

"I appreciate the honesty," Mitch said.

Cassie slammed her wineglass down on the table. "Well, I don't."

The Queen of Deflection. Leave it to Cassie to muscle her way into a conversation and misdirect it. Ruthie saw the obvious behavior for what it was now—manipulation and ass covering. "That's shocking."

"Okay, no." Sierra shifted to the front of the cushion and threw her arms wide as if refereeing a fight. "Before you two launch into Round Two . . ."

Mitch sighed. "We're way past two."

"What about Jake?" Sierra asked. "Did he know where we were meeting this weekend? Did he have this address?"

Ruthie knew the answer and it didn't help them. "No."

"Actually." One word and Will commanded everyone's attention.

This asshole. Fake engagement or not, she'd spent weeks with him. She didn't love him because what they had was based on a lie, but she'd underestimated how limited he was when it came to relationships. She continued to be stunned at his lack of self-awareness.

Ruthie tried to rein in her fury. "You told me you didn't know how to reach Jake."

"I had his number and called." Will skipped over acting contrite and moved right to *this is no big deal.* "He doesn't want to be part of the group. I get it. The memories are harsh, but I was hoping, since this was about our engagement, he might show so I told him where we'd be."

Once again Will refused to take responsibility for anything, to dig a little deeper and understand the result of his choices. His inability to react or demonstrate having an emotional pulse tested her. "So, you lied."

"Not that it isn't important for you two to figure this out for your marriage, but . . . later?" Sierra winced as she asked. "I'm assuming Jake can travel. He has the ability to get here, yes?"

"He lives in Vermont," Will said in a voice now thick with tension.

"Shit." Alex shook his head. "I thought you were going to say somewhere overseas."

"Let's not assume Jake is to blame just because he was smart enough to avoid getting trapped on an island with us and a dead body," Mitch said.

"But how—" Sierra's comment ended on a squeal when the lights blinked out.

"Stay calm." Alex got up and went to the window. "Must be the storm. The wind is actually bending the trees. The electricity is probably out all along the coast."

"Sure," Cassie said as she snuggled tighter into the blanket wrapped around her.

"It will click back on," Will said.

Ruthie knew better. She'd studied the house. She knew about the alarm and the sprinklers. She also knew one very important thing the rest of them didn't. The house had a backup generator and for some reason it hadn't turned on.

CHAPTER TWENTY-SIX

SIERRA

The mood of the room shifted from strained to chaos. The mix of darkness and uneasy questions gave way to frenzy. They all stood up. The unspent energy had them milling around and bumping into each other like startled cattle. Will used the lighter on the mantel to light the decorative candles there and on the coffee table. The flickering added to the precarious ambience.

A few of them turned on the flashlights on their phones but then decided they needed to conserve the batteries. They agreed to wait to use phones if the lights didn't come back on within the hour.

A crack of thunder rang out. It sounded close enough for the next one to be a roof strike. They all stilled and waited. For what, *who knew?* The tension clawed and batted at Sierra until she shrugged off the blanket Mitch had thrown around her shoulders. She needed to be agile. Ready to run.

Mitch started to say something, but a flash of lightning cut off his words. The sky lit up the world outside the window in a hazy diorama of misshapen forms before plunging into darkness again.

Alex leaned in until his forehead almost touched the windowpane. "Did you see that?"

Four haunting words Sierra never wanted to hear. She dreaded the answer even more.

"A shadow or . . . Hell, I don't know." Alex put his hand against the glass. "It looked like someone running."

An icy chill moved through Sierra. She closed her eyes and she tried to hum the idea of an unknown attacker out of existence but screaming panic filled her brain. Thoughts jumbled until all she could do was mentally beg for mercy.

"It's nothing." Definitely not, she thought. Only pieces of debris blowing across the island. Nothing was out there. Just water and leaves . . . despair and isolation.

"This isn't the time for jokes, guys," Ruthie said in a clipped voice.

"He's not kidding." Will joined Alex at the window. "There was something. It streaked across the lawn."

"A tree. Nothing more than a tree." Sierra's body listed to one side, forcing her to fight for balance.

"Where was this?" Mitch took a step toward the other men, but Sierra pulled him back to her side. Latched on to his arm in a clench that made him glance at her.

"We all need to stay in here. Find weapons." She looked around for that fireplace poker. Did she leave it at the garage? *Where the hell did it go?*

Cassie picked up her wineglass but put it back down again without taking a drink. "It's okay."

"It's clearly not okay." Mitch took another step toward the window, this time dragging Sierra along with him. "Do you see the person out there now? Show me."

Instead, Alex looked at Ruthie. "What's in that oversized shed?" When she didn't immediately answer he snapped his fingers. "Ruthie. Talk to me. Boats? Gardening equipment?"

She shook her head as if trying to clear her mind. "What are you—"

"We toured the island yesterday, just to see what else was here, but the shed was one of the locked buildings. We couldn't look inside and none of the keys the owners left us would open the door," Will said.

Mitch blew out a ragged breath. "Just like the garage and look how that turned out."

The owners. The words touched off a memory. A question Sierra wanted to ask but the thought slipped out again. Her mind was too scrambled to latch on to anything logical right now.

"Everyone, stop." Cassie stood in the middle of the room, looking every inch the calm, in-control mom. "We're all on edge. I feel it, too, but it's just the storm. Bad weather makes things extra creepy." Thunder picked that moment to crackle and drown out her voice. She waited until it died down again. "Don't let your imaginations run wild."

Alex glanced at her. "But, Cas. There's a dead—"

"No." Cassie's voice rose and bobbled. "You heard me. It's only a storm. A little rain."

Fissures. Cracks. Sierra watched Cassie's slick outer shell break then disintegrate. The frazzled tone and pleading in her eyes. Fear tugged and pulled at her even as she fought it.

Ignoring the last few hours of bickering and bossiness, Sierra extended her hand. Cassie stared at it for a few seconds then grabbed on to it.

The cacophony of wind and thunder rolled over the island.

The shrieking melody had them crowding closer together. They jumped at every lightning strike and creaking noise.

During a brief lull Alex looked at Cassie. "I'm going out there."

"Have you lost your mind?" Sierra could hear her rising panic. The terrible idea didn't help to put her at ease.

Sierra felt a tremble move through Cassie, who stared back at her husband without saying a word, as if silently begging him not to play the hero. That made sense to Sierra. Before the storm and nightfall—maybe they should have done a quick look around outside. Gone out as a group. They'd had a fighting chance back then. The uneven terrain and the roiling cold water were enough of a deterrent now without adding in the horrifying reality of a stalker lurking out there.

"Don't be a dumbass." Mitch's tone matched his words. "Do we even know how Tyler died? I didn't do an examination, did you? A person could be out there with a knife or a gun."

Alex exhaled in a way that suggested he was about to do something really not smart. "Someone is playing games with us."

"Yeah, and that someone killed Tyler," Ruthie shot back.

"Come on, man. You can't out-macho a bullet." Mitch's voice took on a just-between-us-men quality. "Really, don't leave this room."

Alex shook his head. "What choice do we have? We can't wait to be hunted and picked off."

"No." Cassie dropped Sierra's hand and reached for her husband's arm. "Alex, no."

"I'm just going out on the porch, Cas. Maybe a few steps into the yard." He stopped for two seconds to kiss her then looked around the room. "With all these windows you'll be able to see me the whole time."

Cassie glanced out the windows on the side of the house then to the one over the sink. "There are blind spots."

"A few seconds while I round the corner." He quickly pivoted. "I'm not a martyr. I'm not wandering far. I just want to know what we're dealing with out there."

That sounded strong and fierce . . . and so misguided. Sierra tried one more time to dissuade him. "Okay, but there's no electricity and you won't see very far with the light on your phone."

"I saw a flashlight earlier." Mitch opened three kitchen cabinets before he found it and turned it on. "If you're going to do this asinine thing I'll come with you."

A screeching noise filled Sierra's head. Every horror movie she'd ever watched while tucked in a blanket on her couch rolled through her mind. "What is with you two and this sudden spark of misplaced bravery? Absolutely not."

Alex shook his head at Mitch as he took the flashlight. "You and Will stay in here. Watch the front door and windows . . . just in case."

Alex opened the back door and the brutal wind swished through the house. Rain pelted the floor. The temperature had dropped again, sending a chill air whipping against Sierra's clothes. The urge to slam the door shut and bolt it, put her body against it, overtook her. But by the time she regained her emotional balance, Alex was gone.

"Shit." Mitch scanned the room and finally picked up one of the three logs sitting in the fireplace. "I'll go get him."

Will was a step ahead. "I'm not leaving you two out there."

"What kind of testosterone bullshit is this?" Ruthie asked.

"Lock the door behind me. Grab some towels because we're

going to get soaked." Mitch issued the orders as he stepped onto the porch. The wind ruffled his hair and plastered his shirt to his chest and arms.

Seeing the storm rage, almost sucking him out there, jump-started Sierra's brain. "Please don't—"

Will's yelling cut off further argument. "Mitch! Get out here now."

Mitch took off. He disappeared into the night just as Sierra heard Will's next words: "It's Alex . . . I need help."

CHAPTER TWENTY-SEVEN

RUTHIE

W e're all going."

Sierra made the announcement just as Ruthie committed to finding the best place to hide until morning. She thought they should all side with her plan. "Screw that."

"No, Sierra's right." Cassie picked up one of the logs but dropped it again in favor of a small fireplace shovel. She held it as she faced Ruthie down. "I don't trust you, and I need to get to Alex. So, you're coming with us. No arguments."

Cassie, all five-foot-seven of her, stood in the middle of the floor with her hair and clothing disheveled, weapon in hand and eyes wild, looking like an avenging angel. Every move she'd made up until then seemed calculated to maintain control of the house and the conversation. This, the monotone threat and the grip on that shovel, showed fear. For her, for Alex, maybe for all of them. It was the first genuine emotion Ruthie could detect from Cassie.

"Or you'll hit me with that?" Ruthie thought it could happen and took a step back until her legs hit the couch.

"Between you and Alex, I pick Alex. Always." Cassie's eyes

cleared but the fury and panic still lingered. "You should never forget that."

Ruthie grabbed her phone and clicked on the light. "You win."

Sierra ducked her head and whispered, "It's going to be okay."

"Is it?" Because Ruthie couldn't see a way out of this that didn't end in more bloodshed.

Sierra sighed. "I have no idea."

Three steps later they were outside, and the storm spun around them. The rain soaked their clothes. Their sneakers at times slipped on the drenched grass and at others sank into the mud. They trudged and watched and stayed together. Even Cassie, who looked ready to bolt back in the house, now slowed her gait.

The howling wind made it tough to hear. Cassie said something but the words turned into muffled nonsense. Incomprehensible. Ruthie didn't try to decipher or clarify. Head down, she leaned into the slog.

The house provided some protection from the battering mix of water and gales. The hurricane-like conditions had them pushing forward, each step heavy and labored, as the storm tried to stuff them back into the house.

When they turned the corner, the whistling drafts came in punches. Each battering blow stole Ruthie's breath. She tried to focus through watery vision. Cassie dropped the fireplace shovel and fell to her knees. She seemed to be crawling. Then Ruthie saw the body. Recognized Alex's shirt.

Cassie reached for Alex. Her hands moved all over him. She was talking to him. Crowding in, Ruthie could hear the rapid *you're okay* being repeated over and over. Blood dripped from a wound on his forehead and his eyes stayed closed.

Mitch and Will pulled at Cassie, trying to lift her. They outweighed her and had leverage, but she lowered her body tighter against Alex's, as if protecting him.

Mitch slipped and fell on his knees beside her. His arm went around her. "We need to get him inside."

"No, no, no." Cassie wailed as she rocked her body back and forth over Alex's still form.

"The branch." Will pointed to a splintered piece of wood next to Alex's head.

Ruthie had no idea what that meant, but she agreed with Mitch. They needed to get inside and check Alex. She hoped he'd passed out but was fine. Dry clothes. A first aid kit. Those were the priorities.

They were all yelling directions that disappeared into the roaring air. Wet hands. Clothing weighing them down. A weeping woman. They shifted and grabbed until Cassie stood up, wrapped in Sierra's arms. Mitch and Will lifted Alex's torso off the ground and started dragging him. His head bobbed as his brown shoes disappeared into the trail they left in the mud.

The return to the house went faster. The wind at their backs propelled them forward. Ruthie hugged the fireplace shovel and one of the logs to her chest. All other weapons and thoughts of conducting surveillance vanished under the need to get Alex inside.

As they neared the porch the shed door flew open and slammed against the side of the small building. The banging sound traveled a good thirty feet and rose above the din. The noise also stopped their final push inside.

"It's the wind." Will nodded, satisfied with his explanation.

They continued. Grunts mixed with Cassie's panicked mewing. The pathetic sound sliced through Ruthie. No matter how little she trusted Cassie and Alex, they were married. Cassie's panic for Alex sure looked genuine. She seemed so self-focused, but she obviously did love him.

Once inside the house again, Ruthie and Sierra dragged supplies out of the linen closet. They had pillows and blankets piled on the couch as Cassie stripped Alex's wet shirt off and the other men laid him down.

"Was he ambushed?" Ruthie asked the question that had been trapped inside since they took off on their thankless excursion.

Will shook his head. "I think it was an accident."

What was it Cassie kept shouting earlier? *Convenient.* "How is that possible?" Ruthie couldn't see it.

Will dried his hair with a towel. "It looked like a tree branch snapped and fell on him."

"While a killer is running around the island? No, it's more likely he was attacked," Sierra said.

Ruthie appreciated the combination of confusion and sarcasm in Sierra's voice. A simple weather-related mishap sounded too easy. But no one had attacked the rest of them out there either. They'd been wet and distracted, basically disarmed and vulnerable, worrying over Alex. The perfect targets. If someone wanted to hurt them, that was the time. Use the storm and the darkness as cover.

Bang. Bang.

Cassie stopped fussing over Alex. "What the hell is that noise?"

"That shed door." Mitch took a towel off the pile as he balanced on the sofa's armrest. "I guess the wind snapped the lock."

Again, convenient. The coincidences piled up and threatened to tumble over. Ruthie didn't know why this group always missed the obvious.

"If there's a portable generator it might be in the shed," Mitch said.

The easy way he offered the comment put Ruthie on the defensive. "Why do you say that?"

"It's where I'd keep it." He shrugged. "It can't get wet. It can't operate in an enclosed space either. So, you drag it out when you need it. Except for the rain, the picnic pavilion near the back porch would be the ideal spot."

She was about to question his sudden wealth of generator knowledge when she remembered his job. He sometimes worked on construction sites. Worked outside. He probably worked with the machines all the time.

"This is all supposition." Will dropped the towel and headed for the kitchen. "Wait, where's the house manual? That should say if there's a backup generator on the island."

Shit. This would lead to more speculation and mistrust, but . . . "There is. A generator . . . on the property."

Cassie stopped drying Alex's face and trying to shake him awake. "Were you planning on sharing that information?"

"I didn't remember seeing anything marked 'generator' and we couldn't open the shed, so it was irrelevant." And that was the truth. Well, part of it. She also didn't know anything about generators and assumed it would come on automatically. That one of the people in this room had sabotaged it. Waiting them out, trying to figure out which one of them did it had seemed like the smart choice. Now it had backfired on her.

Cassie stared at Ruthie. For a few seconds Cassie didn't say a word. "We need it now. I'm not sure about the rain part, but we don't have enough light and we might need to hunt down medical supplies and—"

"I'll go." Mitch's voice cut through the growing tension in the room.

Sierra made a choking sound. "Since when are you so big on volunteering?"

Mitch glanced at Alex's still-unmoving body. "I saw a bag blowing around out there. That explains the person they thought they saw."

"And the dead body in the trunk? Does a bag explain that?" Sierra asked.

"We need power." Mitch moved closer to Sierra. Acted as if it were just the two of them as he tried to convince her. "I also want to look for anything that might help us get off the island as soon as morning comes."

Cassie turned back to Alex. She checked his pulse and buried him deeper in covers.

Sierra watched it all before unwrapping the blanket around her. "I'll go with you." She shot Mitch a look that suggested he should concede. "It's not negotiable, so don't whine about it."

"The four of us will go," Will said before anyone could complain.

"Please hurry." Cassie sounded desperate as she fidgeted and fussed over Alex. Not her usual angry, bossy self, but like a woman worried about her unconscious husband.

Ruthie didn't have the strength to argue with this new dangerous plan.

"Right." Mitch pointed to the discarded weapons. "Grab the log and the shovel."

They all headed out, shutting the door behind them and leaving Cassie and Alex alone.

Alex's eyes opened a second later. "We have a new problem."

CHAPTER TWENTY-EIGHT

SIERRA

Trudging outside for the second time wasn't any easier than the first. The wind caught Sierra's shirt and flipped it up her back. Her hair whipped around, blinding her until she yanked it away and it happened all over again.

Every exhausting step stole a bit more of her energy. The mix of panic and exertion had her gasping. Her anxiety burned through the few calories she'd eaten on the drive to the island, leaving her with only hope and adrenaline to propel her on the trek.

Her muscles ached as the four of them stomped and slid and wandered farther from the relative safety of the house. She glanced back at the dark windows with the wisps of light from the candles burning downstairs, but not for long. The gusts knocked her sideways and into Mitch. He steadied her by winding his arm through hers, linking them together.

Bang.

She tried to focus on the shed, on getting to the building and that damn slamming door. She used up most of her concentration staying upright, except a tiny part. A voice in her head that asked the same question over and over—was Alex's wound from an accident or something else? She thought about an attack by an unknown killer on the island. But a stray thought turned to a different answer, one much more devious. What if Alex had faked the whole thing?

Convenient. Convenient. Convenient. The word played on a loop in her head and refused to stop.

Bang.

They pushed forward. All four of them stood in a huddle as they made the journey that would have taken a minute in good weather. Her gaze bounced from the uneven path beneath her feet to the flapping door. Anything could be in there. Someone could have broken the lock, or even just opened it.

The flashlight Mitch had found and the light on Ruthie's phone guided them. The beams bounced as they walked. Ruthie mumbled something as she buried her head in Will's shoulder.

The closer they got, the faster Sierra wanted to move. Prolonging their time outside came with a myriad of dangers. Check for the generator, get what they needed to start it, secure the door. That was her plan. The bit of logic that broke through her fear.

Bang.

Mitch slipped on the grass right before the entrance. The swinging door almost smacked into his side, but he grabbed it in time. The move balanced him and sent her skidding. The thin sole of her sneaker careened with what felt like ice. She tried to hold on to Mitch but knocked the flashlight from his hand instead.

Down she went, hard on one knee. The landing thudded through her. It was like running full speed into a wall. The immediate shock of pain doubled her over.

"Shit!" Mitch's yell echoed through the empty landscape.

"Are you okay?" Ruthie reached down to help Sierra up.

As soon as the rush of nausea moved through her, Sierra closed her eyes. She struggled to stand as the rain soaked through to her skin and the wet ground drenched her knee. She inhaled, trying to drag in enough air to calm her racing nerves, but a sick smell hit her. Blame the tension tightening her body or the adrenaline high, but she hadn't noticed it before. Now it scalded the inside of her nose.

She opened her eyes and saw the flashlight on the ground. The beam aimed right at her leg.

"What the hell?" Will asked.

Mitch crouched down next to her. "Did you land on something?"

Her knee ached and every muscle screamed for relief but none of that explained what she was seeing. What they all saw. So much red. Too much for falling down. It puddled under her, making the grass extra slippery.

She lifted the hand she used to brace her fall. More red. Dripping down her palm. Oozing between her fingers.

The red flashed in her brain until she gagged. "It's not my blood."

CHAPTER TWENTY-NINE

ALEX

Don't panic. I needed to talk with you before I said anything to the others." Alex held on to Cassie's wrist. He didn't want to scare her but the way she jumped when he'd looked at her suggested he'd failed.

She shook her head as if confused. "You were faking?"

"No. I was out but only for a few seconds. The rest of the time I was listening and trying to think around this killer headache." A sharp pain sliced through his skull when he tried to shimmy his body higher on the pillows piled behind him. "Shit."

"You're really hurt. There's blood." Cassie switched back into nursing mode as she balanced on the sofa cushions beside him. "I don't understand. Did you fall?"

He tried to think of a way of delivering the news without scaring her. The thick fog in his brain prevented that. "Someone hit me."

"What?" She pulled back but didn't stand. "But they were all in here with me. Except Will, but—"

"There's only one possibility. Jake. This, all of this, has to be him." Alex made the mistake of lifting his head or talking too loudly or something because he got hit with a second shot of pain. "Damn. It hurts to move my head."

"Just lie there." She got up. "You could have a concussion."

That was the least of his worries. He wanted to tell her that but shutting his eyes and staying silent won.

He could hear her moving around the kitchen. Then came a rustling sound. A familiar one. The sound of her searching through the giant bag she carried everywhere she went. When he opened his eyes again she stood over him with a damp cloth, a glass of water, and two pills he hoped were pain relievers. He welcomed all of it.

Her warm palm slipped behind his neck and steadied his head as he drank the water. The idea of letting her wrap him in comfort and drifting off to sleep tempted him, but he couldn't risk the rest.

She made a face. "Are you going to be sick?"

"I sure as hell hope not." He decided not to shift or look around, or even think while she cleaned the blood around his head wound. "Fucking Jake."

He'd been their friend. One of the gang. They all hung out, they grieved . . . they made bad choices. But no one forced him to go along with the pact to stay silent. He might pretend now, but his right to revenge wasn't based in reality.

She lowered her voice despite their being alone in the house. "Did you actually see him?"

"I thought I picked up on something. The wind feels like it's hitting you from every direction out there." It had been more of an impression than an actual sound. He sensed someone hovering nearby, hiding. "Next thing I know I hear this crack and my vision blurred. I went down hard. I opened my eyes and saw men's boots . . . I think."

"You're saying Jake is out there right now with the others?" Worry showed on her face.

Alex put words to the worse-case scenario. "Maybe he finally snapped."

"This can't be happening. Why now?" she asked.

Guilt. That had to be the answer. Alex spent his days mired in it, getting sucked down and battling his way out. Jake had struggled from the beginning. A few months after graduation, he begged them to let him break their pact. He promised to take the fall. Over the years, Alex would visit with him as he unraveled, listen to him cry, then try to put him back together again. Anything to reinforce their bond and that promise of loyalty to each other.

He and Cassie paid for Jake's expenses during those extreme emotional downturns. That stopped when Jake cut off all contact a few years ago. After everything, being alone might have been too much.

Before Alex could lay out his reasoning Cassie started shaking her head. "But how do you explain Tyler? His murder links to Mitch, not us. Certainly not to Jake."

"All of this links to us. Mitch is one of us. Killing Tyler like this, with Mitch here, is the perfect way to aim law enforcement at him. To put pressure on him." Because Mitch would crack. He'd been through too much, wallowed in so much fear and confusion that when the truth finally slipped out it would rush out of him . . . and ruin them all. "The rest is obvious."

He turned his head without thinking, hoping to get a good look at her face, but the surge of pain stopped him.

She sighed. "You're going to do real damage if you don't stay still."

She had to understand how dire the situation was, right? "Jake cutting off contact. The revenge. Emily. All of it goes back to that night."

She hated talking about graduation. She claimed it only took a few words to mentally take her back to that place. The *we were too young to know better* excuse, already dubious as college students, lost all potency as time ticked by. Shock, confusion, alcohol might explain the immediate aftermath but not the ongoing lies needed for the cover-up.

Hell, he'd tried for more than a decade to block out the images. Nothing worked. Not sex or work. Not Zara or exercise. The memory would recede, slip into a dark corner, and sit there so long as he didn't poke at it. But then, without warning, it pounced. Crept up and played in such vivid color in his mind that he felt twenty-one and helpless again.

"I still think Ruthie is the director of this horror show." Cassie sounded firm.

But he knew his wife. They'd been together long enough that he could read her tells. The way her gaze shifted slightly to the left and her voice deepened but lacked emotion. She was trying to convince him, maybe convince herself, about a line she didn't quite believe.

"Where would Ruthie fit in?" He wanted to be careful with the words he chose because he'd picked up on Cassie's underlying distrust of Ruthie. The whole house had because Cassie didn't hide it. "Emily had brothers and we've watched them. From afar, sure, but the one on the West Coast doesn't seem to be looking for revenge for his dead sister. Same with the one in North Carolina, who just got married. Emily's family thinks Brendan killed her. Most people do."

"Okay, but—"

"Jake knows the truth." They couldn't outtalk or outrun that fact.

"I need to think." Cassie stood up again. With a hand on her head and her mind clearly elsewhere, she walked around in a circle.

"If he's on this island—"

She stopped and did that thing where she held up a hand in front of him. "Don't."

Alex couldn't back away from this topic. Not this time. "If he's here, he's looking to take us all down. We need to be ready."

"How?"

Even without the head injury Alex had no idea. He tried to come up with something—anything—then he heard a shrieking sound. High-pitched and loud enough to carry over the storm.

He glanced at Cassie again. "That was a scream."

CHAPTER THIRTY

RUTHIE

So much blood. Ruthie stopped screaming when Will put an arm around her. She could hear the noise and feel it vibrate through her, but until his touch she'd blamed the screeching sound on the wind.

"It's okay. There's an explanation," he said.

She almost lashed out at her useless fiancé and his useless platitudes. She might have if she hadn't seen Sierra's face. All of the color drained from her cheeks, leaving her ghostly pale in the flashlight's beam. Then Sierra bent over. Her body shook and bucked as she gagged. Mitch rubbed her back while scanning the area, likely readying for the next attack. Ruthie turned away because seeing someone else lose it like that would set her off.

The acrid smell wiped out the scent of rain. Ruthie held a hand to her nose as she stepped back. Will's body blocked her. He stood right where she planned to run.

"Is that from an animal?" Will asked.

Ruthie's mind had jumped to a much darker place. She grabbed on to his hopefulness now. *Please let it be an animal.*

"I can't see a damn thing." Mitch reached up and pulled on the cord hanging in the open doorway of the shed.

Will scoffed. "That's not going to—"

Fluorescent lights buzzed to life, highlighting the blood puddled at the doorway and streaked across the shed floor.

The unexpected blast had them all blinking. Ruthie glanced back at the house. No lights there or anywhere else on the property. Just the shed.

"Wait, did a breaker blow? Is that why these are on here but not elsewhere?" Such a simple answer. Why had none of them thought of that? They hadn't even checked. The tension had them flailing and skipping over reasonable explanations in search of dangerous ones.

Sierra lifted her head and looked at Mitch. "How did you know the lights would work?"

"I didn't." He sounded stunned. "It was habit. I go into a garage or whatever and see a string and assume it's a light and pull it."

That made sense . . . or did it? Ruthie was struggling to decide when she heard Sierra's sharp intake of breath.

"What is that?" Sierra asked.

The shed turned out to be part workshop and part storage. The blood smears formed a path inside. A battered rowboat laid on its side on the dusty floor to the left. There was a workbench with a few tools on the right. The basic stuff, like a screwdriver and hammer. Directly in front of them was a longer table, maybe six or seven feet. A large mass sat on top of it wrapped in a blue tarp.

"Animal?" Will asked but didn't sound confident of his guess this time.

Ruthie wanted to blame the panic bubbling inside her, but she thought she saw the outline of legs under there. Human legs. The size looked off, as if the legs had been tucked or placed into a fetal position. She hated all of those options, so she focused on the most innocent explanation she could think of. Supplies. A pile of house or boating supplies.

"Not an animal." Mitch stepped into the doorway and faced them. "You all should go back to the house. I'll handle this."

Ruthie refused to give in. "I have a hundred questions about why this light works and whatever that is." Ruthie pointed at the tarp. "The blood . . ."

Blood. The horrors fell like dominoes. One careening into the next.

"It's a body." Sierra didn't ask. She sounded shaky but sure as she gave voice to what they all suspected.

"Someone moved Tyler?" But Ruthie doubted the words as she said them.

"It has to be, though that won't make any of this better." Still pale but with a stronger voice, Sierra took a deep breath. "We need to know."

"We need to get the hell off this island," Mitch said.

Ruthie agreed with him. She thought that hours ago. Leave. Swim. Scream. Anything.

Sierra walked past Mitch but kept her hand on his arm as she moved toward the table. The bright light showed off the soaked-in patch of red on her knee. Blood stained her khakis and arms, even her hands, as if she'd rolled in it.

I can't do this anymore. Ruthie wanted to call Sierra back. They could grab that boat and get out of here. The lightning and thunder had stopped. If Ruthie had believed running would let her put all of this behind her and go back to the person she was even a year ago, she might have tried. Might have begged Sierra, the one innocent party in all of this, to escape.

Mitch and Sierra held hands as they glanced around the shed. With a nod from Mitch, they approached the tarp, tiptoeing around the pools of blood, and let go of each other to stand on opposite sides of the table. Bungee cords held the material on, binding the object into a shape that mimicked a folded body.

Tyler's killer wanted to torture them. Move the dead body around, keep them guessing. Every confusing move chipped away at their feeling of security until they doubted and bickered. Ruthie's skin itched at the thought of a killer watching them even now, plotting and wallowing in their fear.

Sierra clenched and unclenched her hands at her sides before unfastening the end of the cord on her side. She and Mitch shared a look before they loosened the binding and freed the tarp. Mitch pulled it back.

A head rolled off the table and onto the floor.

Human. Very human.

Sierra tried to take a step back but in the small space fell against the workbench. A second later she doubled over again and dry heaved.

Ruthie watched the horror unfold and grabbed the door for support. A body on his back with legs curled to one side. A hole in his chest. Not the same clothes as the guy in the trunk. And the head. Ruthie didn't look at it as she silently begged the universe for forgiveness for starting all of this. *Please let that be a mannequin or . . . anything but a headless human being.*

The sound of Sierra's retching filled the small room. The horrid noise touched off Ruthie's gag reflex.

All of the color left Mitch's face as he stared at the floor. Focused on the closed eyes and matted hair. "Son of a bitch."

"Please . . ." Will sounded unsteady. "T-tell me that's not a person."

"Not anymore." Mitch visibly inhaled as he reached for something tucked into the pocket of the guy's shirt. Ruthie didn't realize it was another note until Mitch turned the paper around for them to read it.

TICK TOCK

Ruthie almost screamed again when Mitch crouched down to take a closer look at the head. "What are you doing?"

He stood up again with a look of pure despair on his face. "He's not missing."

Ruthie didn't get it. "What are you talking about?"

Mitch glanced at the floor one more time. "That's Jake."

CHAPTER THIRTY-ONE

BOOK NOTES: EMILY'S FRIENDS

I t's impossible to investigate Emily's death without looking into the people who mattered to her while she was alive. A deep dive into her social media and diary focused the search. She obsessed about a certain professor early senior year. The poor bastard got an unexpected visit from the police during a midday lecture in a packed hall. Whispers about an affair started right after, but it turned out he had no clue about Emily's interest and had a solid alibi that included being out of the country for a family wedding at the time of her death.

The other players in the game of Who Knew Emily Best neatly matched the list of people she spent time with during her last hours alive. A finite list of best friends. One other woman and four men. Will Mayer, Mitch Andersen, Alex Greene, Jake Parker, and Cassie Holder, now Cassie Greene. An indivisible group that for four years traveled as a pack and shared most meals. They met in classes or bricks, the nickname for first-year housing at Bowdoin. In later years, they spent weekends hanging out either at each other's apartments, in town, or on weekend getaways.

They came from different backgrounds and had varying dreams. Anyone who knew the members of this little group viewed them as inseparable. But the look from outside the window rarely reflects the reality behind the walls. Friendships, like expensive houses, have an outward shine. Get an invitation inside and you'll see the imperfections. Dig around and you'll find the cracks.

With this friend group, every flaw and every argument took on the heightened ferociousness reserved for twenty-somethings looking at an uncertain road ahead without a map to guide them. Technically adults but vulnerable from their four-year cocoon in an environment meant to shelter, educate, and launch them.

Emily loved with a fierce sense of loyalty. Between the pages of the diary she thought no one would ever read, she described her friends both with terms of awe and disdain. In language that could be overly dramatic and romantic, or empathetic and mature, depending on her mood, she set out her thoughts, letting them form the final, biting statement about the person she was.

I told Cassie I'd been thinking about Mitch, about that dream I had, and she jumped all over me. Told me to leave him alone. Why does she get to decide? I guess turning Alex from a hottie to a simpering loser who all but wipes her ass makes her think she's in control of every other guy on campus. I get it. She has this big life plan. With her, it's all about a job and money but SHUT THE FUCK UP, CAS. Nobody cares about your sad mom or your sister who turned out to be a washed-up teen mother with three kids, living in a trailer at twenty. I love you but you're exhausting!

With every line, Emily slashed into her friends to reveal what she viewed as their faults, at times embellishing them and at others forgiving them. She examined every hurt inflicted on her and others in the group both petty and significant. She assessed these moments through a black-and-white lens because she hadn't yet experienced the world of gray.

I've decided! Mitch and Jake are the most attractive of our group. I was watching them the other day. Jake does this thing where he has to be the funny one, but he's messed up. Can't blame him. My brothers make me want to hide in my room, but I can't imagine losing one because my drunk ass mom drove a car into a lake. And Mitch. He had no chance of being ok with that mom.

If the police hadn't focused on a killer so early, been so determined to put a period on the report that wrapped up the investigation, some of Emily's words could have been twisted. Inferences could have been made. Leaps taken. All of which might have pushed the search for the murderer in another direction and back to the original one. To a search of Emily's inner circle.

Maybe I just find guys with a dark side sexy. It's tempting to push them and see how far you can go. Discover how bad they really are underneath it all. Imagine trying to contain that!

CHAPTER THIRTY-TWO

SIERRA

Sierra wiped the back of her hand over her mouth as she stood up from a second round of vomiting. The quick change of direction knocked her off-balance and sent the small room spinning around her again. Between the dizziness, lack of fresh air, and suffocating closeness, her equilibrium vanished. She gripped the side of the table for support. Her fingers landed so close to the dead body.

The hours of fear and uncertainty had caught up with her. Her personal motto of *I can get through this and thrive* faltered. Any momentum, every ounce of calm, abandoned her.

"I have to get off this island." She didn't wait for agreement or an argument. She didn't want to see questioning looks, or worse, faces that showed only a mild discomfort at the sight of a decapitated person.

She raced around the other side of the table and grabbed the end of the rowboat while the others watched in stunned silence. Her sneakers slipped on the blood and the strain of pulling the thing burned through her energy reserves. She thought a few tugs would get it moving, but it weighed more than she thought.

It bumped along, smacking against the concrete floor as she yanked with each fumbling step.

"Sierra, no." Mitch put a hand on the boat, stopping what little forward movement she'd accomplished.

"Don't just stand there. Help me." Her arms ached and her muscles clenched. What felt like a permanent case of airsickness buzzed through her, but she kept pulling, trying to maneuver the boat to the door. "We can use this."

That was the new plan. No details or set destination. Just get in and leave. Figure out the next move once they were in the water and away from the pile of dead bodies.

A head rolled onto the floor.

She would never be able to unsee that.

"There's still a storm," Ruthie said.

Sierra would take her chances on the choppy water. "It's not safe in here."

Her cell phone. The thought popped into her head. She didn't have it with her because she couldn't get a signal. She hadn't eaten in hours and didn't have food or supplies. Alex's keys to the rental car could be anywhere. The weight of what she lacked nearly knocked her over.

"For now, we need to get back to the house." Mitch gestured somewhere behind her.

His expression was stark but he sounded so reasonable. So reassuring. But she couldn't trust anything right now. Fear held her in a stranglehold. She had to suck in big gulps of air just to stay on her feet. She'd never experienced a panic attack . . . until now.

She let the words floating through her head tumble out. "I'm not going in that house. I'm not staying on this island another second."

"I know we have to get away but not like this. Not in a panic in the dark." This time Mitch put a hand on her shoulder. "We'll go in the morning, low tide or not."

She wanted to scream at him, to shrug off his calming touch, but the last of her energy drained out of her. "Please. I can't wait."

The wind whistled through the shed's wooden boards. Another reminder of the dangers waiting to devour her on this island. Sick, winded, terrified. She needed to harness all of those into an adrenaline rush that might save her.

"Is a rowboat strong enough to get us off this island?" Ruthie asked.

A potential ally. Not a trustworthy one but right now Sierra didn't care. "It should float."

"Stop," Mitch snapped at Ruthie. "Don't encourage her."

"No, she's the only other person thinking around here." The revving inside Sierra wouldn't slow. She dropped the boat and pleaded with Mitch to listen. "If we use the location of the causeway as a guide, we'll be fine."

He looked at her like he thought she'd lost all sense. "It's flooded. Totally underwater."

"We have a general idea of the area. We can figure it out." The words flowed out of her now. Some of them made sense. Most of them didn't. "The water won't be as deep in that area. We'll travel and have the causeway a few feet under us for protection."

The actual depth and the temperature of the water were unknowns. A rampaging killer . . . that head . . . gave her no choice but to abandon logic and run.

"You know that won't work," Will said.

Fine. She'd rescue herself then come up with a way to rescue them later. But she needed Mitch with her. Needed him safe and away from this life-sucking crowd. She could barely stand without her sore knee thumping, but they'd manage.

Survive. The word played over and over in her head.

She picked up the rowboat again and yanked it toward her. The tip slammed into her chest, but she kept shuffling and dragging. A rough inside edge of the fiberglass dug into her palms. A nail or screw—something sharp—cut into her skin. She'd barely gone three more steps when Mitch shifted to stand behind her.

"Sierra, stop. God, please."

The tiny flicker of hope inside her danced as it closed in on extinction. She ignored his pleading and expressions of concern. Refused to look at Ruthie again to see her confusion or Will's skepticism. They could all rot here.

Sierra's muscles begged for mercy even as her mind continued to race. All logic gone, she moved on pure will. She dropped the rowboat and it landed with a crack. "I'm leaving."

Swim. So dangerous. The worst option and the least likely to work. Blackouts and notes, dead bodies and stupid games. Had they really been on the island for less than a day? Memories ran together in her head, crowding out every thought until only one remained. *Go!*

She pivoted around Mitch. Ignored the bile rushing up her throat and the way her sneakers slipped and slid. She ran out of the shed and into the night. The darkness closed in on her, but she could breathe again.

The driving rain had her turned around and twisted. "Which way?"

Mitch's voice rose over the howling wind. "No!"

"Stop her," Ruthie said at the same time.

Sierra zigged and zagged. She'd read somewhere about not running in a straight line if you're being attacked. Her eyes adjusted to the lack of light. The whole world plunged into a deep navy blue, filled with shadows and shifting shapes. She could smell the grass and the trees. The air carried the intoxicating scent of nature cleansing itself. Cold but clean.

Footsteps thundered behind her as she grabbed on to a tree trunk and used it to navigate a hill. One step then another. She picked up speed, but one unbalanced choice and her feet flew out from under her. Instinct told her to curl to the side to protect her sore knee. She smacked against the ground on her hip. Her body all but bounced down the slope.

Not knowing if her leg would hold her, she slithered from there. Kept her body close to the ground and used her elbows to move as Mitch called out behind her. Every thud against the muddy earth vibrated through her.

"Sierra, stop!"

The grass got swampier and the yelling behind her grew louder. Another wiggle and shift and gravel dug into the fleshy part of her palm. Water lapped and roared around her. She was close enough to dip her fingers into the bay or ocean . . . she didn't even know where they were anymore.

Mitch swooped in. Her body lifted off the ground and landed on his lap. She tried to squirm out of his hold, but he yanked her against his chest as he sat there in the mud.

Freedom loomed just out of her grasp. A sense of failure crept in. Rain pounded on her head and all around her. Desperate for relief, she buried her face in the folds of his wet shirt and cried as his arms closed around her.

"I can't . . ." She didn't even know how to finish the sentence.

"I'm so sorry."

"I should have listened to you." Stayed away. Never met these people or walked down the road to their shared and sordid past. She sensed Ruthie and Will huddled behind them. Sierra said the truth anyway. "We're going to die out here."

Mitch rocked her in his arms, as if oblivious to the downpour. "We're leaving as soon as the storm breaks and the sun comes up. We'll swim if we have to."

She didn't believe him. "Please don't let them kill me."

CHAPTER THIRTY-THREE

RUTHIE

Watching something as painful and intimate as Sierra's unraveling and Mitch's gentle coaxing started an ache thumping inside Ruthie. Seeing practical and determined Sierra brought to her knees, willing to risk drowning rather than be hunted, ripped the last of Ruthie's control away. Screw her plans and all that time spent dissecting them, crawling through their histories, and stepping through their collected lies. Survival was the ultimate goal now.

The way the head dropped. It had been unreal and horrifying, and every time she thought about it her mind blanked. Probably a protective mechanism her brain created to help her survive, and she was thankful for the brief reprieve from reality.

Will and Mitch lifted Sierra to her feet. She didn't fight them. She didn't say anything as she limped her first few steps.

The wind had died down to a normal storm-like heavy breeze. Annoying but it no longer knocked Ruthie sideways or held her in its grip. The rain continued to fall but they were already drenched so trying to outrun the drops seemed futile. They needed to keep Sierra up and moving. Between the limp and unruly wind-tossed hair, the clothes caked with mud and patches of blood, she looked feral. Eyes wild and searching the area with every step.

Ruthie fought to find normal. Her muscles shook and her dry throat made it tough to swallow. Danger lurked all around them. She didn't know where or when it would strike, but she understood the inevitability of another round. The faceless attacker was on a killing streak. He wouldn't just slink away. Not until he had what he wanted.

"We'll go inside and dry off. Check on Alex." She'd almost forgotten about his injuries while they were out collecting new ones. Every time they ventured away from the relative safety of the kitchen something huge happened. They'd been stumbling over dead bodies and strained explanations all day. Trying to make the inexplicable, the horrifying, understandable.

Will joined her at the head of the pack, constantly scanning the landscape for trouble. "Are you okay?"

He didn't sound shocked or scared. *How was that possible?* She wondered if he schooled his emotions or if he didn't have any at all. "No."

He continued as if he hadn't heard her. "We should look for the electrical panel. We assumed the worst when the power went out but maybe the storm tripped the breaker."

Ruthie didn't believe that. She still blamed intentional human interference. A deliberate attempt to shake them up and keep them off-balance.

"If it's innocent then explain the body," Mitch said from right behind her. "Actually, bodies. Plural."

"I don't understand who would want to kill Jake. And like

that . . . it was brutal." Will made the comment in a faraway voice, as if his mental wanderings had slipped out.

He and Mitch hadn't had a second to mourn for their friend or reason out the *why* behind his violent death, but now was not the time for this discussion. Not while they were out in the open.

Ruthie was about to make that declaration when Mitch answered. "The real question is who wants to kill all of us?"

"I can't believe our engagement party weekend turned into this." Will tangled his fingers in hers. "I'm sorry."

She didn't want comfort from him. The voice in her head whispered to keep her hands free *just in case,* so she let go of his hand. "Inside."

The distance between the couples grew. No one lingered, but Sierra's listlessness slowed Mitch down.

Will glanced back at Sierra. "Is she okay?"

Such a ridiculous question. None of them were okay. Ruthie couldn't believe he was trying to hold a rational, *normal* conversation under the circumstances. "Trying to leave might make her the most sensible one here."

"Will."

Mitch's voice made Ruthie jump.

Will slowed down. "What is it?"

"Grab it." That's all Mitch said then he fell back into position with Sierra.

"What are you talking about?" Sierra asked.

Ruthie wondered the same thing.

"Nothing. Just keep walking." Mitch had his arm over Sierra's shoulder and all but carried her across the lawn. "I've got you."

Ruthie felt sick for Sierra. Her love for Mitch had snarled her in this mess. She'd disintegrated in an epic, unguarded way. The breakdown had provided a peek into her desperation. Letting others see her that way, so vulnerable, probably felt risky now that she was beginning to stabilize.

"You two keep this pace. We'll get the door." This time Will grabbed Ruthie's hand close to her wrist. He walked at a faster clip, taking her along with him.

She jerked her arm, trying to break free. "Why are we running?"

"See the note on the door? That's what Mitch meant."

Ruthie saw it now. The small familiar square of paper tucked into the edge of the screen door flapped in the breeze. "The wind has been fierce. How could it stay on there?"

But she knew the answer to her own question—because it hadn't been there long. Someone put it there with little worry of being caught by the two people in the house or the four of them outside.

"I think he's afraid seeing another note will put Sierra over the edge," Will whispered.

Uh-huh. "What about me?"

Will ripped it down. Mitch was talking to Sierra, keeping his side of an inane conversation so as to hold her focus. Reading the note made Ruthie wish someone would care enough to protect her from all of this.

Who's next?

Another one? She crumpled the paper Will was holding. Balled it in her fist and mentally ran through everything she knew about this weekend. Finding the notes here, like this, didn't make sense, yet this was the fourth one.

Ruthie stared at it. It looked like all the others—same print and same paper—even though that wasn't possible. The notes had more than one creator.

She knew because she didn't write this one.

CHAPTER THIRTY-FOUR

ALEX

The door shot open and Will, Mitch, Sierra, and Ruthie walked in. Remnants of the storm clung to them. Each wore a grim expression as they shuffled lifeless and defeated inside. Dripping on the floor, leaves in their hair, soaked to the skin. Huddled together.

Alex tried not to move his head too much but what was all over Sierra's pants? The red streaks and patches looked like blood.

What happened out there?

"Are you okay?" Cassie sounded like a concerned mother as she rushed to Sierra's side. Whatever comfort she might have offered stopped when Sierra shrank back, as if trying to burrow into Mitch's side.

Before Cassie could say anything, Mitch shook his head. He headed for the stairs without stopping. "I need to get her in the shower."

Ruthie slipped past Cassie and walked up the steps on Sierra's other side. "I'll help."

"We need to check the electrical panel," Will said, calling after Ruthie.

"You do it."

Three sets of footsteps clunked up the steps. Alex waited until they were out of sight to ask the next question. "Sierra looks like . . ." God, how did he even describe that look? Glassy-eyed and lost. Beaten up and resigned. "Was she attacked?"

Will grabbed one of the towels they'd gathered earlier. "No."

Alex looked at Cassie. She was frowning, and assessing every move since the others had walked in the door.

"What kind of answer is that? What happened to Sierra out there?" she asked.

Will dropped the wet towel on the floor like a teenager who assumed other people would clean up his mess. He wrapped a blanket around his shoulders and sat on the coffee table in front of Alex. "Did you really slip and fall?"

Truth or no? Alex decided he needed to trust someone other than Cas. "I thought I heard someone then got hit in the head before I could turn around. It felt like a deliberate strike."

Will nodded. "The fireplace poker was out there."

"Where?" Cassie sat on the sofa's arm. The move put the three of them in a tight circle, but they whispered anyway.

"On the ground. I saw it a few feet away from Alex's body but was too busy checking on him to grab it."

Made sense to Alex. It never occurred to him that Will would take a swing. He didn't have a reason to. But there was one person who could have done it, and it was time to clue Will in. "Do you think Jake hit me?"

"Jake?" Will shouted the name, earning a round of frantic shushing from Alex and Cassie.

"It's the only explanation," Cassie replied.

Will frowned. "You're absolutely wrong."

Alex's head pounded hard enough to force his eyes closed.

"I know you don't want to hear this or think about graduation night, but it makes sense."

"Listen to me." Will leaned in closer. "Jake is dead."

Cassie's face fell. There was no other way to describe it. All animation vanished along with most of the color in her cheeks. Her mouth went slack, and those bright eyes dulled.

Not asking seemed safer but Alex didn't have that choice. "What are you talking about?"

"He was in the shed. He'd been . . ." Will made a strangled noise. "Someone cut his head off."

Cassie jumped to her feet. She paced along the back of the sofa without saying a word.

The pain in Alex's head turned sharp and stabbing now. The combination of surprise, sadness, and *what the fuck* had him reeling. "That's not possible."

"Trust me. We saw him. Sierra lost it and tried to swim off the island after, so yeah. Beheaded." Will's shoulders slumped. "But how did you know he was on the island?"

"We didn't," Cassie said.

"We assumed he tracked us down. That he couldn't live with what we did back then." Alex spent most days trying to forget. He didn't deserve forgiveness, but he craved it. Hoped like hell to earn it one day.

"We all live with it." The snap had returned to Cassie's voice. She stopped moving around and faced them down. "If Jake . . . God, I can't believe . . ." She shook her head. "The point is, if he hasn't turned on us and isn't running wild on the island, then who's doing this?"

"Whoever killed Tyler and later moved his body." Will's words slowed as he watched Cassie shake her head. "What is it?"

"I moved the body. By accident. Alex watched while I snuck out there to make sure the guy was dead. Because I thought maybe he followed us here and was torturing Mitch by pretending to be dead. Now I wish that was the answer."

Alex listened to her deliver the excuse and it rang hollow. The problem could be the thumping in his head or the fogginess of his thinking, but he would have sworn her explanation made more sense hours ago when she told him to cover for her.

"When was all of this?" Will asked.

"It doesn't matter." Cassie waved off the question and drove right to the topic she wanted to discuss. "The point is, there was no one else out there. Not that I saw. I picked up the fireplace poker at the garage. Sierra must have dropped it. I put it on the back porch. Then it disappeared."

Alex didn't understand that part. Why would a roving killer be looking for new weapons for his attacks? He should have what he or she needed on him. "Until someone struck me."

The entire house whirred to life as the lights clicked on.

"There's some good news." Cassie went over to check her phone but shook her head after pressing a few buttons. "Still no signal, so that damn signal jammer still works fine."

"The lights in the shed were working earlier. That means we either overloaded the circuit and tripped the switch or someone flipped it on purpose to keep us in the dark. Literally." Will suddenly frowned. "I was going to go check the breaker, but Ruthie must have done it."

Cassie dove in. "How much do you really know about Ruthie?"

"We're going to be married."

Cassie rolled her eyes. "That's not really an answer."

"You can't believe she's running around killing people." Will didn't pretend to be confused as he sometimes did. He liked to hide behind the practical and one-track-thinking engineer stereotype. Not this time. He jumped right to the defensive.

"Her story doesn't make much sense." A huge understatement but Alex didn't want to get bogged down, walking through each instance where her story had failed. The rest of them could come downstairs at any minute.

Cassie flipped back to in-control attorney mode. "How much have you told her about what happened at Bowdoin?"

Will shook his head. "I would never tell her or anyone."

"It might slip out." Secrets did that. Holding them chipped away at your decency, at your strength, and worse, at your memory. The lies expanded. New lies got piled on top of old ones until the line between fiction and fact blurred and the secrets found room to weasel out. Alex knew because he lived it.

"Never." Will's voice remained firm. "We made a promise."

Alex wasn't convinced. "And now one of us is dead."

Revenge was a nasty bitch.

CHAPTER THIRTY-FIVE

RUTHIE

And now one of us is dead.

Ruthie hesitated at the top of the steps when she heard the words. She debated storming into the room and confronting them about their covert conversation and dire words. But what did the sentence really tell her? They had secrets. Hell, so did she.

Theirs were about murder. She'd bet everything on that.

She thumped a little louder on the stairs, warning them of her impending arrival. "You fixed the power."

Will shook his head. "No. I thought you did."

She almost tripped and fell down the last few steps. "How? I've been upstairs, helping with Sierra and taking a quick shower to wash away the . . . you know."

Cassie took over the topic. "We're going to act like the electricity went off due to the storm and is now back on because the wind died down."

That amounted to a lot of denial. Cassie wallowed in it. Ruthie tucked that information away for later.

Will had other ideas. "Okay, but the shed always—"

"How's Sierra?" Cassie practically shouted the question over Will's voice.

Ruthie didn't want to think about an attacker wandering around outside or near the electricity panel. She didn't want to think at all, so she focused on the discarded towel on the floor. That looked like Will's handiwork. He lived in a perpetual state of emotional stagnation. A poster child for arrested development.

He was a grown man and could pick up his own wet towel. Being his fiancée was enough of a sacrifice. She refused to be his babysitter or his mother.

Since everyone in the room was staring at her, she flipped back to Cassie's question. "Not great. Sierra slipped and landed in a puddle of blood out there and then fell apart. I don't blame her. It was a miracle she stayed as calm as she did for as long as she did."

"Wait a second." Alex's voice grew stronger. "How was there a puddle when it was raining outside? Shouldn't the blood have washed away?"

Will shrugged. "It depends on where and when Jake was killed."

Ruthie refused to dissect the questions and comment. Their recluse friend Jake being massacred only a few feet away while they'd said hello and drunk wine was bad enough.

"We're done with that topic for now," Cassie said.

"*That* topic?" Alex frowned. "We're talking about the murder of one of our oldest friends."

"Another murder," Will said under his breath.

About time someone remembered. This group sucked at mourning. Only Sierra, who didn't even know Jake, broke down at his loss. The rest of them . . . frenetic with a distinct lack of debilitating sadness. Ruthie wasn't sure what they meant but she questioned their humanity. Of course, that wasn't new. She'd been dissecting and studying them for months. The way they forged ahead, not noticeably racked by guilt, disturbed the crap out of her.

"Let's make some tea. You all need to warm up." Cassie didn't wait for a response. She walked into the kitchen, clearly expecting Ruthie to follow.

Caught off guard by what sounded like a hint of genuine concern, Ruthie followed. The two of them buzzed around the kitchen, gathering mugs and heating water, and generally ignoring the fact someone was out there killing people only a few feet away. Cassie hummed, and probably didn't realize it, but the sound cut off when Mitch and Sierra walked downstairs.

Like Ruthie, they'd showered, dried off, and changed into clean clothes. Mitch handed Alex a new shirt.

Cassie broke the silence by holding up an empty mug. "Coffee or tea?"

"Anything warm. Thanks." Mitch guided Sierra into the kitchen before turning back to Alex. "You okay?"

"Killer headache but getting better."

Ruthie winced at the use of *killer*.

"No." Cassie pointed at her husband when he lifted his upper body off the pillows stacked behind him. "Don't even think of getting up."

"Just putting on the dry shirt." Alex nodded at Will to help him. The two struggled while Alex closed his eyes in obvious pain.

Mitch watched over Sierra as she settled on a barstool, then he sat beside her. "You could have a concussion."

"Probably." Alex's voice sounded deeper than usual, likely because it came slicked with pain.

They all sat there, pretending to relax, as they waited for the water to warm, the coffeepot to finish, and a new round of death to paralyze them.

"We need sugar." Cassie opened a cabinet door and started searching.

"I didn't see any earlier." Mitch likely meant when he went on the hunt for the flashlight, which now sat on the end of the counter.

Ruthie joined the sugar search because it gave her hands something to do. If she concentrated hard enough she might be able to trick her brain into thinking they were fine. That this had all been a disturbing dream or game gone wrong.

"I think you're out of luck on the . . . oh, wait. Found it." Cassie held up a small plastic container with a piece of tape on it that identified it as sugar. In the other hand she held a bunch of papers. "And reading material."

"What's that?" Mitch asked.

Cassie gave the first page a quick look. "It's titled 'Book Notes.'"

Book Notes. Everything inside Ruthie froze as a wave of new panic swamped her.

Sierra sighed. "I'd welcome any opportunity not to think for a few minutes."

"I vote with Sierra." Cassie gestured at the empty mugs. "Ruthie can pour. I'll read."

A strange ache started in Ruthie's chest. Anxiety, possibly? A blaring warning signal, definitely. This wasn't possible. "Maybe we shouldn't—"

"*Emily Hunt disappeared on Saturday of graduation weekend. No one noticed until Sunday afternoon.*" Cassie flipped through the pages. "Wait, what the hell is this?"

Those words. So familiar. Ruthie's stomach fell. She almost dropped the mug in her hand. In her mind, she saw it hit the granite and shatter into a thousand tiny pieces.

"Where did you find that?" Alex asked.

"It was in the cabinet." Cassie didn't look up as she continued to read. "*The recent college grad dreamed of becoming an investigative reporter, of breaking big stories, getting awards, and doing splashy interviews. Even ignoring her questionable talent . . .*"

Sierra put up a hand. "Okay, stop."

Will frowned. "That doesn't sound like Emily."

"It's not *her*. The notes are about her." Cassie's voice almost demanded that Will keep up. "Papers about Emily in a house she's never been to. About her death." She looked at Will. "I thought you searched the cabinets earlier."

"There weren't there, or if they were I missed them."

The conversation took off and Ruthie had no way to stop it. All of her hard work shredded in front of her. That well-thought-out plan went from practiced and studied to superfluous.

"Where did the papers come from? They're planted here for us to find, right?" Cassie shook the crumpled stack in her fist. "Someone needs to come clean and do it now."

Cassie looked at Ruthie. Ruthie forced herself not to look away.

No one said a word. Ruthie couldn't. She held the right answers, but only some of them. The notes shouldn't be here. The fact that they were meant someone else in the house was playing a game, and she'd become a target.

CHAPTER THIRTY-SIX

BOOK NOTES: DID BRENDAN CLARKE TAKE THE FALL?

Brendan Clarke was an easy target. He had few friends. While it might look like he fit the role of quiet loner, he had the love and steadfast support of his parents. A few fellow students and more than one professor vouched for him. People who really knew him insisted *but, he's really a nice guy* and *I can't imagine him doing this.*

We're all cynical. We hear those denials so often in cases like these that they ring hollow. Not genuine. Easy to discount. Sitting on our comfortable couches and scrolling on our computers, we think we know better. We've solved the puzzle, acted as jury, and moved on.

Brendan proclaimed his innocence loud and often. He survived hours of interrogation without coughing up an admission. He held tight to his story. He was home, alone, playing an online game. He wasn't a graduate, so he had no reason to roam around campus that night. He'd packed and was waiting for his father to come get him early the next week.

The friend who was online with him verified the gaming story. The other players verified. The company who ran the game could probably have verified if anyone bothered to ask them. No one did. That lone text to Emily sealed the case. Brendan's perceived oddity shored up the allegations. His suicide settled all doubt.

The ending was so clean, so quick, that few questioned it. But they should have. The case is notable mostly for what didn't exist. There was no discernible motive. No evidence, forensic or otherwise, to tie Brendan to Emily's murder. No witnesses. No one saw him at graduation, near the museum on campus where Emily's bag was found, or by the New Meadows River.

The police believed Emily was killed and left in the river. Brendan didn't have a car. He traveled by bike and there's no record of him renting a vehicle. So, how did he move the body? And where was the primary crime scene? None was ever located.

What the police did find was a shoe imprint in the mud on the riverbank next to where Emily's body tangled in the weeds. The size didn't match Brendan's.

Brendan lived in a campus apartment with an entry card access system. His card logged him coming back to his place from a food run around noon on Saturday, while Emily was very much alive. Parking lot security footage, while not conclusive, didn't show him leaving the building again.

The pieces, when taken together, painted a picture of a gamer guy staying in on Saturday night. Not an unusual thing for him. He dreamed of writing games for a living and viewed playing them as homework of sorts.

If he didn't kill Emily, which seems the more likely scenario, the pressure of being questioned and accused could have driven him to suicide. It's also possible Brendan and Emily were bound by more than a text. Both could be victims of killers who walked free.

CHAPTER THIRTY-SEVEN

SIERRA

Sierra's mind refused to clear. She'd been focusing on the rhythmic drumming of the rain against the house, letting it ease her back to reality. Now she heard raised voices and saw Cassie waving papers around. As much as Sierra wanted to fall into a blissful state of nothingness, that couldn't happen. Not when this group's secrets and lies kept crawling out and demanding attention.

"Let me see those." Sierra held out her hand and for some reason that stopped Cassie's agitated shifting around. Sierra wished she'd known something so simple would work earlier.

Her vision had barely cleared from the pounding shower. She'd let hot water wash over her, knowing it could clean the outward grime but never block the horrors she'd seen. She didn't even have to close her eyes to see that head roll across the floor. The body had been cocooned so that unwrapping the surprise would provide the kind of haunting memory that never went away.

The room fell silent as she scanned the papers. Not autobiographical, clearly. This was by someone who knew Emily or thought they did. Honest to the point of being sharp and mean in places. Written on a computer and printed out, so no hand-writing to test. No obvious markings to identify the author.

One thought struck her: this could be the note left to explain a rampage. Kill everyone on the island and drop this on the way out. Let it stand as the *this is why they deserved it* answer.

"Well?" Mitch asked.

She decided to lead off with a few facts. "I didn't know Emily. I didn't know Tyler or Jake. I know exactly one person here. You."

Alex shimmied higher on the pillows, this time with more agility. "That makes you more of a suspect, not less."

"Do you want to get hit again?" Mitch asked in a low voice.

Alex scoffed. "Did you hit me the first time?"

"Yes, please engage in nonsense instead of having a real conversation." Sierra shifted on the stool so she could see the room in one swoop. "That's what you all do, right? You derail the honest conversation, ignore the tough facts."

Cassie poured a cup of coffee. "I know you're upset, but—"

"Shut up." *Damn, it felt good to say that.* Sierra repeated the comment to see if she liked it as much a second time. "Just shut up."

"Excuse me?" Cassie's indignation filled the room.

"Your suddenly not-so-addled husband seems to think I've played the long game. That I masterminded all of this and have been, what, waiting for the six years I knew Mitch before making a move?" The last of the brain fog burned off and Sierra's energy returned full force. She would not let these people get her killed. "Do I have that right?"

Alex stared at her. "My point was, you might have an underlying motive. One we don't know about."

"Do you hear how ridiculous you sound?" Mitch asked.

Sierra appreciated Mitch jumping into defender mode. Most times she felt pretty secure in speaking her own case, but it was nice to have support, especially when the risks were so immense.

Will shrugged. "He does have a head injury."

Cassie and Alex both intrigued her and repelled her. They fit together. Sierra just didn't like very much about them. They seemed to love their daughter but barely tolerated each other . . . except for the few times when they stood solid and inseparable and clearly concerned about one another. They were a mess.

An underlying pulse of dishonesty emanated from them, and not just because they were lawyers. She couldn't read them, but she understood them. Their type—pretty on the outside, ruthless on the inside—slithered all around Boston. She'd been tripping over seemingly well-meaning-but-not-really people her entire life.

But Sierra didn't get Will at all. He should be horrified about how his weekend had unfolded and demanding answers. This was his party, after all. He'd lured them all here to introduce Ruthie, the woman he seemed willing to throw to the circling wolves every chance he got. He bumped along, going from one danger and horrifying incident to the next without much of a change in affect. Not fighting for Ruthie or for anything else. Not questioning anything about Ruthie, and he should have questions. The only word Sierra could think of to describe Will was *useless*.

Part of her wondered if his moves really were benign. "And you. Why here? Why this house? The house with murder victims littered around the property and strange notes about vengeance for long-dead friends."

Will nodded in Ruthie's direction. "She picked it."

Ruthie shot him a look that bordered on venomous. "Thanks for that."

"Anything you want to tell us?" Cassie asked Ruthie.

"I'm here to host an engagement party."

A nonanswer. Sierra noticed Ruthie excelled at those.

"And how's that going?" Mitch asked with his usual load of sarcasm.

"I'm not the one who knew where to look to find those papers." Ruthie smiled at Cassie in a way that said *gotcha*. "What's the word you used before? Oh, right. *Convenient*."

Sierra wasn't in the mood to indulge any of them right now, including Ruthie. "More derailing. Did you all learn that in college? Is there a class you have to take freshman year?"

"You've made your point." Cassie toasted Sierra with her coffee mug. "Clearly someone wants our attention. They have it, so they can say what they want."

"And tell us without killing anyone else," Mitch added.

Sierra was in mid-eye roll when she saw it. "There's a light out there. Down by the water."

Will nodded. "Yeah, the electricity is back on."

Sierra slid off the barstool and walked toward the back door. She could see the small bouncing beam. "I think it's a flashlight."

That got Alex on his feet. He stood up and immediately fell back down on the couch with his hand on his head. "Shit."

"Where's that fireplace poker?" Cassie looked at Will when she asked the question.

The side looks. The whispered comments. Sierra had enough of all of it. She unlocked the back door. Only Cassie's outraged voice stopped her.

"Where are you going?" Cassie was looking at Ruthie, who now stood on the steps.

Ruthie shrugged. "Upstairs."

"Absolutely not." Cassie put her mug down with enough force for it to make a cracking sound. "If you try it I will tackle you and drag your ass back down here."

Sierra looked outside again. The light was closer. She could see the flashlight now and the person holding it. A rush of relief left her light-headed. "It's the police."

Timing had not been on their side . . . until now.

"It's this guy . . ." Sierra reached for the card in her pants pocket, but she'd changed clothes. "What was his name?"

Mitch loomed behind her. "The guy from the garage?"

"Yeah." *A police officer. A way off this hellscape of an island.* "Thank God."

Cassie held up both hands, trying to direct the conversation and movements, as usual. "Wait a second. We need to think about this."

"Not this time." Sierra fell for that once with Alex. She'd learned her lesson.

She opened the door and could feel the rush of people crowding in behind her.

Cassie reached over, as if to shut the door again. "Sierra, stop."

Done with all of this, Sierra body-blocked her. "You can all tell the friendly officer your theories and let him figure it out. I'm done."

"How did he get here?" Ruthie asked.

Sierra opened the screen door and waved. "He had a boat."

"Blurting things out is too dangerous." Cassie's words rushed together. "What about Mitch and Tyler? Their shared past?"

Alex joined in. "You don't want Mitch to get in trouble."

The questions and arguments sounded rehearsed, which made them easier for Sierra to ignore. "You two are trying too hard to avoid the police."

He was close now. Maybe thirty feet away and walking under the pathway lights. Sierra recognized the hair and the face. He wore his uniform and a serious scowl that suggested he was not happy to be there. That made two of them.

"I appreciate the concern about my well-being but that was a valid argument when we had one dead body," Mitch explained. "Now we have two. I'll take my chances."

"Right. We're doing this." Sierra stepped onto the porch as a healthy portion of her panic drained away. She'd taken two steps when she heard Ruthie's voice from her position on the stairs.

"Guys? I don't see a police boat."

CHAPTER THIRTY-EIGHT

ALEX

Alex's mind raced with a tragic mix of fragmented thoughts and pathetic excuses. He'd spent so many years dreading the knock at the front door, worrying about seeing the blue flashing lights in his driveway and being hauled in for questioning. To invite the police into his world now, after only recently beginning to indulge in the fantasy that he didn't need to panic every single day, struck him as dangerous. But he couldn't come up with an alternative or a way to stop the inevitable.

Sierra and Mitch crowded the doorway. Ruthie hadn't moved off the first step to the second floor. Will blocked Alex's view to the outside, but he could feel the anxiety buzzing through Cassie. Not the sort of thing anyone who hadn't spent more than a decade reading her moods would notice, but he did.

The blinding headache kept Alex from moving too fast or stepping into the lead. Just standing up set off a new round of banging against his skull. He grinded his teeth together to force out the truth he needed them to realize. "We're going to be blamed for all of this."

Will didn't look impressed. "You're safe. You were injured."

"That's not going to help." Because Alex knew better. The killings now would shine a light on the deaths back then.

"If you have nothing to hide you shouldn't be so worried," Sierra said.

That just pissed him off. "Don't be naïve. That's not how the criminal justice system works."

Ruthie let out a harsh laugh. "Says the white guy who's spent a lifetime benefitting from the system and now dreams up ways to ensure his clients can maneuver around in it."

Alex's brain couldn't form a single response that wouldn't start an argument. He didn't have the strength or the time for that right now.

"No, no, no." Sierra almost leapt off the porch. "Where's he going? Not that way."

Mitch caught her arm and eased her back next to him. "Take it easy."

"I just rolled around in your dead friend's blood, so no." Sierra waved her arms. "Hey!"

The screaming screeched right across Alex's last nerve.

"What's happening?" Ruthie moved off the stairs. She was at the back of the group up on tiptoes, bobbing and weaving to get a better look. "I can't see."

"He's headed the wrong way." Sierra's shoulders fell. "Why can't he hear me?"

Alex could see the retreating figure now. The officer turned off the path and stalked toward the shed. The one place guaranteed to ratchet up everyone's anxiety. "He probably saw the blood."

Mitch frowned. "From over there?"

As if on cue, the officer glanced down at the grass, hunched down to take a better look, then stood up with his hand on his gun. He hesitated at the shed door before disappearing inside.

The rain continued to stop and start and the dark sky promised hours more, but the time for thinking and planning had passed. Any minute now an armed policeman would storm out, demanding answers, and pick away at every carefully crafted defense they'd manufactured and shored up for more than a decade.

"Where is he? I can't see anything but the open doorway." Sierra looked at Mitch as if begging him to do something.

"Unfortunately, there's a lot to look at in there," Mitch said.

Ruthie pushed her way to the front of the group. "I didn't have a chance to meet him before. I am this time."

"Ruthie, no." Will tried to catch her before she stepped outside but missed. "Come back in here."

"Why?" She turned and stared. Her gaze bounced from Cassie to Will to Alex. "What is it with the three of you and your need to hide things?"

"This isn't the time for drama."

Alex agreed with his wife.

Mitch snorted. "Seems like it is."

"Ruthie, don't make the situation worse than it is," Will said.

"Do you and Will even like each other?" Cassie took the verbal shot at Ruthie.

Alex guessed Cassie's goal was to throw Ruthie off, derail her from running out there, spouting theories and launching accusations. The longer they stayed inside, the longer they had to come up with a way to survive this mess. Alex hoped his brilliant wife was working on a solution because his brain couldn't keep a thought for more than a second before the pounding pain moved in again.

"You know." Ruthie took the bait. "Comments about being a healthy couple are interesting, coming from you."

Cassie spread her arms wide as if to say *come get me*. "Meaning?"

"You two are exhausting." Sierra shook her head before turning to Mitch again. "Let's go get him."

No one was thinking clearly. That was the only explanation Alex could come up with for that ridiculous suggestion. "That's an invitation to accidentally get shot. He's going to find the body and come out, gun firing."

Sierra groaned. "You watch too much tele—"

Bang.

Will actually ducked as the noise cut through the storm and traveled across the island. "What the hell was that?"

Alex knew. Not a door this time. A gunshot.

A body moved into the shed's doorway, blocking most of the light. He faced inside the enclosed space, but from this distance it looked like the policeman. He stumbled and hit the wall. His body rested there then slid. His knees buckled and down he went.

"Was he shot?" Cassie sounded stunned by the idea.

The body crumpled into a heap on the ground. The light slashed across his unmoving form. Definitely a police uniform.

"Get inside." Mitch jumped into action. He had Sierra and Ruthie corralled back through the door and into the kitchen within seconds. "Everybody, move. Now."

They all retreated to the false safety of the house. The door slammed shut and Cassie locked it. Without a word, they scurried around and checked the obvious locks before gathering again at the nearest window to stare out into the darkness. A crescendo of heavy breathing filled the room as they each shifted, trying to get a better look.

"Can you see anything?" Ruthie asked.

Cassie pressed her hand to the glass. "The body."

"Let's think." Will stepped back. "A shoot-out? He fired at the attacker and vice versa."

Mitch shook his head. "There was one shot and he's not getting up."

"No one else is coming out of the shed." Alex focused on the beam of light shining in the shed's doorway. He waited to see a shadow, a movement . . . something.

"Is it possible we were in the shed with the killer and didn't realize?" Sierra seemed to be asking herself more than anyone in the room. "Maybe the killer was hiding."

Cassie answered. "The shed isn't that big."

"You didn't see the body. Once we did, everything else stopped." Will's voice got smaller. "At least it did for me."

Trapped. Hunted. The words floated through Alex's mind. The closeness combined with the panic radiating off them and bouncing against the walls magnified every lurid thought. He needed to sit down. Find more meds. Grab Cassie and swim.

"What do we do next?" Cassie's attention shifted as she asked the question. "Where are you going now?"

They all glanced up, looking for the source of her renewed anger.

Ruthie stood on the stairs again. "We need weapons."

CHAPTER THIRTY-NINE

SIERRA

Sierra wanted to believe Ruthie was overreacting, but all the evidence pointed toward more violence. Someone out there had gone from killing to prove a point to killing anyone in their way, even someone with a badge.

They needed to be armed and ready.

Sierra headed for the steps to follow Ruthie. "I'll go with you. There might be something we can use on the third floor. I admit I didn't spend much time up there after seeing those photos."

"Okay, but there were tools in the shed. The garage would be the other place for anything sharp," Will said.

The frenzy of activity stopped. Only Ruthie kept moving. She disappeared onto the second floor.

Alex leaned against the breakfast bar, clearly still feeling the effects of whatever happened to him outside. "No one is leaving this house. We stay in here. Together."

Sierra didn't often side with Alex, but this time, yes. "Agreed."

Cassie nodded. "We'll take the kitchen."

She started opening cabinets, shoving useless items aside and stacking pans on the counter. Alex went to the knife block. Will, as usual, stood there, as if he needed a few more minutes to process the plan.

To Sierra, the rules seemed simple: there were none. Anything they could swing, throw, or stab with needed to be collected. They had to be ready to unleash them all.

"Hey." Mitch's whispered voice stopped her from taking another step. "If you hear anything start to go sideways down here, you stay up there and hide. Sneak out on the roof if you have to but then go."

"I'm not—"

"Listen to me." He moved to the step right below hers. Since he was a few inches taller that put them even with each other. "Do not try to save anyone, including me. Don't hang around for low tide to use the golf cart. Wait it out until morning or the storm clears, whichever comes first, so you have light and then swim."

He was trying to save her. She got it. In his head, he brought her here, but in reality, she'd insisted. Maybe not exactly, but she'd pushed him and landed them both here.

She touched the side of his face. It might be her only chance before their worlds exploded, so she gave in to the need. "We go together. I'm coming right back down."

"Don't." He leaned into her palm. Just for a second, but it was enough. Then he trudged down the steps and shoved Will. "Don't just stand there. Do something."

She'd always joked that she'd be the first to die in a horror movie. She'd curl up in a ball in the closet and wait. Go out first and save the heartache of running and watching people die. Now she knew better.

She blocked the panic from seeping in as she jogged up the

last few steps. She walked past the partially closed door to Ruthie and Will's room. The sound of Ruthie rummaging around floated into the hallway. Nothing unusual under the circumstances, but Sierra doubled back and pushed the door open. Ruthie sat on the floor, half in the closet, with a bag open on her lap. A bag Sierra didn't remember seeing earlier.

That's not what caught her attention. "You have a gun?"

Ruthie jumped as she reached for the weapon wedged under her thigh. "Sierra . . ."

Run. The word flashed in Sierra's head, and she didn't ignore it.

Ruthie got to her feet and lunged. She beat Sierra to the door by seconds. Threw her body against it to block Sierra's exit.

"Sierra, no. Please listen," Ruthie begged in a harsh whisper.

A gun. They came to talk about wedding plans and this woman brought a gun. Ruthie had been playing a deadly game this whole time, and Sierra still didn't know what it was.

She inhaled, trying to get her rebelling nerves to relax. She held out her hand, ignoring the small tremor running through it. "Give me the weapon."

Ruthie's grip visibly tightened on the gun. "You're the only person in this house I trust, but no way."

Sierra heard the tremble in Ruthie's voice. Not the sort of thing she'd expect from a cold-blooded killer who'd managed to subdue and kill men who outweighed her. Sierra didn't understand any of it. How did Ruthie manage all of this with five other people milling around? She couldn't have shot the policeman. Did the shed door open by accident? None of the pieces fit together. Not in a logical way that Sierra could follow.

She stepped back. Tried to use the panic flowing through her as fuel. The only thing that kept her from screaming for help was the pleading in Ruthie's eyes. Probably a ruse, but Sierra let this play this out while she tried to make sense of it.

She nodded at the gun in Ruthie's hand. "Why would you bring that to your engagement party weekend?"

"Look at what's happened. It's good I have it."

The dodge didn't build trust. "That depends on which side you're on."

Ruthie shook her head. "I'm not the one killing people."

She acted like her word was good enough. Like she hadn't lied her way through this weekend. Sierra's loyalty ran to exactly one person in this house. Ruthie had tried to build camaraderie. Sierra saw it all as bullshit now.

"You're the one with the secret gun at a celebratory event, which you have to admit is suspect." The scheme, whatever was happening here, had nothing to do with a wedding. Sierra hoped she didn't get stuck betting her life on that fact.

"You're smart, Sierra." Ruthie's tone changed. Gone was the panicky bobble in her voice. She sounded firm and genuine. "The smartest one here. Probably the only honest one."

Such complete bullshit. "There's nothing subtle about this suck-up job."

"Fine." Ruthie visibly changed again. This time back to the same woman who could out-argue Cassie, or at least take a good run at it. "I brought the gun for protection."

Sierra guessed that was the first honest thing Ruthie had said since coming upstairs. "From what?"

"That doesn't matter."

"It does."

"My only request is that you don't tell the others. Just for now." Ruthie gestured with her free hand. Adopted a friendly back-and-forth tone that ignored reality. "I don't want to get into a battle with Cassie over which one of us should hold my gun. The answer is me. It doesn't leave my side."

"One question. Did you kill those men?"

"I already answered that. No."

Not a violent protest. No long-winded explanation about how she couldn't or wouldn't. The brevity almost convinced Sierra. Except for one thing. "Was this weekend ever really about celebrating your engagement?"

Ruthie didn't say anything for a few seconds. "That's two questions."

"Answer anyway. Did you bring us here for a party?"

Ruthie didn't hesitate this time. "No."

CHAPTER FORTY

ALEX

Fifteen minutes later they reconvened downstairs. A pile of knives and heavy house furnishings, like a decorative statue and lamps, sat on the coffee table, guarded by Alex. He didn't trust anyone else to do it. Not even Cassie. He needed to be able to reach and throw without warning.

Everyone else stood guard at a window or door. They kept watch, blinking but not moving, waiting for the danger lurking on the other side of those walls to strike.

No one said much. Now and then one of them would throw out a question or a one-liner to stop their attention from drifting. Alex had lost his watch outside and the electricity going out meant every clock within viewing distance, most of those on kitchen appliances, blinked with the wrong time. He could check his cell phone, but he didn't want to move for fear the shifting would set off a bomb in his head.

They hadn't eaten or slept. He guessed it was around two or three in the morning, which meant they had hours before the sun came up and even that might not help because the storm raged on. Less intense but still hovering over the island, trapping them in their worst nightmare.

Cassie nodded to Will, leaving him as the lookout for two windows while she stepped away. She walked up to Alex and put her hand on his head. "How are you feeling?"

"Useless." He could stand but not for a long time. The room shimmered in front of him if he lifted his head for too long. So, he sat on the couch with a knife in one hand and a load of makeshift weapons within reach.

"Maybe we should take turns sleeping." Will made the suggestion as he glanced at the sectional.

He missed Mitch's eye roll. "Who could sleep through this?"

"A psychopath," Sierra said.

"Any chance you want to run through what we know again?" Alex expected Sierra to reel off the facts and get them all talking.

"No." That was it. That was all she said.

A sense of edginess blanketed the room. For a few seconds there the idea of a policeman wandering around the island had both scared him and given him hope. Now the guy was out of commission. The only possible positive outcome was that the one officer radioed others. If the storm ever died down they might still have that chance . . . but they had to survive that long. And after that? Alex didn't even want to think about what came next.

"Who did you rent the house from?" Cassie stared at Ruthie as she asked the question. "We need a name."

"As we wait to die," Mitch mumbled.

"Becky." Ruthie sighed. "She's a friend."

Will frowned. "Wait, who?"

"A woman I know." Ruthie stared out the window, acting as if she could hide from the questions. "She comes into the gallery."

Alex and Cassie shared a look. Cassie's said *I told you so* and

Alex thought she deserved to gloat. He tried to gather more intel this time. "Does this Becky have a last name?"

"Have you met her?" Cassie asked Will.

But Will's focus stayed on his fiancée. "I don't remember you talking about anyone named Becky. I thought this place belonged to a friend of your parents or something."

They barely knew each other. Yeah, that was Will's style. Find someone, overcommit, and drive her away. He'd confided a few weeks ago that he proposed to Ruthie so fast because he felt like she was dropping hints about needing more from him and he'd panicked.

The whole messed up relationship pissed off Alex because it meant Will had dragged them out here to celebrate another wedding that likely wouldn't happen. In Will's desperation to create a life that might lead to happiness he'd inadvertently put a target on their backs.

Will's comment hung there along with Cassie's question. Ruthie didn't fill in any blanks. Sierra didn't say a word. Alex tried to figure if those two things were related.

"Have any of your friends met each other?" Alex really wanted Will to say yes, to describe parties and dinners, so this weekend would feel less like a setup.

"Of course." Will made a dismissive sound. "There's Tara. That's her partner in the gallery."

One name. One friend. Alex could name Cassie's friends through Zara's school, or as she called them, The Mom Squad. He also knew the names of most of the women in Cassie's yoga class. The neighbors she liked. That's how a relationship worked. You talked about other people, exchanged stories, found ways to stay engaged.

Ruthie still didn't say a word.

Will seemed to take the quiet as license to fill them in on the gallery. "You should see the place. Ruthie sets up shows and works with artists."

"No one wants to hear about that now." Ruthie's sharp voice cut through the room as she glanced at Will but only for a second. "What time is it?"

As far as conversation pivots went that one sucked. Alex was not about to let her off that easily. "Why did we change subjects?"

"Yeah, I'd like to hear about the gallery," Cassie said in a voice that could only be described as too bright and too happy for the circumstances.

Mitch shook his head. "Maybe when we're not being hunted?"

But Cassie didn't back down. "We need to stay alert but be able to concentrate. A talk about the gallery and Ruthie's friend who owns the island strikes me as the perfect listening material."

"I'm not this evening's entertainment," Ruthie said.

Cassie made a humming sound. "But you are defensive."

If Cassie meant to ruffle and unsettle Ruthie, she'd failed. Ruthie just shook her head. "Probably because an increasing percentage of people on the island are dead."

"Has he moved?" When Will didn't respond, Alex tried again. "The police officer."

Will frowned. "What?"

"Jesus, Will!" Mitch shouted from across the room. "The guy on the ground. Is he moving? We're trying to figure out if he's dead or just passed out or injured or what."

Will glanced over his shoulder at the window. "No."

Not a surprise but Alex still hated the news. "Then he's probably—"

"I mean he's gone." Will backed away from the window as he delivered the news. "He's not out there."

"But you've been watching." Cassie took over Will's stakeout position. "How could you miss that?"

"I looked away for a few minutes." Will spread his arms wide. "You walked over there, leaving me with this whole side."

Never his fault. Will always blamed. Always had an explanation that absolved him. He stayed detached to avoid conflict. Alex could probably recite some psychological reason relating to Will's past for all the avoidance or parrot Cassie's thoughts on Will's blunted development but after a while making excuses for a grown man's behavior became exhausting.

Alex was two seconds away from strangling the guy. "Are you saying you didn't see someone drag a body—"

The doorbell chimed before Alex could finish his sentence. The noise paralyzed him. They all stopped doing anything other than staring at the locked front door.

Then the banging started.

CHAPTER FORTY-ONE

RUTHIE

Ruthie never thought she'd need the thigh holster when she bought it. Now she was grateful for that specialized shopping trip. Despite all the safety classes and all those hours spent at the shooting range learning how to handle a weapon, she didn't feel one bit prepared for the turn this weekend had taken.

Getting drenched going out to the shed had given her a reason to change clothes. She'd picked a flowy skirt for exactly this reason, but the strap hugging her leg felt so confining, like it was cutting off the blood to her leg. The suffocating sensation wasn't real. She blamed the people in this house for crowding her mentally and physically.

The unspent energy inside her ramped up as she waited for Sierra to spill what she knew about the gun. She'd ended the bedroom confrontation by walking out. She didn't say a word or make any threats. She calmly backed away, leaving Ruthie confused and spinning, dreading the moment the situation would implode into a rain of emotional shrapnel and forced secret-sharing.

But Sierra and her worries didn't matter to Ruthie now. The

door mattered. How fast she could pull that gun and fire mattered. Practicing on a stationary target without a pulse differed from this hellish experience. The former marines who owned the range and had trained her insisted there was nothing worse than being forced to fire on another person. Wrong. Waiting to die and fearing you wouldn't be able to defend yourself was worse.

They'd left their lookout positions around the room and crowded by the sectional. Everyone held a makeshift weapon. They looked like a mismatched neighborhood watch group ready to defend their rosebushes from invaders. All they needed were the pitchforks and shovels.

The banging started again. This time the sound of muffled talking seeped through the door. "Let me in."

"Do we?" Will asked.

Ruthie couldn't believe he'd survived in the world this long.

Mitch also looked stunned by the question. "Seriously?"

Sierra, who had been stoic and mostly silent since their run-in, shook off her stupor. "Can anyone get a good angle and see who's standing out there?"

"Not from here." Cassie had fallen into a sort of *protect what's mine* stance with her legs slightly apart and a log in her hand, ready to swing. She'd positioned her body in front of Alex's. He was on his feet but listing, depending on the back of the sectional to keep him upright.

They stood about twenty feet from the front door. Mitch shot glances behind them at the much closer back door. Rain pinged against the porch roof and spattered the windows. Streaks of water clouded their view, and the lighted path didn't provide any hint about who was out there.

Will should do it. Ruthie felt fine sacrificing him. He was the one person in this house she didn't trust fighting beside her in a battle because he'd reason out the angles while she got stuck protecting them both. She at least stood a chance with the rest of them.

She stared at him then nodded toward the door. "Try it."

"What if someone shoots through it?" Will's voice rose as he spit out the question.

"This is ridiculous." Sierra shoved her way to the front of the group and took a few hesitant steps toward the door.

Mitch reached for her. Even Cassie tried to stop her.

Ruthie didn't want Sierra hurt. Not the one innocent person in all of this. "Sierra, no."

Sierra ignored the shuffling and made it to the small foyer. She stood pressed against the wall to the side of the door and peeked out the thin strip of glass there. In theory, the reflective film allowed her to look out but blocked anyone from looking in.

The tension in her face relaxed a bit. "It's the police officer. He must have been unconscious at the shed."

"Is he alone?" Alex asked from the back of the crowd.

Sierra looked again, taking a longer peek this time. "I don't see anyone else."

"Wait a second." Mitch stalked up behind her. He gently maneuvered her behind his shoulder as he took a turn peeking out. "He keeps looking around, as if expecting to be jumped."

"I wonder why," Sierra said as if she'd borrowed some of Mitch's sarcasm for the response.

Boom. Boom.

They all jumped at the renewed banging on the door. Sierra grabbed the back of Mitch's shirt and seemed determined not to let go.

"Open up." The voice sounded far away but the order was clear.

"Right." Mitch motioned for everyone to move back and lift their weapons. "Be ready."

Ruthie wanted to ask *for what?* but she doubted Mitch had a better guess than anyone else.

Sierra stretched up on her tiptoes, using Mitch for leverage, and looked outside again. "He's holding his side. I can see dark blotches on his shirt. Probably blood."

"Move back." Mitch's hand hesitated over the lock. He closed his eyes for a second then opened them again and undid the bolt.

The door bounced open, bringing in a sweep of wet, cold air on a burst of wind. A figure stepped inside and slammed the door shut behind him. The lock slipped back into place as the officer leaned against the door, looking out the side window with his back to the room.

Ruthie tried to shift to get a better look at him but he wore a raincoat with a hood. The mix of grass stains, mud, and blood on his pants confirmed he'd been knocked down.

Sierra and Mitch stood the closest. Mitch hadn't lowered the log he held. Sierra seemed more concerned with other issues. "You were shot."

The officer didn't turn around or give up his position at the door.

Mitch's gaze moved over the officer. "And you were on the ground."

"Anyone have a weapon?" The officer got the question out through a round of coughing.

Sierra glanced at Ruthie but didn't say anything.

Ruthie barely noticed because the question hit her the wrong way. Her trust, already waning, performed an unexpected nose-dive. "Did you see your attacker?"

The officer stiffened before answering. "Only a shadow then the gun went off and I went down."

That voice.

"You should come in and let us check your injuries." Sierra gestured toward Cassie's purse and the piles of medicine and assorted mom things inside. "Sorry, I can't remember your name."

The officer dropped his hood and turned to face the room. "Dylan. Dylan Richter."

He had dirt-streaked cheeks and disheveled hair that had long ago lost the battle to the wind. His hand moved to his gun as he stared right at Ruthie.

Only one thought ran through her mind—*Not a police officer. Not law enforcement of any type.*

Now she knew what this game was . . . and more people were going to die.

CHAPTER FORTY-TWO

BOOK NOTES: THOSE SEARCHING FOR THE TRUTH

You can smother the truth. Bury it deep in a hole and cover it with rocks and dirt. Plant trees. Build houses and highways over it. Let the years pass and tendrils of memories grow up and around for cover as the earth devours the shattered pieces left behind. But the truth's tattered edges still pulse with life. Faint and carried in hints and promises to others, it survives. Through strength of will or out of pure audacity, it's there. Waiting to be uncovered.

Who would dig up the truth about what happened at Bowdoin and shine a light on it? There were, of course, those left behind. The ones who knew and grieved, as well as those who viewed the ongoing investigation as a calling. Family members, friends, detectives, and in modern times, keyboard warriors. People who spent their days and nights sleuthing and dissecting, watching and devouring true crime, questioning and analyzing. In groups or as a movement, they ban together and try to give that tiny flicker of truth air and breathe life back into the quest.

The truth-seekers never gave up on Emily and Brendan. They viewed with skepticism the packaged results that bound their deaths together. They poked at the holes. They asked questions and more questions. Over smirks by some outsiders and whispers about their "questionable" motivations, the murderinos persisted until the drumbeat of doubt grew louder and seeped out of their insular online world and into the general consciousness.

They had theories and timelines. Photos and a copy of Emily's leaked diary. Many pointed to Mitch and Jake as the *real* suspects. A few threw out names not previously mentioned in the public space. Nothing and no one were off-limits.

They got others interested in their findings and theories, and their ranks increased. They spent hours looking into the private lives of those who knew Emily and Brendan back then.

They drew attention. People who knew Emily and Brendan, and some who pretended to know them, crawled out of their dark spaces. The dedicated started a conversation . . . and woke a beast.

CHAPTER FORTY-THREE

SIERRA

Dylan. For some reason the name hadn't stuck in Sierra's head before. She bet it would now. She'd never been the type to expect someone to ride into trouble and save her, but this weekend—today—the concept sounded good. They needed an advantage and Dylan provided that.

His arrival meant two people in the room had guns. Sierra debated spilling Ruthie's secret and eliminating more surprises. They'd had enough of those. But, despite every new bit of information she'd collected, Sierra didn't think Ruthie was a killer. She wasn't a fiancée who ran lukewarm on the guy she planned on marrying either. No way was that relationship real. Sierra couldn't figure out how to make those two ideas fit together.

"Everybody, back up," Dylan said. "Those weapons you're holding? Drop them. Nice and easy on the table."

Will frowned. "Why?"

"A precaution until I understand what's happening here."

They obeyed him with varying levels of reluctance. Sierra didn't want to drop the pan in her hand, but she did. She'd grabbed a knife earlier and palmed and pocketed it. Just in case.

"Step over here." Dylan waited until they all walked around the sectional, away from the table with the makeshift weapons, to talk again. "The way I see it either one of you hit me or someone out there did."

Cassie nodded at the door. "Out there."

"You." He pointed at Sierra. "This is the second time I've seen you. Both times you looked just this side of frantic. Tell me what's going on."

Where do I start? "I honestly have no idea."

His eyebrow lifted. "But . . . ?"

Instead of waiting for an answer, Dylan leaned against one of the barstools. Not really sitting, more like preparing to pounce. He wore a ripped strip of cloth around his arm as a bandage but otherwise looked steadier than the rest of them. The injury and the earlier gunfire suggested either the killer was a terrible shot at close range or the killer had been toying with Dylan. Toying with Dylan and the rest of them.

Cassie and Ruthie didn't move closer, and Alex probably couldn't. Still, they all managed to stand about eight feet from Dylan, crowding him but not answering his question.

"The important thing is you're here." That sounded like nonsense. Sierra knew the minute she said it. But he expected them to explain the unexplainable.

"There's a body in the shed, so I'm betting you're not that happy to see me." The officer's gaze traveled over them. "Anyone want to tell me what's going on?"

"We should leave the island. We can answer your questions and sit down with your entire department once we're back in whatever town has jurisdiction." Sierra barely knew where they were, but she knew they'd need legal reinforcements. She refused to let Alex and Cassie act as her lawyers in this disaster. Not for a second. "Which is it?"

Dylan pointed the gun toward the back door. "In case you missed it, there's a storm out there. No one is leaving."

"What about your injury?" Sierra could see the arm bandage but he didn't act like a guy in pain.

He shrugged off the concern. "I'm fine."

"Our cell phones don't work. Does yours?" Cassie took a step toward the table with their abandoned phones. "I'd really like to call my daughter."

Dylan looked stunned by the comment. "Don't you think you have bigger worries right now?"

The way he delivered the line set a new wave of anxiety spinning through Sierra. She understood his point. This looked awful. The whole situation *was* awful. The bodies, though it sounded as if he'd only found one. The shifting and fidgeting. The way they ignored his questions. They all sounded and acted guilty. The tension clogging the room had her fighting for breath.

"We didn't touch the guy in the shed." Will's words came out rushed and panicky. He pointed at Mitch and Sierra. "Well, they unwrapped him, but we didn't do it."

The outburst sucked away the last of the calm.

"Okay, I've heard enough." Dylan reached into his pocket and pulled out a handful of white zip ties. "Each of you put one on. Behind your backs. Help each other."

Cassie scoffed. "No way."

"Is this necessary?" Alex asked.

"It wasn't a suggestion." Dylan lifted his gun a little higher as he stared at Ruthie. "You, too."

"Just do it." Mostly Sierra didn't want him to start shooting. If he searched them and found her hidden knife or Ruthie's gun he just might.

They all complied but not without grumbling. The officer ignored most of the muttered denials and Alex's insistence that they were the victims.

With their hands bound behind them, Dylan directed them back to the sectional. They sat on the edges of the cushions while he moved their gathered weapons to a chair on the other side of the room, out of reach. He picked up discarded knives and studied them. Then he walked toward the kitchen.

No limp. No dripping blood. She'd hurt her knee and hadn't stopped rubbing it and wincing. He'd been shot and moved as if the bullet had passed right by him. "Where's your boat?"

Dylan stopped in mid-stride and turned around to face her.

"You need reinforcements. The weather stinks, but we could pile in your boat and just go before anyone else gets hurt." That was the only logical plan. Sierra's skepticism spiked when she realized he hadn't suggested it.

Dylan smiled. "What boat?"

CHAPTER FORTY-FOUR

ALEX

Alex's worst fears had come true. Dylan showing up had been too easy, too convenient. He came off too steady for a guy who'd walked into a massacre and got shot. He stayed too calm for someone facing off against a bunch of strangers with a dead body they couldn't explain. And the voice change. It morphed from low and serious to more natural sounding and almost amused.

His manner, his tone, could only be described as chilling.

"How did you get to the island without a boat?" Alex balled his hands into fists and turned his wrists behind his back, trying to get enough leverage to move his arms and break the tie. Even that little bit of jostling turned up the pounding in his head.

Dylan's smile grew wider. "I didn't need a boat. I was already here."

Alex felt the cold delivery vibrate through him. *Already on the island.* What did that even mean? Actually, he knew but he couldn't believe it. This man was a total stranger . . . wasn't he? "What are you—"

"Everyone stop shifting around." Dylan aimed the gun that time. Right at them. One by one. "No one is going anywhere."

"I don't understand what's happening." Will sounded lost.

Dylan cocked his head to the side. "Story of your life, isn't it, Will?"

The whole room froze. Ruthie, who had barely said a word, sat wide-eyed, her focus never leaving Dylan's face, as if she was trying to read him.

Alex struggled to keep up, but he had an excuse for his delay. His brain, usually his strongest asset, had gotten stuck in neutral. He strained to make even sluggish connections and logical leaps. But the *oh shit* look both Mitch and Sierra wore told Alex they'd realized how dire this situation was and how much worse it could get.

Will swallowed a few times. "How do you know my name?"

"Will." Dylan pointed the gun as he spoke. "Mitch." Moved it around the couch. "Cassie and Alex."

Mitch shook his head. "Sonofabitch."

"How do you know who we are?" Cassie asked at the same time.

"We'll get to that." Dylan glanced at Sierra. "I'm sorry you're here. You could look at this as an important lesson about what happens when you love the wrong man. If you survive, of course."

Mitch looked like he wanted to get up. "What the—"

Sierra rushed in, probably thinking Mitch could say the wrong thing and get himself shot. "Where's the boat you were driving before? The one you had when we were at the garage."

"Safe. Off island."

"But you're here." Sierra's voice had gone flat.

He winked at her. "Yes, I am."

Who the hell is this guy? Alex searched his memory, tried to come up with an answer. When that failed, he tried gathering more intel. "You're not injured."

"Of course not." Dylan removed the scrap of material tied around his arm and held it up. "Not my blood. I needed an easy way inside the house and went with *act injured*. It's all part of building trust and getting you to talk."

Cassie made a noise that sounded like a mix of impatience and terror. "Talk about what? What the hell are you saying?"

"Actually, the 'trust' thing was a line from a seminar I attended a long time ago." Dylan shrugged as he continued using a light tone that didn't match the dark vibe pulsing through the room. "Doesn't matter. The point is I'm here. You're here. Now we can chat."

"No one else is on the island." Sierra said the words as if she was saying them right as she thought them. "There isn't a dangerous killer running around out there."

Dylan's annoying smile fell. "It's fair to say all the killers on the island who are still alive are in this house."

Ruthie finally spoke up and said the one thing they all knew. "He's not a policeman."

"Wasn't that clear?" Dylan laughed this time. A deep, grating sound without one ounce of amusement. "No, I'm not."

CHAPTER FORTY-FIVE

SIERRA

Not a policeman. The three words ran through Sierra's head nonstop. He looked like one, dressed like one, carried a gun like one, but he wasn't. On this island, if you weren't a killer you were prey, and nothing about this guy said *prey.*

Her mind whirred back to life after that bombshell. Every nerve inside her screamed in terror. Anxiety rushed over, through, and around her, dragging her down into a sucking void.

She forced her voice to stay steady as she battled the panic that threatened to drown her. "You killed Tyler and Jake."

"Now, now." Dylan made a clicking sound with his tongue. "Let's not jump ahead."

The maniacal taunting tone of his voice promised more pain. He sounded as if he was enjoying the game he'd trapped them in. She'd always expected murderers to seethe with anger. This one was too busy toying with them to wallow in rage, setting them up to gleefully knock them down.

"What do you want?" Cassie asked.

"Don't pretend to be clueless. It doesn't suit you." Dylan frowned at her. "I'm here for answers."

Sierra used the few minutes of diverted attention to move her leg. A few inches. Nothing that would put the spotlight on her. Just enough to hide her pocket from direct view. She couldn't move her arms much, so she leaned down and let the inside of her forearm do the work.

Push. Push.

The blade jabbed into the fleshy part of her thigh. She flinched but didn't make a sound. One more push and the knife fell out of her pocket and onto the cushion.

Dylan's gaze shifted and landed on her.

"Not everything is about Emily." Alex almost shouted the comment.

His loud voice had everyone turning to him, including Dylan. "Damn right."

Well done, counselor. That was exactly the distraction Sierra needed to grab the knife, tucking it behind her as she shifted to her original position.

"He's here about Brendan," Mitch said.

Dylan smiled. "Ah, I see it on your face. You finally remember."

What the hell is this? She assumed Mitch was stalling but now she saw his expression—focused, concerned. Mitch knew this Dylan guy.

"Dylan Richter." Mitch said the other man's name nice and slow, almost as if he'd rolled it around in his head and found a memory. "I remember the name. Now. It didn't register before, if I even heard you or Sierra say it back at the garage."

Ruthie had been inching her skirt up on one side. Cassie's arms had been tensing and relaxing, as if she'd been pulling on the binding behind her. All that movement stopped. Every gaze locked on Mitch and Dylan, waiting for them to divulge whatever recognition they had of each other that remained a mystery to the rest of them.

"That was a test. I wanted to use the real name to see if you were all still self-important assholes, too busy saving your own pathetic lives to take a minute and think about someone else's." Dylan shook his head in a sort of *aw shucks* kind of way that came off far too light for the circumstances. "The answer? Yes."

"It's been a long time." Mitch's voice stayed calm and devoid of emotion.

Dylan clapped. He seemed to be relishing the conversation and being totally in control of it. "It's coming back to you, isn't it? It was nice of you to come to the funeral."

"What funeral?" Alex asked.

"Brendan's," Mitch answered without breaking eye contact with Dylan. "But you weren't there. I looked for you, trying to figure out what you looked like and expecting you to speak."

"The police suggested I keep a low profile due to the death threats. See, telling the truth about Brendan pissed people off. And that's what I did. Unlike all of you, I told the truth about where Brendan was when Emily died, so I had to hide. No photos or personal information about me in the news. I was referred to only as 'the friend' or 'the cousin' for my protection."

"You challenged the findings about Brendan's guilt and about his death," Mitch continued, filling in the rest.

Dylan's smile faded. "His murder."

"That's not true." Cassie leaned forward, looking desperate to drag Dylan's attention toward her but failing.

Mitch had attended Brendan's funeral. Of course he had. The information didn't surprise Sierra. Mitch's life revolved around trauma and death, and going might have been a way to deal with the newest emotional blow. He also likely saw a bit of himself in Brendan, someone the press referred to as a loner. Someone, like Mitch, who she guessed retreated into a safe world he'd created to avoid the real one that beat him down.

Whatever the reason, the ongoing talk gave her chance to cover her movements. She pricked her thumb with the knife. Annoying, but now she knew how to hold it to saw through the binding cutting into her wrists.

"Mitch, here, was the only one who bothered to show up. He hid in the back. I saw him because I was hiding, too." Dylan let out a dramatic exhale. "I could never figure out if your unexpected and unwanted attendance showed a hint of decency or if it spoke to your guilt. Want to solve that puzzle for me?"

"You can't hold our refusal to go to a memorial service against us. Brendan killed our friend," Alex said.

Dylan turned away from Mitch just long enough to point the gun at Alex. "You would be smart to stop saying that."

"You were Brendan's alibi." Mitch's voice never rose or slid into a whisper. He lulled Dylan in with a discussion the man clearly longed to have. "The online friend."

"As I said, friend and cousin, and the one person who knows for sure where Brendan was that night." Dylan looked around the room. "And the answer is *not with Emily*."

Sierra needed him calm. Pissing off the man with the gun struck her as the wrong strategy. The longer he talked, the greater the chance one or more of them could get their hands free. She saw Ruthie's skirt shift again and Alex, who'd been mostly quiet, appeared to be concentrating on something other than Dylan. The only person she couldn't read was Will, but that wasn't a surprise. He'd been almost comically frozen since Dylan gave up the cop pretense.

"You don't really want answers. You wouldn't believe them anyway." Sierra shrugged her shoulders, hoping the move came off as genuine and not as a way of getting a better grip on the knife. "All of this is about revenge."

"You're a smart one." Dylan winked at her again before glancing at Mitch. "You were really going to let her get away?"

Cassie and Alex seemed to pass a silent message between them before Cassie started talking. "You have to understand. We were young and confused. Those days were so bleak. We were all mourning and not at our best. Nothing seemed real."

Dylan groaned. "Stop trying to win your opening argument, lawyer lady."

She didn't give up. "I know this is hard to hear. Believe me, I do. But Brendan killed Emily then killed himself."

"No part of that sentence is true." Dylan's jaw clenched as his anger visibly rose.

Sierra tried to ratchet the tension down before it exploded. "You've proved your point."

Dylan scoffed. "Not yet."

"You know what happened to us in college. And now, all these years later, you somehow set all of this up. With Ruthie's help." Cassie glanced at Ruthie. "What do you have to say?"

Dylan made that annoying clicking sound again. "I'll ask the questions."

"Fine," Cassie snapped back. "Now what?"

Sierra wanted to grab Cassie and tell her to stop. Taunting a homicidal psychopath was a terrible strategy. Unless Cassie had some big secret plan, she was bringing them closer to the brink, and if she had a plan, she should either clue the rest of them in somehow or deploy it.

Dylan rubbed his thumb over the side of his gun, almost caressing it. "Simple. You're going to admit what you did twelve years ago."

"There's nothing to tell," Alex said.

"I'd rethink that response because the first one to tell the truth gets to live."

Sierra hated that answer. She had a feeling she'd hate the response to this question even more. "And the rest of us?"

Dylan didn't hesitate. "Are you familiar with the term *bloodbath*?"

CHAPTER FORTY-SIX

ALEX

With every sick comment Dylan uttered the walls closed in on Alex. He'd been so busy trying to concentrate and follow along over the slamming in his head that he'd almost missed it. Sierra's arms. They were no longer tight against her sides. She'd shifted and shifted, moving every time Dylan looked away from her.

She'd done . . . something. Loosened the ties somehow. Alex kept trying and couldn't get the plastic to budge, but Sierra had figured out a solution. The flash of relief in her expression hinted at her progress. But outrunning a bullet sounded impossible. All Alex could do was keep the conversation going, try to ease it away from the topics that could get him killed and away from Sierra.

"The notes. The lights going out. The Emily photos. All you." *Damn.* Even if he did survive this trip the things Dylan knew or had stumbled over could steal Alex's freedom and that thought took over every inch of extra space in his head. "And the dead bodies."

Dylan took a dramatic little bow. "Most of that list, yes."

"Most?" Cassie asked.

Mitch shook his head. "You're insane."

"Angry, not insane," Dylan responded before turning to look at Ruthie. "And you should stop moving."

Her skirt. Alex saw it now. It rode up higher on her leg. Alex had no idea what that meant, but a part of him believed the women might save them all. Ruthie and Sierra. Both of them. The outsiders. The ones with everything to lose because they'd had nothing to do with setting them on this path.

"Ruthie and Sierra weren't at Bowdoin. Let them go," Alex said, knowing the words would bounce right off their attacker.

"A good argument but not a persuasive one." Dylan turned on the stool. The gun bobbled but stayed aimed in the direction of all of them. "All Sierra had to do at the garage was admit there was a dead body in the trunk and ask for help. When she didn't she showed me that she's as corrupted as the rest of you."

"No. Please." Mitch spoke through a voice laced with pain and guilt. "She only knows me."

Dylan's eyebrow rose. "Then you're to blame for whatever happens to her."

"You waited twelve years to exact revenge." Sierra whistled. "That's a hell of a long game."

Not the direction Alex wanted them to go, but at least Dylan hadn't started shooting.

"Years of tracking. Of feeding information to online chat groups. Of pressuring the police." Dylan sighed. "I thought one of you would crack by now. There are some obvious weak spots in this group. At the very least, I thought the police would wake up and do their job. But nothing. It's all fallen to me."

"There's nothing else to find," Will said, speaking for the first time since the room's calm imploded.

Dylan hummed. "That's not quite true, is it? Reading your emails and listening to your phone calls, waiting to hear you slip up, has been enlightening."

"Listening to . . ." Alex's insides turned icy cold. "What are you talking about?"

"Dylan Richter, computer genius." He nodded as if to congratulate himself on his self-designated title.

"You should work on your low self-esteem," Mitch mumbled.

All the amusement vanished from Dylan's face. "I see you're still hiding behind that smart mouth to avoid dealing with sad things. This is going to be a rough few hours for you."

Alex still couldn't wrap his head around the piece of information Dylan had just dropped. "You couldn't possibly have—"

"It's so easy to get people to click on a link and let me in. Even careful people, like Mitch." Dylan's gaze switched to Cassie. "Disguise the malware as an invite to a legal conference." That gaze zipped to Mitch. "A request for a bid on a hotel project." Dylan's attention landed on Will. "Porn."

He'd been watching them. Following. Learning about them. Alex tried to remember if he'd messed up. If he'd said the wrong thing at the wrong time and admitted his role in the horrors that still haunted him.

"I did the same thing here." Dylan pointed to the fire alarm then to a decorative model ship sitting on the fireplace mantel. "Watched. Listened in. Very interesting, by the way."

"No." Cassie shook her head. "You're bluffing."

"Should I recite the conversation you and your husband had

with Will earlier right on that sectional?" No one said a word as Dylan continued. "Don't doubt me, my skills, or my determination to see this through. I've been stalking your lives, learning your secrets."

Alex stared at his wife, but she wouldn't meet his gaze. She knew how much they stood to lose. How much they'd buried and what it had cost them.

"I made a promise not to let killers go free. Innocent people need someone to protect their memory. Someone who will make sure the guilty parties pay." Dylan's voice was softer now, less gleeful in the destruction he'd wrought but no less determined. The way he sprawled on that stool looked relaxed but his white-knuckle grip on his gun suggested otherwise. "Brendan's parents are good people and you broke them."

"They wouldn't want you to kill us," Cassie said.

Dylan's eyes actually darkened. A lethal vibe bounced off him. "Don't act like you've spent one second thinking about them or what you did to that family when you killed their only child."

Alex didn't like the glint in Dylan's eye or how easy it was for him to ratchet his rage up and down. Alex fell back on stalling. Sierra's arm moved easily now. She'd gotten loose. He bet everything on that and dragged Dylan's attention away from her one more time. "How did you even get Jake and Tyler here? And why them?"

"All good questions, and maybe I'll answer a few, but I'm not going first. See, we're all here for a reason."

No, no, no. Alex tried again. "Did you set up the party?"

Dylan nodded in Ruthie's direction. "She did."

Cassie groaned. "I knew it."

"You don't know shit," Dylan shot back. "I hacked her emails, like I did to all of you. Genius, remember?"

"It's not as impressive if you have to keep telling us," Mitch whispered.

"Do you want to go first? Tell me what I want to know and maybe I'll have mercy on you . . ." Dylan pointed the gun at Sierra. "Or someone you care about."

"You're going to sit there and interrogate us then shoot us, one by one, if we fail your little test?" she asked. "You can't possibly think that will work."

"I have you trapped on an island. I've proven I can kill two grown men without breaking a sweat."

Desperation surged through Alex. "This revenge plan won't bring Brendan back."

The barrel of the gun moved around the room, pointing at each one of them in turn. "Stop with that bullshit. You don't get to kill someone, stain their memory, then use their good character as a shield for your sick behavior. And you don't get to hide. Not anymore."

"You won't get away with this."

Alex feared his wife was absolutely wrong.

"Ah, the lame response to the inevitable." Dylan's laughter ended with a shake of his head. "No one knows I'm here. My computer and phone will show me sticking around home all weekend. No forensics. No DNA. No direct line back to me. Tricks I learned from you all."

Sierra looked around the sectional. "Take them to the police. Present your evidence and make them answer for whatever they did."

Alex couldn't allow that to happen. "Sierra—"

Dylan talked over Alex. "Sensible but they've had years to come clean. Years to perfect their lies. They have no intention of doing the right thing. They have to be forced. That's my job."

Alex felt the end racing toward him and rushed to deflect one last time. "We're all going to tell you the same thing. We don't know who killed Emily, but, like everyone else who knows anything about this case, we assume it was Brendan."

"I have another idea. I'll kill one of you at a time. I'm betting, eventually, I'll pick a person at least one of you cares about and then we'll see some self-sacrifice in the form of an honest answer."

"What happens if someone does admit to doing something to Brendan?" Will asked.

"They die." Dylan's smile returned. "Admittedly, this isn't a game you can win. And if you think that's unfair, imagine how Brendan felt."

CHAPTER FORTY-SEVEN

BOOK NOTES: THOSE LEFT BEHIND

Brendan had friends. All of them vouched for his character and insisted he'd never hurt anyone. Law enforcement had heard it all before, so they gave little credence to those statements. But it was harder to write off Brendan's alibi. The person whose story never wavered. The one who passed a lie detector test without trouble.

Dylan Richter. Two years older than Brendan. They shared family ties, a passion for online gaming, and a dream to work with computers in some way. Dylan at Cornell, seven hours away and in the first year of graduate school, communicated with Brendan almost every day.

Dylan showed the computer logs and explained the reality of Brendan being in his room all night when Emily died. Dylan also knew about Brendan's dream for his upcoming senior project. A beta of a video game he wanted to create. A video game with a role he wanted Emily to narrate. That was the reason for the supposedly damning text. Simple. Uncomplicated. Not violent.

The police believed Dylan's high IQ and computer talent provided an opportunity to create evidence to support the alibi. In other words, those in charge thought Dylan lied.

After graduation, Dylan landed a job with a small gaming company that eventually sold to a very large company in a lucrative deal. Instead of going on vacation or jumping into a new area, Dylan took time out for a personal project. Clearing Brendan's name became an obsession. It took months to collect data and build online connections. To put Brendan's name, life, and alibi in front of a group of sleuths who dedicated huge amounts of energy to investigating crimes.

The plan worked. Dylan got people talking about Brendan and poking holes in the case against him. Dylan aimed information and misinformation at the problem in equal measure. Whatever it took to get people to listen, to make them doubt the version they'd been told about what happened at Bowdoin.

Dylan decided to confront the people at the heart of the Emily and Brendan mysteries. The goal morphed from clearing Brendan's name to controlling the fate of those who'd destroyed him, all while ignoring the real costs of digging into the past.

In the worst of all outcomes, Brendan's murder became a rallying cry for a few to justify more killings. A rage-filled, grief-stricken genius turned into an emotional black hole who thrived on chaos.

Another killer was born.

CHAPTER FORTY-EIGHT

RUTHIE

Thanks to a combination of panic and inexperience, Ruthie had placed the gun too high up on her thigh. Covertly reaching up under all that material to grab it proved tricky. She needed to time this perfectly and not attract Dylan's attention, not provoke him, before her finger hit the trigger.

She knew too well what he was capable of doing because she'd created him.

"Who wants to confess first? Any volunteers?" Dylan looked around the room as if he expected someone to raise their hand.

The gun remained trained on them. He handled the weapon like the expert he was. They'd spent hours together at the shooting range under the guise of teaching her how to defend herself. He'd been obsessed with her safety and determined that she never become a victim. Now who lived and who died might be determined by which one of them possessed the better shooting accuracy and if he still believed she deserved saving.

Ruthie felt the uncomfortable tick of someone staring at her. Sierra forced eye contact before her gaze wandered down to Ruthie's leg and back up again. When she did it a second time,

Ruthie got the message. The gun. She dreaded using it but responded with a tiny bob of her head.

Sierra cleared her throat, silently demanding Dylan look at her. "You're asking someone to step up and make themselves a target."

"Exactly."

That voice. The singsong quality, so amused and in control, toying and playing with them, told Ruthie that he'd tipped over the edge. Gone was the hopeful computer nerd who thrived on finding answers. A man confident in his beliefs and driven by an unmet need pounding inside him to find the truth. Brilliant but socially awkward. A guy who experienced pain and slowly, over months of burying himself in online theories and conspiracy nonsense, now wanted to inflict pain on others. Despite who he once was and all that promise, he now presented as an evil shell of a man consumed by a stark determination to kill.

She'd started this. She'd failed to understand how loyal he was to his idea of justice and how deep his vein of rage ran. She'd unleashed this horror. Now, she had to rein it in or risk becoming a target.

"You can walk away. Stop this right now." Ruthie jerked at the lack of strength in her voice. She'd aimed for confident, but a squeaky tone came out. She could not show fear no matter how much it bubbled up inside her.

Dylan finally looked at her. The full intensity of his focus knocked the breath out of her. She stumbled over her words, searched her mind to find the right ones. He'd blown her well-structured plan to hell. Used her notes and her life until nothing was left but a twisted carcass of a plan. He introduced a level of danger she couldn't control.

She'd spent the last half hour desperate to stay under the radar, trying to figure out a way to hold her scheme together while minimizing his. But that wasn't possible.

"You've scared the hell out of everyone. You've proven you're more powerful. Smarter. No one questions your abilities or your will." She spoke directly to him on a private level she knew he'd understand if he could snap out of this role. "They now know they can't hide from you. That you'll be watching, and they'll spend every day of their lives waiting for you to come after them. You've won."

"Have I?"

She refused to get sucked into this mess any deeper. She needed control. There was no way to fix the hellish damage he'd done, but she could contain the carnage going forward. Stop the bleeding . . . literally. "You can leave now and disappear."

Cassie made a noise that sounded like a gasp but, for once, she stayed quiet. They all did. Ruthie had their rapt attention. More important, she had Dylan's.

"Why should I do that?" he asked in a deadly quiet voice.

She'd started their relationship by appealing to his sense of fairness. After a month of watching his online interactions, she'd fed him a line about being a decent man who'd lived through the unthinkable. He gave her a small opening and she moved into his life. She told him what she needed and, in a short time, his compulsion fed off hers. She thought that meant they were in sync, but his thoughts grew disjointed. All those conspiracies other sleuthers offered twisted and turned in his head. His rage grew as his thin and fraying tie to reality stretched then snapped. He talked about killing without remorse.

She'd had no choice but to cut him off after a few months and ignore all those plans they discussed, some possible and some too ridiculous to try. She moved. Changed her number. Pushed aside his needs and focused on her own.

Instead of working with him, she went right to the source and insinuated herself into Will's life. He was the easiest target of the Bowdoin group because he was so clearly floundering when it came to interpersonal relationships. She'd studied and knew that Will, unlike Mitch, welcomed companionship.

She figured Dylan would cry foul but then slink back into his own life. Find another person to latch on to. She thought he had because he stopped all contact, but now she knew better. He'd been waiting and creating his own ending to her story. This. The "bloodbath" he'd referenced, only in this version he stole the spotlight.

"You're not really a killer." At least he wasn't until he'd met her.

He smiled. "I think I've proven I am."

"You're talking to him like . . . I don't . . . it sounds personal, right?" Will asked.

The question made Dylan laugh. "Yeah, Ruthie. Care to explain to the group?"

"I'm begging. Don't do this." She knew her comment could be taken so many ways, and that was on purpose.

Will inched closer. "Ruthie, stop. He won't—"

"Shut up." The demand came out rougher than she planned. All those weeks of pretending to care about Will had worn her down. She was tired of cooing and calming. "I don't need you to help me."

Will jerked back. "Hey, I'm trying to support you."

Ruthie ignored his whining. Ignored him. Tried to wipe out

the unwanted memory of every time he'd touched her and focus on the danger in front of her. "You want the truth. Right, Dylan? You want the person who hurt Brendan to—"

"*Killed* Brendan," Dylan shot back.

"Okay, who killed Brendan to face justice."

Up until then he'd been leaning and lounging on the barstool, acting mostly unaffected by the fear pulsing through the room. Now, he stood up, fully in control and clear in his intentions. "I am justice."

Air rushed out of her, but she tried again. "No, you're a man."

He aimed the gun at her without blinking. "I could kill you. Prove I'm serious and feel nothing."

Everyone shifted in their seats. Alex told him to lower the weapon. Sierra's left arm slipped behind Mitch.

Ruthie didn't move. She needed all of Dylan's focus on her. "Killing me won't get you what you want."

"Maybe it will make your weasel of a fiancé finally talk about what he did." Dylan continued to look at her, but the barrel of the gun moved toward Will, who started to stand up. "Try it. I fucking dare you."

"Will, don't. Sit down." Ruthie's voice vibrated now. She couldn't keep the thread of panic out of it. "He will kill you."

Dylan nodded. "Yes, I will."

The confusion hadn't cleared Will's eyes. "How do you know so much about him?"

"Because they know each other." Cassie words came out slowly, as if she realized the truth as she spoke it.

Dylan's head tilted to the side. "Do we?"

That amused voice had come back. Ruthie tried to block the

mocking tone as she performed a mental countdown in her head. If she shot first maybe they'd have a chance. At least some of them.

Will's mouth dropped open. "Wait . . . what?"

"Poor clueless Will." Dylan walked around to the other side of the kitchen island. He now had a shield of sorts between him and the rest of the room. He could shoot and duck.

The move made Ruthie wonder if he knew about her gun.

"What are you saying?" The strain in Will's voice suggested he might have a clue after all.

Dylan shook his head. "Ruthie, honey. Don't you think it's time you tell these people who you really are?"

CHAPTER FORTY-NINE

ALEX

Alex blamed Will. His pathetic need to be loved and taken care of had caused this. He'd been desperate in his search to find *normal* and opened the door to a person who blew up the patchwork past they'd created.

Cassie shook her head. "I knew it."

She did. Alex had to give his wife credit. She'd been skeptical of Ruthie from the start. Alex had chalked up Cassie's spiraling mood to a mix of mistrust and misplaced worry, but he'd been too quick to jump on a stereotype and write off her warnings as part of a *strong women can't get along* vibe when he'd known better. Cassie could read people.

The rushed engagement. The party in the middle of nowhere. Ruthie had been luring Will in . . . luring them all into Dylan's waiting and deadly hands.

"They're working together," Cassie added.

"No. She's my . . ." Poor Will, as usual, three steps behind, refused to believe the obvious. "This can't be happening. I would have known."

Some of Ruthie's usual confidence seemed to wash away,

leaving her alone and wilting in the middle of the sectional. "Will, listen—"

"The things we said to each other. All that talk about your family living overseas and wanting to meet me."

"What the hell was the plan here?" Alex asked as his emotions seesawed between frustration with Will and sympathy for his failure to move forward from his mess of a life.

"My goal was to win Will's trust and eventually the trust of all of you then get you to talk." Ruthie tripped over a few unintelligible words before speaking again. "You deserved being lied to because you're liars. You've hidden so much about Emily's death and everything that came after."

Will shook his head. "Nothing between us was true?"

"Good God, man. You're not really this clueless, are you?" Dylan asked.

"Shut the fuck up." Will's anger whipped out, overtaking his confusion.

"Be careful." Dylan's playful mood vanished. "While I find your distress enjoyable, I still have a gun and a temper."

Ruthie shifted to the front of the sofa cushion. The move pushed her skirt up higher on one side, but he didn't seem to notice. "Most of the threatening notes were mine, but I didn't intend for them to be used that way. To be planted the way they were."

Dylan winked at her. "I thought printing those out and using them the way I did was ingenious."

"Of course you did," Mitch mumbled.

When Dylan started to respond, Ruthie talked faster, dragging Dylan's gaze back to her. "How did you get them? How did you know about this weekend? I assume at some point you got my computer password and could see what I was doing and decided to crash, right?"

He shrugged. "You fall asleep after sex. That made it easy to search through your condo."

Will stood up. "You cheating bitch."

"Language." Dylan snapped his fingers. "And sit."

"You're fine with killing but not name-calling?" Mitch asked.

Alex almost warned Mitch to be quiet, but Sierra wasn't trying to tone down his usual sarcasm. No, something else was happening here. Something intentional and baiting that Alex couldn't decipher. Every time Dylan looked away, Sierra studied him, as if trying to figure out his reaction time.

"Call me sentimental." Dylan smiled at Ruthie. "We have a past."

"You're partners in this?" Alex knew the answer, but he needed Will to hear it this time and be more careful.

Dylan nodded. "Yes."

"No, we're not. I had nothing to do with the killings or any of his plans this weekend. When you found Tyler, I assumed the violence related to Mitch's past, not Emily's. I was as surprised to see Dylan as you all were," Ruthie said at the same time. "I brought you here because I'm writing a book about Emily. Beautiful, funny, bright, fun, and flawed. Neither a saint nor a villain."

Cassie frowned. "What the hell are you talking about?"

"Those notes you found. The Book Notes. That's what they're for. Emily and I grew up together. We went to the same school. Our families were friends. We were inseparable. Best friends." Ruthie labored over the words, trying to get it all out and build her case. "When I said I wanted to go to Amherst and major in journalism, so did she. That's the kind of thing she did. Tagged along. Stole other people's thunder. It was never a big deal until it was."

"The best friend . . . You're the one she said betrayed her," Mitch said.

"That's ridiculous, of course. No one stole her place in the Amherst freshman class." Ruthie waved off the suggestion. "But she was furious at not getting in and . . ." She seemed to run out of energy. "Honestly, the specifics don't matter."

Dylan hummed. "Sounds like Emily was a spoiled brat."

Ruthie leaned forward on the cushion, as if trying to reason with Dylan. "Don't do that. Don't judge her. She was a kid. That's what kids do. They make bad choices and act immature. None of that means they deserve to die."

Alex couldn't make the Dylan piece and the Ruthie piece fit together. The way she described the timeline the two of them *happened* to meet. Dylan *happened* to lose control. She then *happened* to stumble over Will and used him to get to all of them.

Too convenient. Ruthie's role had to be bigger. Sidekick, partner—something.

Will's expression bounced around from furious to confused. He kept emotionally circling and landed back on lost and disoriented. "I don't understand any of this."

"He's a prize." Dylan whistled. "You really dumped me for him?"

The overlap. Dylan's clear goal of revenge. Alex's brain refused to take it all in.

"I needed the truth for my book. It's that simple," Ruthie said. "Will, you were my way in. I needed to get close to you all to get you to talk."

"To destroy us." Cassie looked and sounded like she was

winding up. No longer a step behind. She'd clearly determined Ruthie's motivations and viewed her as the enemy.

Ruthie shook her head. "You didn't need my help for that. Your secrets couldn't stay hidden forever."

Alex didn't agree. They'd spent so much energy and to have it implode now, like this, was almost too much to take.

"My goal was to write a book about Emily and Brendan." Ruthie shrugged. "None of you would answer questions if you knew that. You'd sidestepped law enforcement with your attorneys and blocked any real attempt to review the case for years."

"That's how we met," Dylan explained. "We went back and forth on online forums. Discussed theories and evidence. Most people concluded Mitch killed Emily and Brendan."

Mitch sighed. "Great."

"Once I started investigating, I couldn't stop. The whodunit shit gets in your blood. Gives you back your control." Dylan set his gun on the counter. "During that time, Ruthie and I started going out . . . or should I say staying in."

"You're disgusting." Will looked at the door, as if he thought he could make a run for it.

Alex needed Will to hold it together. Admittedly, the last few minutes had been a mess of admissions and threats, but Dylan had a gun and an agenda. No matter what Mitch and Sierra were planning, a bullet moved faster.

"I thought we both wanted the same thing. The truth. But Dylan started talking about the need for a big show. For revenge." Ruthie looked at Dylan's gun then over to Sierra. "Talked about inflicting pain without one ounce of guilt."

"I own that. I'm not ashamed of how much I want this college gang dead," Dylan said.

"Do you hear yourself?" Ruthie sounded frustrated.

Dylan shrugged. "It's a good thing I'd already installed the programs I needed on your computer. They allowed me to watch you track them all down, see your plans, read the threatening notes you'd written to spook this fine group. Most importantly, I got a look at that draft book of yours."

An explanation. One Alex almost believed. This little scene made Ruthie another victim of Dylan's plans. It all sounded too wrapped up and easy. Alex didn't buy that part at all.

Will leaned forward, sounding more lost than ever. "We met in an art gallery."

"A setup." Ruthie seemed to ignore the danger and her ex to focus on the man she'd tricked with a mountain of lies in a tone that hinted at regret. "Will . . . I . . ."

"Fine." This wasn't the time for an emotional dump. Alex pushed them in another direction because he needed Will angry and ready to fight. "You led us all here. For what?"

"Answers." Ruthie's serious tone suggested that her response was true. "But I swear I didn't know Dylan was here or that he planned to come."

"I'm persistent," Dylan added.

Will stared him down. "Insane."

"That's the second time y'all have thrown that word around." Dylan's voice turned deadly cold. "I warned you."

The screaming started the second after the shot rang out.

CHAPTER FIFTY

SIERRA

Sierra ducked as the bang echoed through the room. One second she was sitting, getting ready to throw the knife, and the next Mitch tackled her, pinning her against the cushions.

She'd cut their hands free while Dylan preened and threatened but in the pushing and diving after the shot the knife slipped from her fingers. Panic swamped her as she patted and fumbled. Her fingers dug into the crease between the couch cushions. Something hard rubbed against the back of her hand. She twisted and shoved at Mitch to slide over. In a weird way, time both moved in slow motion and sped by. She grabbed the hard plastic and . . . the broken zip tie. No knife.

Find it. Find it.

Mitch's weight pinned her down. She could hear Ruthie yelling and saw someone slump over and fall. Alex, maybe?

Desperation scratched and clawed at Sierra. She struggled and shimmied, trying to get a better view of the room. Her hair had escaped its ponytail to hang in front of her face. Mitch's chest trapped her, pressing her into the couch in a move that likely was meant to protect her but left him exposed.

"Stop moving." Mitch whispered the order into her ear.

She ignored him as she wiggled around and shifted. She needed to find that knife before Dylan did. Once he figured out they'd broken the zip ties he'd shoot again, and Mitch provided an easy target.

"Nooo!"

Sierra heard the wail and a grating sound that might be Dylan's laugh. The sick bastard loved this. Enjoyed seeing them scurry and beg.

"What did you do?" Cassie yelled the question.

Mitch lifted off Sierra. His knee pressed into the couch cushion for leverage before he stood. The dip caused Sierra to roll. Something hard dug into her hip bone. Had to be the knife.

She sat up in the middle of the unrestrained chaos. Alex rocked back and forth in his seat with a grimace on his face. Cassie hovered, unable to touch him but trying to comfort him.

Will looked frozen and Mitch was on the move, heading toward Dylan and that damn gun. Sierra didn't hesitate. She aimed and hoped all those years of playing darts while her dad drank in the bar would pay off.

The knife soared across the room, narrowly missing Mitch's head. The blade grazed Dylan's cheek. He flinched and ducked but not in time. When he stood up again blood trickled from a slice on his skin.

His eyes filled with rage as he let out a battle cry. A guttural roar that sent everyone jumping and running. They headed for those confiscated household weapons.

Sierra couldn't move. She saw Dylan's jaw clench. Watched him raise the gun.

"Sierra, no." Mitch pivoted and flew toward her, ignoring his own peril.

"Move!" Ruthie yelled.

A series of thunderous bangs exploded around Sierra. Mitch tackled her, rolling them to the floor as she covered her ears and closed her eyes. Bullets shattered a crystal lamp and knocked pictures off the wall. Sierra heard an odd *pfft* noise and opened her eyes to see a hole in the cushion above her head.

Footsteps. Crashes. Not the sounds she expected to hear right before death.

As quickly as the banging started it stopped. An acrid smell filled the room. Sierra did a quick pat-down of Mitch.

He groaned as he rolled off her. "I'm not hit."

She scanned the once beautiful room now plunged into disarray. Nothing left but a mass of shredded couch cushions and broken glass thanks to Dylan's shooting. Ruthie stood with her skirt hitched up on one side and her hand holding the material in an awkward position because of the stretched-out tie still binding her wrists. She blinked but didn't try to uncover or grab her gun.

Sierra swallowed as she forced her mind to reboot. Then she saw the blood on Alex's oxford shirt. It soaked the area around his biceps. Cassie pressed her body and a blanket against him, but her hands hadn't been freed.

Sierra tricked her mind into believing it was a superficial wound. Bloody but not serious. "Are you okay?"

But Mitch was the one to answer. "Where's Dylan?"

They all looked around. Will slowly stood up. Mitch got off the floor and reached to pull Sierra up. The room was awash with nervous energy and careful shifting but no talking. Saying something could conjure Dylan up again, but not knowing where he lurked struck her as even scarier.

The table with the cell phones had gotten knocked over in the melee. Sierra righted it. She stared at the two sets of keys on the floor—one for the buildings on the island and the other for the rental car across the water.

She peeked around the breakfast bar. Her knees buckled as she walked. She grabbed on to the counter to keep from falling and felt Mitch's hand at her back. They both searched and he retrieved her knife.

Seconds, minutes, hours passed. She wasn't sure which, but probably more like a minute or two. She glanced into the family room and saw the four others still locked in a haze of panic and confusion.

Sierra said the words that made a shudder run through her, stealing the last of her confidence. "Dylan is gone."

CHAPTER FIFTY-ONE

RUTHIE

He wouldn't disappear." Ruthie whispered the words as Sierra cut the zip tie locking her hands together.

Cassie snorted. "You would know."

Once free, Ruthie rubbed her sore wrists. All the stretching and pulling had carved deep red grooves in her skin. Not her biggest issue right now, but it was easier to look at the bruises than to glance up and see the judgment on the faces around the room.

Sierra cut them all free. "Now isn't the time for—"

"Why did you say yes?" Will sat on the edge of the cushions with an unreadable look on his face. "You never felt anything for me. Clearly. So, why say yes when I proposed?"

Everyone stopped moving, as if waiting to hear Ruthie's answer.

The quest for a concrete solution, for a way to assuage her own guilt over not pushing harder, had brought her here. Every move, every decision, had gotten bound up in a confusing mix of *anything for the cause,* a need for closure, a drive to define this new career path, and unresolved trauma. Her judgment clouded and the line between good idea and bad got so blurred she'd sacrificed her personal life—and Will's—for the truth.

Ruthie had given different excuses to different people. Her friends and colleagues viewed her relationship with Will as book-related research that grew into something else. The *too busy* excuses to dinner invitations and limited contact helped her carry off the charade. She never let the separate parts of her life touch for fear someone would ask the wrong, or right, question and figure out the dangerous game she was playing then try to stop her. Her best friend knew, even encouraged the dangerous stunts, right up until the time Will proposed, when she shifted and declared the whole setup had gone too far.

Ruthie had promised herself to end the lies after this weekend, but she never expected another person with goals more twisted than hers to get in the way. If she'd been more aware, less tied to sticking close to Will in the hope of stumbling over the truth, maybe Dylan wouldn't have blindsided her.

Instead of letting any of those thoughts rise to the surface, she fought back. She ignored the disappointment and hurt in Will's eyes and went for the killing blow. "Why did you propose after six weeks? Who does that?"

"That's pretty fucked up, coming from you." Alex's voice sounded breathy and pained as Cassie dabbed and fussed over his wounded shoulder and covered him with a blanket. "You used him."

The guilt Ruthie had so strategically pushed aside and buried under a pile of he-deserves-this excuses smacked her. Every time the *maybe he didn't do it* and *he's a human being* thoughts crept in, she'd stomped those doubts out. She focused on the end goal and not who she had to become and how much decency she'd sacrificed to get there.

All of the lies and months of deceit twisted inside Ruthie.

She wanted to scream at all of them to, for once, tell the truth, but had she sacrificed that right? She was an imperfect vessel for gaining justice. Breaking Will, a man she knew lacked the emotional skills to avoid her manipulation, made her into someone she pretended not to be. Constantly reminding herself of his faults and setting him up to fall in the wake of any Emily and Brendan revelations allowed her to take away his humanity and reinforce her self-designated right to be his judge.

The echo of how cold and ruthless that sounded had her questioning if she and Dylan were more alike than she wanted to believe.

"I messed up." The words came out as a whisper.

Cassie didn't miss it. "That's all you have to say?"

"I was trying to get to the truth."

Will stood up. "By lying to me."

"Okay, enough." Sierra stepped into the middle of the group and fell into the practical leader role that fit her so well. "We can all interrogate Ruthie later. Right now, we need to find Dylan."

"She's his partner." Will shrugged. "Not me. Him."

Ruthie wanted to kick Dylan for binding them together in that way. "In case you missed it, the man threatened to kill me."

"How convenient for your little game." Cassie finished wrapping Alex's shoulder and dropped discarded scraps of material on the table.

"What about this is convenient?" Mitch asked.

Before anyone could answer, Sierra took the lead again. "He has a boat."

That got everyone's attention.

Cassie frowned. "What?"

"Dylan came to the island by boat." Sierra looked to Mitch

and Alex. "Remember when we were at the garage? He then left on it. We saw him go. It wasn't a trick. Now he's back. So either that boat is on the island or it's parked somewhere and he used a smaller boat or some other way to get to the island."

Ruthie thought about the islands she'd researched for this weekend. All the information about boats and travel and weather. She hadn't been looking at this island, at this house. She thought it was too remote but then it kept popping up in her searches. The reviews were great. The owners were so accommodating in their emails and . . . all Dylan. Had to be. He'd had access to her computer the whole time and drew them here.

She decided not to share that revelation with the group and focused on the boat. Having one meant he had to be holed up nearby. Close enough to get on and off the island without being detected. His policeman sham wouldn't have worked for as long otherwise . . . and wouldn't have worked at all if she'd been at the garage or seen him sooner.

"Let him leave the island. We'll be safer," Will said.

Alex winced. "We can't let him go."

"He's not going to leave," Sierra said. "He's not done with us."

Cassie picked up one of the knives and turned to Ruthie. "Tell us his plans."

Her distrust wasn't misplaced but Ruthie still hated this woman. "I have no idea."

All but Alex stood around, talking this out. Being out in the open, easily viewed through the windows, struck Ruthie as a terrible idea but no one cared what she thought.

"What about your injury?" Mitch asked Alex.

Alex. Yeah, the man looked like crap. Between the glassy eyes and bloody shirt, Ruthie thought, he couldn't be of much help in a fight except for possibly arguing someone to death with his lawyer nonsense.

"Hurts like hell but I think it's a flesh wound." Alex touched his shoulder then hissed.

"But you have a concussion," Cassie added.

"Right. You stay with your wife." Mitch pointed at Will. "We'll go find Dylan."

Will shook his head. "That's ridiculous."

"He's going to come back here. Reload and continue killing." Mitch shoved a knife and a hammer into his pockets. He looked around the fireplace for additional, informal weapons but quickly gave up. "Sierra's right. He hasn't gotten his answers."

Cassie groaned as she sat on one of the barstools. "I'm tired of this topic. We don't know anything."

Sierra and Mitch were right about hunting Dylan down. But the lack of urgency among the others made Ruthie more anxious. Talking about tracking Dylan, debating the pros and cons, only gave him a chance to regroup and attack. She didn't think Sierra had done much damage with that knife, except to piss him off even more.

"We need to go on the offensive." Sierra turned to Ruthie. "Is it loaded?"

Ruthie realized the gun was still strapped to her thigh. She unfastened it and held it in a tight clench. "Yes."

Cassie rolled her eyes. "Loaded? You have a gun? What am I saying, of course you have a gun."

Alex went a step further. He held out his hand. "Give it to me."

The wind kicked up, rattling the windows. Ruthie tightened her grip on the only weapon they had that could take on Dylan's gun. "Never going to happen."

"She keeps the gun." Sierra didn't give any of them a second to argue with her. "We go out there and track Dylan down. We have knives and a gun. We attack, search him, strip away that weapon of his, and tie him up."

"Come on." Alex shook his head. "I want him stopped, but this plan is too risky. This is real life. He'll kill you."

Sierra sighed. "He's going to kill us all anyway. The question is if we go out fighting or just surrender."

Alex turned on Ruthie. "You did this."

Ruthie refused to take the blame for their terrible decisions. "No, you all did. Not Sierra, but the rest of you. You know what really happened to Emily and Brendan. Your lies birthed this."

Mitch ignored the bickering and kept moving. He stood by the back door. "Ready?"

"Wait." Sierra sniffed then made a face. "What's that smell?"

Mitch backed away from the door. "Fire."

CHAPTER FIFTY-TWO

ALEX

Flames licked up the front door. Flashes of orange and red appeared in the thin window before being overtaken by rolling gray smoke. Wisps seeped under the front door as the smell of burning wood wafted across the room.

Reality pressed down on Alex, forcing him to grab for the kitchen counter to stay upright. "He's going to kill us."

"Not by fire." Sierra looked from one end of the room to the other. "He's trying to lure us outside. Check out the back door. No visible flames. No smoke."

Mitch reached for Sierra. "He wants to shuttle us out there to—"

"Pick us off one by one," Will said.

They all shifted, moving to the middle of the room and farther away from the most pressing danger. The small window next to the front door cracked. The crunching sound had them all on edge. The collective inhale turned to screams as the glass shattered. Shards blew in through the ragged hole and skittered across the floor.

The smoke poured in now, setting off rounds of coughing and

garbled talking. The whistling wind dragged in a cold, damp air but the fire still blazed. They scattered, searching for cloths to cover their noses and mouths. Like frightened animals, they foraged only to meet up again in a panicked huddle by the refrigerator.

Will pulled down the blanket he'd wrapped around his head. "What about the rain? That should put the fire out, right?"

"Some but the rain died down. The storm is more fog and wind now." Rain wasn't a firehose or a miracle cure. Depending on the weather was a losing game. Every muscle in Alex's body slowly shut down, but his brain still worked . . . for now. "We have to get off the defensive and strike."

"The windows." Mitch nodded in the direction of the window on the other side of the room by the fireplace. "I can slip out there and—"

"Die." The stark delivery had everyone staring at Sierra and her grim expression.

Mitch turned to her as if begging her to understand. "I'll go out and see where Dylan is. Try to find a path for us to get to the garage or one of the other outbuildings. Our best recourse is to hide until we can find a way off this island that doesn't result in us drowning."

Ruthie shouted through the towel covering her mouth. "Don't you get it? He's planned all of this. He's waiting for you."

"Is he half as smart as he says he is?" Cassie asked.

Ruthie nodded. "Smart and devious. For him, this is a matter of survival. He's convinced the only answer is for all of you to die."

"Then he would have contemplated a possible window escape," Cassie said.

Mitch's shoulders lifted in question. "I'm open to any other plan."

Smoke billowed into the room, blanketing it in a heavy gray film. They all crouched and yelled to be heard over the fierce rumble of fire as it ate away at the front of the grand house.

The crackle and bangs drew Alex's attention. The walls seemed to shift and groan as flames curled into the room and snaked up the walls. "We have to move."

"I'll be the diversion." Ruthie dropped her towel and lifted her gun. "Everyone gets down and out of the way. We'll open the door to draw his fire. Mitch can escape through the window."

"I'm going with him." Sierra held her hand in front of Mitch's face. "No arguments."

Mitch nodded before turning to Will. "You need to back up Ruthie. Pull her out of Dylan's line of sight and slam the door shut if this goes sideways."

Ruthie winced. "I don't think—"

"Fine," Will said.

Alex refused to put any trust in Ruthie. If he had more strength he might wrestle that gun away from her. With that not being an option, he had to hope her will to survive outran her desire for answers. "Do you know how to use that?"

Ruthie's grim expression didn't give anything away. "I'll shoot Dylan if I have to."

"You two." Mitch nodded toward Cassie and Alex. "Cas, can you get him out?"

Alex hoped he could walk to the window. Jumping out of it sounded impossible.

Cassie didn't hesitate. "Yes. We'll be right behind you."

They all moved into position. Cassie and Alex stayed close behind Mitch and Sierra, but everything depended on Ruthie . . . the person who'd dragged them into this hellfire.

She did the countdown on her fingers. "Go!"

Her shout broke through the crashing roar of the fire. The back door flew open, sucking the flames deeper into the house. Will and Ruthie flattened against the inside wall on either side of the door. Mitch and Sierra were already moving. He went through the window first, sliding into the opening and ignoring the wind trying to shove him back inside. He did a quick look around then reached for Sierra. Her feet were the last thing Alex saw before she disappeared into the foggy night.

Dylan didn't rush inside or shoot. If he hovered just beyond the back door he possessed the patience to hold his ground and wait.

"I'm going out." Ruthie waited for Will to nod and then they ducked low, almost at a crouch, and slipped outside.

Alex didn't like her with a gun so close to Will. "We need to—"

Cassie put her finger to Alex's lips to cut him off. "The boat."

"What?"

"Those are for the car, right? Grab them." She pointed at the keys on the floor. "We're going to find Dylan's boat and get out of here."

He pocketed the key ring without thinking, his focus solely on his wife. Her eyes were wild and her movements frantic as she raced around the room. She grabbed the only knife left.

The smallest one. She mumbled to herself as she picked up her cell . . . then took the others, too.

But that would strand everyone else. They couldn't. Little got through to his brain right now, but that did. "That maniac is going to kill our friends if we don't help."

She put her hands on his forearms, careful not to touch his wound. "You're injured and can barely function. I need you off this island and safe."

He couldn't do this again. He had so much blood on his hands already. "Cassie . . ."

"The best thing we can do for the people we love is get to a place where we can call the police."

But he knew that wasn't really her plan. This was about survival. About Cassie looking out for Cassie and the life she'd created and fought for.

"Leave them a phone," he said.

She dragged him toward the back door and peeked out. "We need to control this."

His knees buckled as she pulled him into the cloudy night. Cold air whipped around him and pelted him through the tiny holes in the blanket. Fog covered every inch of the island. Combined with the darkness, he couldn't see the water or land in the distance or anything more than a few feet in front of him. Behind him? Flames eating through the house.

"Lean on me," Cassie whispered.

The burning smell filled his nose, and he started choking. He needed to sit, to lie down, but Cassie didn't give him those options. She tugged and heaved. Her shoes slid on the wet grass. Her strained breathing echoed around him.

They turned the corner of the house and kept going. His head spun. He couldn't figure out which direction they were headed in. Then they slammed to a stop.

Alex's head bounced up and he saw the only person they needed to avoid standing less than three feet away. Alex couldn't really make out his face. He didn't have to.

Dylan laughed. "Where do you two think you're going?"

CHAPTER FIFTY-THREE

RUTHIE

The maniacal laughter stopped Ruthie. The steam ran out of her run. Will kept walking but slowed down. She glanced at Sierra and Mitch, who'd also stilled at the sound. None of them said a word, but they had to go back.

After all the research and interviews, Ruthie suspected Cassie and Alex had played pivotal roles in the killings twelve years ago. Having met them and had personal experience with both of them, her dislike had grown, but she couldn't walk away now.

"He found Cassie and Alex." Ruthie whispered the horrible truth when no one offered a different explanation.

Will turned to stare her down. "*He* as in your boyfriend."

Sierra groaned. "Don't do this now."

But Will stepped in front of Ruthie. Got in her face and hurled his anger straight at her. "You're the reason my friends are in danger."

Ruthie was done with his shit. He glossed over his responsibility for landing them here. Blamed everyone else. Slunk into a corner as others stood up and fought. No more. "You and your friends are the reason my friend is dead. So I guess we're even."

Will grabbed her arm and squeezed. "Emily never talked about you."

The unexpected force of the grip stole Ruthie's breath. She tried to pull out of his hold but couldn't. His anger, so carefully banked until now, flared, increasing his strength until her arm went numb. "Let go."

"What is wrong with you?" Sierra shoved Will away from Ruthie. "Stop manhandling her."

"Thank you," Ruthie mumbled. The protection humbled her. She genuinely liked Sierra. Betraying her had been difficult despite the fact they barely knew each other.

"No. Don't be grateful." Sierra's exasperation bubbled over. She held up her hand, standing like an avenging angel with her hair unbound and her gaze scanning the landscape for incoming danger. "Your behavior has been crap, but that doesn't change the facts. Dylan is not your responsibility, and you are not Will's punching bag."

Sierra wasn't wrong. Ruthie could admit that . . . just not out loud.

Wound up and ready, Will didn't slink away chastised. "Of course this is her fault."

Ruthie saw the comment for what it was—annoying bluster. He'd been quiet most of the day and happy to blend into the background whenever difficult topics arose. Now, when she was the proposed target, he found his balls and came out fighting. She was about to tell him what she thought of his refocusing when Mitch jumped in.

"Shut up. Not another word."

Will frowned at his friend. "Why are you turning on me?"

"Ah, the moment I've been waiting for. When you start chewing off your limbs in an effort to escape. There's nothing as satisfying as watching you sacrifice each other." Dylan materialized, came around the corner of the house holding a gun to Alex's head. Cassie walked in front of the pair with her hands in the air. "Please carry on. I'm in the mood for a fight to the death."

Will's shoulders fell as the indignation ran out of him. "Damn."

Ruthie was done with Dylan most of all. This vengeance-soaked version of him had stolen enough of the limelight. "Put the gun down."

He scoffed. "I know it sounds childish but make me."

"Did you really think ordering him would work?" Mitch asked.

"Everyone, drop your weapons." Dylan waited for compliance but none of them moved. "I need to see knives hit the ground."

"We can't see anything," Sierra said.

"I can solve that." Dylan reached into his pocket and took out his phone. One press of a button with his free hand and the pathway lights brightened. The fog still plunged most of the area into a shadowy gray stillness, but they could see a few feet in front of them now. "I'm a problem solver."

The jagged cut across his cheek reminded Ruthie that he could be defeated, if only temporarily. But temporarily might be all she needed to take back control. She had the gun hidden in her skirt pocket, but could she use it? She brought it in case things grew rocky with Will and his friends. She'd never contemplated this situation, of being forced to defend them.

Right now, Dylan didn't seem to realize she carried a gun. Ruthie knew if she took the weapon out things would escalate, meaning she'd be a major player in an unwanted shoot-out. She needed to put the possibility off as long as possible. The man on a rampage now meant something to her once. They shared a profound loss that upended and unbalanced their lives . . . and a part of her feared she wouldn't be able to fire. Not at him. Not when a part of her still grieved along with him.

"I'll ask one more time." He waved the gun around until the knives plunked against the wet ground. "Well done. Now, everyone, kneel. Hands on your heads."

Ruthie refused. She needed to stay upright. To be able to reach and aim. "We can't—"

"Don't push me. I have you to thank for being here but a stockpile of information will only win you so much favor." His eyes narrowed. "Any weapons you have need to hit the ground, too."

Did he know about her gun? He seemed to be a step ahead on everything else, but she doubted he expected her to carry, so she kept the weapon right where it was.

Will's knees didn't bend. He took a step toward Dylan, but Sierra stepped in front of him, clearly trying to drag the attention toward her and away from whatever inciting thing Will might say. "The house. The fire will draw attention."

Dylan frowned. "From where? Look around you. There's no one out here. The island is isolated. That's why this location was so perfect for this little reveal party."

The words crashed through the last of Ruthie's calm. Every part of her shook while her insides bounced and twisted. He knew . . . something, and she dreaded it, but she needed to know what it was. "The owners have a security system. The fire will trigger an alarm. You're running out of time."

Cassie gasped. "Are you trying to make him shoot us faster?"

"Me." The single word cut through the gusts of wind and black night.

The look of satisfaction on Dylan's face had Ruthie bracing for the shocking news ahead. "What does that mean?"

"I've taken over every system. Alarm. Fire. Rigged the entire place with the cameras and microphones I needed then disconnected the alarm system, so no call will go out to any police or fire department. Also blocked your cell phones, just to be safe." He shrugged. "I've even set up and paid for a series of reservations so the owners think the island will be occupied for the next month when really it's just us. No one will come here or find the bodies for a very long time."

That wasn't possible. She remembered the light back-and-forth about renting the property. The charming messages from the woman she thought was the owner. Not Dylan's style at all. "I was emailing—"

"A nice older woman? Yeah, still me." Dylan smiled. "See, I needed to guarantee our privacy this weekend. I needed to buy time to bury the evidence and erase you all forever."

He'd spent so much time cannibalizing her plan and creating a meticulous one of his own. He steered her to this house and controlled all communication about it. For every move she made to get the group there and box them in, Dylan was two to three moves ahead. He snuck into her computer and remembered their conversations then redrew her plans to suit his needs. It was amazing he hadn't killed them all already, but she guessed the delay only added to his amusement. He enjoyed toying with them, watching them spin as they fought and devoured each other.

"You planned to burn down the house," she said, looking for any way to put off the inevitable.

"It was a contingency plan that Sierra forced me into when she threw that knife." His gaze lingered on Sierra. "Nice shot, by the way. It's a shame it will be the only one you get."

Tension swirled and danced around them like a living, breathing thing. The night crawled toward dawn, but the dark clouds and waning storm plunged them into what felt like never-ending blackness.

He was forcing her to take her gun out and kill him. Despite all the horrific things he'd done and how far over the edge he'd gone, every cell inside her balked at ending him and giving the rest of them an easy way out.

"Since I need your attention, I'll resolve this problem, too." He tapped against his phone again, never letting up on the threat to Alex. "The sprinklers will turn on and put out the fire. Still no call out, but fire remediation will begin. Again, genius."

"More like demented." Mitch shook his head.

Sierra joined him. "Sweet Jesus."

"He's not going to help you." Dylan's hold tightened around Alex's neck. "So, who wants to start talking and save poor Alex here?"

"Please don't." The pleading in Cassie's voice bordered on pain.

Dylan dug the barrel of the gun into the side of Alex's head. "Wrong answer. Say goodbye to your husband."

CHAPTER FIFTY-FOUR

SIERRA

Stop. Just stop." Cassie arms shook. She'd barely raised them and now they looked too heavy to hold as a wariness washed over her. "We don't know any more about what happened to Brendan than you do."

"Apparently she doesn't care if you die." Dylan said the words right into Alex's ear.

Cassie stood up, or started to, but the fierce bleakness in Dylan's eyes had her dropping down again. "I'm trying to explain."

"Unless you have a revelation to make or guilty details to spill, you should stop talking."

Sierra sifted through the thoughts bombarding her brain, searching for the right words to stop this madness, but nothing came to her. She wished she knew what really happened years ago. That would at least give her some leverage.

This time Ruthie tried. "Dylan, please listen to me."

"If you plan on trying some sex thing, save it. Not in the mood."

Ruthie closed her eyes as if even broaching that topic cost her something. "I'm trying to keep you from killing."

"Too late." Mitch whispered the comment, but the wind

shifted and carried it through the circle of desperate, panic-filled bodies.

"You're not wrong." Dylan stared at Mitch. "But, technically, Tyler was your fault."

"How do you figure that?"

Stay calm. The words echoed in Sierra's head. She needed Mitch to stay calm, to not match Dylan's ire or shove him into a new round of threats.

"He was following you around, trying to get your attention. I kept tripping over him. At first, I figured he was looking for payback for your sending him to jail." Dylan's wide smile suggested he was enjoying every minute of this. "Imagine my surprise when I confronted him and he babbled about needing your forgiveness."

Mitch's jaw clenched. "That was never going to happen."

"That's what I told him. I know only too well that you can't forgive someone for killing the person you love most. For smashing your family into pieces and sucking every ounce of love out of your parents. For destroying your hope and your future. For turning your life into an endless battle to gain leverage then lower the boom, even though you know engaging in a slaughter won't ease the screaming in your brain." Dylan's eerie words echoed over the island.

Mitch nodded. "Agreed."

Sierra hated all of this.

"See? Look how much we have in common." The singsong cadence of Dylan's voice had returned. An amused, almost inhuman sound.

Sierra close her eyes on a new punch of despair. She needed Mitch not to be lured in or let his mind travel to a place where he grouped his life and his behavior with Dylan's, but she had no way of shoring up Mitch's self-esteem right now.

"Tyler was my test case. His guilt had been established. He killed your dad. He didn't deserve sympathy. I killed him and planted him in the car, waiting for you all to arrive so I could unlock the garage and you could find him." Dylan's grip on Alex eased up while he talked.

"But Tyler had nothing to do with you." Sierra shifted her weight as she looked for a vulnerable spot to lunge at Dylan, to knock him off-balance just long enough for the others to attack him, which was a thing she hoped they'd know to do, and for Ruthie to finally pull out that damn gun.

Inviting his attention was a risk and made her a target but killing her wouldn't give him the satisfaction he craved. Sierra was betting on the fact that every vicious act on this island was about settling an old score that didn't concern her except in the most tangential ways.

"Tyler served a purpose. And Mitch isn't exactly sad the guy is gone. Are you, Mitch?" Dylan kept on baiting. "I figured if everyone on the internet was wrong about you being a murderer then killing Tyler would be sort of an apology for stoking so much online anger at you."

A few seconds of silence passed. The rustling of the trees and hissing of the fire as the sprinklers finished their work provided background, but no one said a word.

Finally, Mitch whistled. "You really are insane."

"Stop throwing that word around." Some of Dylan's amusement faded, and his arm tightened against Alex's throat again. "Back to your friend here. Anyone want to save him?"

Cassie's voice softened. "You have the wrong guy."

"Then tell me who the *right* guy is. I promise to give him a nicer death than your buddy Jake got. What a fucking mess he was. Damn. I thought he'd crack but he kept saying he couldn't tell me what happened."

Poke. Poke. Poke. Sierra could hear Dylan chip away at the group's collective resolve. The dark energy bouncing around them ratcheted up. The stakes could not be higher as Dylan dropped one verbal bomb after the other.

"*Couldn't.* That's the word he used." Dylan shook his head. "As if I was giving him a choice. I admit his obstinance ticked me off after I went to all the trouble to lure him here. Hence the overkill."

"How did you get him to come here?" Mitch asked.

Dylan shrugged. "More fake emails. I made you sound very desperate. He came, thinking he needed to save you. That's a thing with your friends, isn't it? They all baby you."

The memory of the shed and that body swamped Sierra. Jake had come to help, which made his ending even worse. She doubted Mitch would ever get over the role he unwittingly played in his friend's death.

"Listen to me." Cassie's voice rose, getting stronger now. "There's nothing to tell. There's no piece of information that will magically make you feel better."

"You done? Because I know you set up Brendan and killed him." Dylan's gaze traveled around the group. "One of you. Some of you. All of you. The details. Now."

Patience expired. Dylan didn't say the words, but his affect changed. A lethal, there-are-no-limits vibe pulsed off of him. He was ready to kill again.

Verbal gymnastics. Trying to outwit Dylan wasn't going to

work. The harder they tried to avoid the inevitable showdown, the quicker it would come.

Sierra needed Ruthie to fire that gun.

She tried to silently signal Ruthie to flash it, shoot it, threaten with it, anything to even the playing field or at least make Dylan see that he was not the only one with power here. Maybe there was a bond between Dylan and Ruthie because she seemed reluctant to take him down.

"You have five seconds." Dylan delivered the ultimatum to Will in a lifeless voice that promised bloodshed.

Ruthie, please. Sierra willed the other woman to look at her, but Ruthie stayed entranced by the scene unfolding in front of her.

"Okay, wait." Will held up his hands in surrender. "The police said—"

"Four."

It was clear Dylan thought he'd discovered the group's weak link. Now he sawed through the last strings tying Will to his old story. Sierra could almost feel the lies unraveling beneath them, ready to drop them into the abyss.

"No . . ." Will gulped in a large breath. "We're not the ones who said he killed Emily."

"Three." Dylan's attention flashed to Sierra. "Stop moving or I put a bullet in him."

"You don't . . . please . . ." Will folded his arms over his head. His body rocked back and forth as if the words pounded inside him, begging to get out. "I didn't mean . . ."

"Spit it out." Dylan's eyebrows rose. "Cassie? Mitch? Will? Last chance to chime in."

But Alex was the one who moved. He pressed against the arm choking him from behind.

"No." Cassie shook her head. "Stay quiet."

Dylan continued. "Two."

Tension whipped around them, pushing against them. Could the air punch and kick? Because that's what it felt like. A collision of the elements and a history that refused to rest. This strangling pressure that closed in and pummeled their defenses, battering against their worn and exhausted bodies in an attempt to force the horrible words to tumble out.

Sierra held her breath as the group struggled in silence. The pleading looks. The uncomfortable shifting. The debilitating fear that coated and corroded everything it touched as the fog rolled over them.

Cassie looked at Sierra. "Do something."

She only knew one way. One possible thing. "Ruthie. Now."

"One," Dylan said at the same time.

They all started talking. Most of them stood up, except Will, who curled closer to the ground. Cassie reached for Alex, who'd lost all color and hung limp in Dylan's hold. Sierra could feel Mitch's hand on her arm, pulling her back from the collective, unconscious lunge forward.

"Stop. God, stop." Will's arms were fully extended now. Stiff and up and in the air as his head dropped forward. "Please don't kill me."

Dylan wore an unreadable expression. "Say the right words."

Will's chest rose and fell as the words rushed out of him. "It was me. Brendan is dead because of me."

CHAPTER FIFTY-FIVE

ALEX

Alex rallied even as his brain and his body begged to shut down. He craved the sweet oblivion of sleep. Anything to make the throbbing at his temples stop. He focused on the wild look in his wife's eyes. He tethered to her mentally, attempting to force her energy into his muscles before the collapse came.

The strained words echoed in Alex's head. Will had admitted to killing Brendan. He'd opened a can they'd promised to seal and bury and never touch again.

"Will, don't do this." Alex meant to yell the words, but they came out as a pained whisper.

"I'd let the man talk, if I were you." Dylan was right there. His voice and his arms. He refused to back away and let Alex fall.

Will's arms slowly lowered until his hands lay open on the soaked lawn by his sides. "It was . . . you don't . . . It was an accident."

"Wrong. Try again."

The rush of angry breath behind Alex intensified the ache running through him. Like every day since that night, he wanted to call it all back, to close his eyes and pretend it never happened.

The way Dylan's arms contracted served as a painful reminder that this retelling wouldn't lessen the damage. Nothing could.

"Will." Ruthie looked near tears as reality crept up on her. "How could you?"

How could he do it . . . how could he live with it? A list of justifications and explanations rushed up on Alex, but he kept silent. Not because he wanted Will to shoulder this burden alone, but because no answer made sense.

Cassie shook her head. "Will, please. Don't do this."

"One more word out of any of you and I shoot. Got it?" Dylan's firm voice suggested he'd do it.

Cassie. His Cassie. God, he'd loved her so much back then. Was so entranced with her drive. This stunning mix of brains and beauty reeled him in until he lost his way. She'd always been so clear, so in charge, Alex understood the pummeling terror she must be feeling as the shored up and carefully reinforced resistance she'd helped Will develop dissolved.

Will shook his head as he stared at the ground. "It was just supposed to scare him. We wanted to take him to the bridge and . . . and . . . I don't . . ."

"What was your real goal that night?" Dylan's voice grew rougher with each demand.

"Get him to talk." Will lifted his face. A mix of tears and rain streaked his cheeks. "We were trying to get . . . closure."

Ruthie shook her head. "You mean revenge."

Alex listened to Will's surrender. A halting voice but the bumbling words all made sense. Will had broken down. Lost it. The promises and the guilt he'd tried to quiet by getting lost in numbers unwound, leaving him mewing and desperate.

Pain dripped from Will's voice. Alex knew he didn't deserve

sympathy. None of them did, but to see his friend, someone so outwardly unemotional, expose the shattered pieces he hid under a thick layer of practicality proved crushing. So did Mitch's dazed expression. His mouth had dropped open as if he intended to say something but was unable to form the words.

Will's admission took them down a road that would lead to a hailstorm of devastation. While Ruthie and Dylan might gain insight, they'd never be able to understand or forgive . . . and the rest of them would be ripped apart. No amount of careful wording and emotional triage would put them back together again if they even managed to survive the night.

Dylan kept his focus on Will. "Tell me about the bridge."

"We went to Brendan's apartment. Told him who we were, but he knew." The words came out as a jumbled mess of heavy breathing and painful hiccups. "He tried to kick us out, but . . ." Will's voice died out but rose again. "We hit . . . we overpowered him. I pulled my car up to the building's loading dock. There was this . . . I don't know, a rolling bin kids used for moving. We put Brendan in there then dumped him in the trunk. We didn't think the police were watching him . . . but . . . no one stopped us or ever questioned us."

There it was. The grab. The first step in a series of decisions Alex would give almost anything to take back.

Sierra huddled closer to Mitch. "Oh my God."

"Who is *we*?" Dylan asked. "Don't look at them. Look at me. Who?"

"Me and Jake."

Will . . . no . . . Alex wanted to view this as luck but being omitted just compounded his guilt. All these years of keeping secrets and this one ached to get out.

Dylan hummed. "Two of you."

"We . . ." Will glanced at Alex but just for a second. "We wanted Brendan to confess. That's all."

Dylan was fully in control now. "And the bridge?"

"The water was out. They . . . the state . . . whatever . . ." Will inhaled, gulping in a big breath. "They dam up . . . The bed was dry."

"Enough with the water lesson. What happened?"

"We dragged him out of the car. He was conscious by then. He kicked and fought. Kept saying he didn't go near Emily, but the police said he did . . . " Will's voice trailed off to silence. He watched Dylan but didn't speak for a few seconds. "There was evidence. You need to understand—"

Dylan didn't lose focus. "What did you do at the bridge?"

Alex saw the end now. The world he'd so carefully built cracked and tilted. The foundation dropped as it crumbled beneath him.

Dylan set Alex away from him. Still held him up and held the gun but there was distance between them now. Alex tried to pivot away but Dylan didn't give an inch.

"We held him over . . . the side." Someone, it sounded like Sierra, gasped and that made Will stop, but not for long. "There was a bar. He shouldn't have gone over, but . . . he was jumpy and yelling. He had to stop yelling." Will covered his head with his hands again. It looked like he fought to keep the truth from seeping in, but the truth leaked out. "He kept insisting . . . you know, saying . . . but we didn't believe him. So we . . ."

"You killed him," Ruthie said in a rough voice.

Will was in tears now. Dragging in deep breaths and throwing out words through his begging. "God, you need to listen to me. We just wanted him to talk but he bolted. One second we held him, and he started thrashing. I don't even know how it happened. He . . . he lost his balance and fell. We tried to stop it. To grab him in time."

Mitch's shoulders fell. "Fucking unbelievable."

Everything stopped. No talking. Hell, Alex could no longer feel the chill air or hear the whoosh of the wind as it raced through the fire-pocked house somewhere behind him.

"It wasn't supposed to happen that way." Will's body slumped as the last of the energy ran out of him. "It was an accident."

Sierra wrapped her arm around Mitch and dragged him in close, but his wide-eyed, sullen look said more than words could. She looked torn between wanting to soothe Mitch and wanting to berate Will with her disgust.

Alex waited for Ruthie to say something, for the gun to go off. None of that happened. The pitter-patter of renewed rain as it hit the leaves came into focus. Alex tried to match his breathing to the gentle ticking sound but then the gun pressed against his skull again.

"Your turn."

A move Alex expected. Dylan believed some of the story, not all. The jolting, ripped-out-of-him way Will told it spoke to its veracity. But Dylan knew there was more . . . and he was right.

"No." Cassie dropped to the ground, digging her fingers into the mud. She rose in a rush, carrying a knife, and lunged right for Dylan.

The pressure against Alex's back disappeared and his body fell. He went boneless and his knees hit the ground with a crack of pain. He cried out as the world above him broke into chaos. He could see them all move and watched Cassie duck then fall.

A gunshot cut through the frenzy, dropping them all to the

ground. He heard screams and grunts. Watched Mitch reach for Sierra as they both slipped into a crouch. When Alex looked up again Dylan was watching him, and the gun was right there.

"Stop!" Ruthie cried out.

Alex waited for the bullet to tear into him. For bone and blood to explode as he took his final breath. When he opened his eyes again, he was struck by the still air and stunned expressions of his friends. His gaze traveled and he saw it. Ruthie standing there with a gun of her own. Did she fire a warning shot or was it Dylan? Alex thought Dylan, but who could tell?

"This is over, Dylan," she said.

A feral smile broke out on his face. "But is it?"

CHAPTER FIFTY-SIX

RUTHIE

Ruthie thought she was prepared to hear the truth, but the last ten minutes had turned her world upside down. The final minutes of Brendan's life had been filled with terror and shock.

Will. Outwardly upright, privileged, quietly wounded, hiding his feelings, desperate for love and acceptance. Will killed Brendan. He tried to hedge by calling it an accident, but he couldn't weasel out of his guilt.

She'd targeted Will and ruthlessly ripped through his past looking for answers. She arranged that meeting at the gallery and planned for at least one more "imagine bumping into you" type meeting, hoping to initiate an ongoing flirtation that would allow her to get close enough to assess him and ask the right questions. Even with his merry-go-round of past marriage requests, she'd never expected he'd flip from nodding as she described her fake job to talk of deep feelings within the span of two dates.

The immediate intimacy was dizzying because it furthered her agenda, but it raised a red flag. In any other circumstance a guy rushing her into a relationship after a few okay dates would have been a *run from him* warning that she'd joke about with her friends over brunch after she broke up with him by text. But she'd needed to stay close to Will, so she allowed herself to get sucked in. She borrowed a page from Emily's diary and disconnected the romance from the sex.

Ruthie played a role, believing it would be short-term pain for long-term gain. Looking back, she realized Will's tamped-down hold on his emotions was the key to unrolling all of this. Until this weekend, she'd never seen a burst of anger . . . but she missed the subtle signs. His reactions stayed steady, almost unnaturally so. Never too much and always too little. Now, it seemed obvious. He'd lost it that night with Brendan then spent twelve years trying to bury the act deep in his psyche so that he never felt anything real again.

And Dylan. In measured beats, through a series of non-idle threats, he'd demanded answers. She could feel his reality shift and tear. His actions had forced her to finally take out the gun. She'd smuggled it out of the house in her skirt, avoiding the problem of wrestling it out of the holster and waiting for the right time. Probably waited too long and now he was laughing at her, amused to find her fighting back.

She had no idea how to read any of the twisted emotions pulsing off him and polluting the air around him. He had a foot on Alex's thigh, trapping him. Dylan switched the targets of his aim often, not allowing any of them time to relax or to dive at him. He moved with an awareness that trapped them in the role of prey. The gun and the swagger with which he wielded it had them frantic yet riveted, unable to look away.

He'd ventured well past the point of being open to reason, but she tried anyway. She didn't have another choice, except to shoot. She could aim to injure him only, but that sounded too risky. He'd become an unstoppable force, equal parts driven and demented, but the need to complete her mission, to find the answers to the questions that had taken over and shrunk her life, burned through her.

As sick as it sounded, his presence kicked a door open to the past. A door she might not have been able to breach without his unexpected interference this weekend.

"You have your answer. We know what happened to Brendan." She glanced at Will, saw a pitiful man dissolved in a pool of his own guilt, and felt the slight buzz of loss for the person he might have been had his life traveled a different path.

She cared about keeping Sierra safe. The rest of them barely registered with Ruthie, which made her question just how much of her decency she'd forfeited in this search. Fake engagements. Weighing people's worth. Lies. Isolation. Violence. Dylan. The pieces ran around in her head until a scream formed in her throat.

"You know that's not all of it. Your honey implicates a dead man, makes up a story about an accident, and we're supposed to say *fine* and walk away?" Dylan shook his head. "We deserve more than that."

He wasn't wrong. Will's story smacked of convenience and antiseptic scrubbing. Nothing he said explained what happened to Emily, but she couldn't ignore Dylan's self-assigned role of judge and executioner. *We deserve* not *Brendan and Emily deserve*. "You've gathered resources. We all heard what Will said. The police will handle the rest."

"Like they did last time?" Dylan wasn't smiling now. He'd reverted to a reflection of the man she'd met months ago. Earnest and broken but not void of humanity. "You heard him. They dragged Brendan out of his apartment. Scared the hell out of him."

"It's sick and they deserve to be punished, but not by your brand of vigilante justice. You're not this guy." She didn't know what he was these days. He'd spiraled in the months since she walked away, but she was willing to say anything to win him over now.

"They made me into this guy."

Sierra and Mitch jerked back as Dylan waved his gun around. Cassie watched each flick of his wrist, her body clearly ready to push up and pounce if the right moment arose.

"You know I can shoot. We practiced together at the range." Ruthie saw Cassie shift and feared a very savvy person was about to do something very foolish. "I shoot you. You shoot me. They all go free. Is that really what you want, Dylan?"

"I will kill anyone who tries to stop me. Including you."

Dizziness filled her head as time ran out. *Aim for the leg. The stomach.* Somewhere that would stop him but still give him a chance to survive. A chance he hadn't granted Tyler or Jake. She gripped the gun tighter.

A smile inched up the corner of Dylan's mouth. "Do you honestly think I'd let you keep a loaded gun all this time?"

Mitch's head dropped. "Shit."

Sierra leaned against him. "This can't be happening."

"I told you about the cameras. About watching every move." He nodded in Sierra's direction. "Including seeing Sierra find you with the weapon."

Cassie's mouth dropped open. "What?"

Mitch scowled at Sierra. "When did this happen?"

"I didn't know who she was back then. An hour ago."

Ruthie blocked the panicked grumbling and the choking sensation as the last spark of hope flickered out among the group. She hadn't fired that last shot but she intended to fire this one, or at least make him think that she would. "I reloaded the gun. I've had it with me every second since then."

Dylan's amusement was obvious. "Are you sure?"

Yes? Waves of fear combined with a numbing sense of failure, attacking her memories. She couldn't separate out the wishes from the reality. She questioned her brain and her hands. Every part of her rejected his gloating but the mental picture didn't become any clearer.

"What are you doing? Shoot him. He can't fire back at all of us at the same time," Cassie said.

"Are you willing to bet his life on it?" Dylan aimed at Will then Alex. "Or his? Because Will and Jake didn't act alone, did they?"

"You heard the truth." Cassie's usually strong voice faltered. "Alex wasn't there."

Will stood up. "It was me."

"Fine. Then you win." Dylan didn't telegraph his moves or his decision. He said the words and fired two shots right into Will's chest.

The loud booms rang out as Will's body dropped. He sprawled on his back, unmoving.

"Wait . . ." Stunned by the sudden move, Ruthie's hand went slack and the gun dropped. Her breathing kicked up as she slid across the grass and landed on her knees beside Will's still body. She grabbed his hand, watching the blood soak through his shirt and his dark eyes fill with pain.

Bloody coughs shook through him as he fought for air. He

didn't try to talk but he stared at her, almost willing her not to let go. But she had no idea how to help. The only way was to rewind the last few months and, this time, not drop into his life.

The group gathered around his bent legs and heaving chest. Cassie fussed with Will's head and Mitch shouted something about stopping the bleeding. Alex laid nearby, propped up on an elbow with his legs stretched behind him. His hand rested on Will's calf as if he needed to touch his friend and forge a bond one last time.

The cold air filled with whispers of encouraging words and soft cries as Will gasped, desperate to draw in air while he drowned in his own blood. The labored breathing went from quick and shallow to quiet. His chest stilled and his eyes stared blankly at the dark sky. Ruthie watched the life seep out of him as his hand dropped from hers.

The man she had silently vowed not to care about and insisted she hated, the one who had delivered so much damage and lied about it for years, vanished. She ached for the imperfect, damaged man he was. One who owed amends but was hunted and executed in isolation so far from home.

They all sat slumped on the wet grass with the rain still pelting them. Only a throat clearing broke the silence.

"Two down." This time Dylan pointed the gun at Alex. "You're next."

Ruthie saw Sierra and realized she hadn't been huddled around Will at the end. She stood behind Dylan, fireplace poker in hand. And swung.

The metal made a sharp cracking sound as it slammed into the side of Dylan's head. His eyes closed and his snarky expression crumbled. The gun tumbled and his knees buckled. He went down in a boneless whoosh. Fell into a heap and didn't move. The gun landed in the leaves a few feet from his hand, but he didn't reach for it.

Mitch got up and approached Sierra with careful steps, like he might approach a wounded animal. "Sierra?"

Ruthie tried to process the last few minutes. The hopelessness. Sierra's bravery and quick thinking. She still held the poker in the air, but Ruthie could see her arms shake.

Sierra finally blinked. "Who needs a gun."

CHAPTER FIFTY-SEVEN

SIERRA

The rampaging noise in Sierra's head refused to die down. A mix of adrenaline and fear crashed through her. After years of loving Mitch and wondering if she could ever take another person's life she had her answer. She could be pushed to a place where she welcomed the darkness, even wallowed in it.

She'd filled that swing with her anger and rage. Let each shaky, panic-filled minute of being on this island fuel her. The crack against his skull was her answer to every smirk, every feral laugh, every life Dylan took.

Standing there, she couldn't stop shaking. Her body felt wobbly and out of balance. The poker bobbled in her hand until Mitch gently took it from her and threw it on the ground.

Sierra couldn't muster a second of relief or lightness. Not when she glanced over and saw Will's lifeless body. She'd only really known a reflection of him through Mitch. He'd viewed Will as trapped by his upbringing. Lonely in a room full of people. Desperately searching for something he couldn't define.

Did one heinous act define a person? Maybe. Probably not. All she knew was that atonement didn't stop with a confession, and it took more than twelve years and profound duress for Will to even muster that.

Most people could go through their entire lives without seeing a dead body. She'd had three thrown in front of her in about twelve hours and watched Will bleed out at her feet. She couldn't process the loss. Her brain balked at every moment, including the dread of what this would do to Mitch. He kept moving, as if compartmentalizing the grief from the danger. Smart, but a person could only live in that sort of fantasy for so long.

"You're right. Heroes don't need guns," Mitch said.

"Well, I do." Cassie bent down and scooped up Dylan's abandoned gun. She checked the chamber and seemed satisfied with what she saw.

Her tone sent a warning skidding across Sierra's already frazzled nerves. "What are you—"

Cassie moved before Sierra could guess her intentions. One second she held a gun. The next second, she bent down and when she stood up again she held two.

"Give me my gun," Ruthie demanded.

Cassie ignored the uncomfortable shuffling around her. "We need to figure out what we do next. What we say to people. It's not as simple as calling the police and volunteering statements."

"This isn't hard, Cassie," Mitch said. "We get off this island, call the police, and have Dylan arrested."

Cassie shook her head. "You know that can't happen."

The sky lightened to a soft gray, hinting at the coming dawn, but Sierra didn't feel an ounce of relief. Just as they'd neutralized one, another hazard roared to life. This one was even more dangerous because she had so much to lose. Cassie's comments weren't about Dylan or the island. They were about hiding the secrets she'd dedicated her life to protecting.

"Because Alex was there when Brendan died." Sierra didn't phrase it as a question because she didn't have to. There was no other explanation for Cassie's fierce hold on her version of the truth. "That's the problem, right?"

"No." Mitch swore under his breath. "Come on. No."

"I swear it was an accident." Alex struggled to his feet with Cassie's help. "We were only trying to scare him."

Cassie put a hand in front of his face. "Stop talking."

Sierra had guessed and assumed as Will divulged his secrets. The group of friends had been inseparable back then, so Alex tagging along made sense. The unspoken part, the idea she refused to acknowledge, was that it would have been normal for Mitch to be there, too. So far, nothing in the conversation pointed to that, but she braced for the admission.

As it stood now, the story was the type that had repeated throughout history without fail. Three young men, high on anger and testosterone, threatened a weaker one. They bullied and berated him until he died. Jake, Alex, and Will might not have pushed Brendan off that bridge, but they contributed to his death. Sierra didn't know much about the law, but she knew Cassie would never tolerate having that sort of information about her past and her husband become public.

"There is a clean ending here. Jake and Will paid a terrible price for the bad decisions they made years ago. Only Dylan has to answer for the carnage today. Not anyone else." Cassie delivered the comments like a closing argument, challenging them all to continue on as reluctant coconspirators to the awful secret.

The wind had finally died down. It kicked up in gusts now

and then but the steady battering had subsided. Sierra almost didn't notice until the quiet fell over the group.

Ruthie was the one to break the silence. "Tyler and two of your friends are dead and you're worried about your legal exposure?"

Cassie's gaze traveled over Will and some of her rigid self-confidence faltered. She didn't cry but her chin bobbed and un-shed tears filled her eyes. She sniffed them back, as if refusing to let them fall. The brief hint of humanity clashed with her tough talk, and in a flash the emotion disappeared.

"We didn't come this far to lose now." Cassie unloaded Ruthie's gun then handed it back to her. "Look at that. Dylan was lying, which makes me wonder why you didn't just shoot him and end this thing. Maybe you were partners outside of bed, just as he suggested?" Cassie continued to her next thought before Ruthie could answer. "But now I have the only gun with bullets. So, unless someone plans to hit me with a stick or the poker, I'm in charge."

Mitch made a strange sound. Sierra thought it might be disgust, or the final door slamming on his loyalty to the past.

Mitch stepped in front of Cassie, facing her. "You need to take a breath and realize what you're saying here."

"Don't patronize me. I'm very aware of what I'm doing."

Sierra worried Cassie would shoot him. "I get that you're worried for Alex, but—"

"Not this time, sunshine," Cassie snapped. "You don't get to swoop in and play the role of peacemaker."

That unbending sense of being right. Sierra guessed that's what had kept the pretense strong and the lie alive for so long. Cassie controlled the narrative, and she controlled Alex. She didn't know how to stop . . . probably didn't want to.

Sierra tried to reason, hoping a sliver would get through to Cassie's supposedly big brain. "Alex can explain what happened to the police. He was a kid."

"He was twenty-one," Ruthie pointed out.

Cassie shook her head. "Alex's age then or now doesn't matter because he wasn't on that bridge."

"This isn't just about Brendan. It's about Emily," Ruthie said.

"Right." Cassie's chin rose. "Brendan killed her."

Alex glanced at his wife but didn't contradict her.

Something in the look he gave her had Sierra doubting. "Do you still think you can sell that?"

"It's either that or tell the truth." Cassie's gaze shifted to Mitch as she spoke.

What the hell? Sierra kept peeling back layers, horrified at the rot underneath. "Which is?"

An unreadable look passed between Cassie and Alex before she spoke again. "Will was drunk and made a pass at Emily. They struggled. It was an accident."

Ruthie snorted. "Another inconvenient accident?"

The story made no sense. Sierra mentally walked through the timeline then tried again and still she fumbled. "Why would Will go after Brendan for killing Emily if he's the one who killed her?"

"To cover his tracks. Will killed Emily by accident and panicked. Will convinced Jake the police were right about Brendan. They went to scare Brendan, and he jumped off the bridge. Dylan is a homicidal maniac who tricked us into coming here and then killed almost everyone on this island." Cassie shot them a see-how-easy-that-is look of satisfaction. "End of story."

Even if pieces of that were true, and Sierra doubted all of them now, none of that explained how Cassie knew what happened to Emily and Brendan and when she knew it. "Not even close."

Cassie shrugged. "You don't get a say."

"What about me, Cassie?" Mitch asked. "You've been lying to me for twelve years."

Alex shook his head. "We've been protecting you."

"I'm a grown man. Protecting me from what?"

"Enough." Cassie held the gun steady now. She'd dedicated her life to this story and didn't show any signs of backing down. "Alex and I are going to find Dylan's boat and go get the car. After Alex gets medical help and we give our explanation to the police, which we expect you to support, then we'll send people here to rescue you."

Her confidence chipped away at Sierra's. Just when she thought she understood the game at play, it changed again.

"What the hell are you talking about?" Mitch asked.

Cassie kept talking. "My story saves us all."

Ruthie glanced at Dylan, who still hadn't moved. "He'll talk."

"Then you should take care of him." Cassie looked at Sierra. "Another defensive swing or two should do it."

Cassie wanted them to roll around in the blood with her. Sierra could see the argument. *You killed Dylan and there's no evidence he was a bad guy, so I'll set you up to be the aggressor.* Sierra refused to play. "You've lost it."

"You're going to be on this island with him and without a loaded gun until we get back." Cassie gave Dylan's body one last shove with her foot. "You need to protect yourself."

Mitch whistled. "Fucking unbelievable."

"Is it?" Sierra asked.

"Hate me. Call me names. I don't care." Cassie's tone matched her words. "I'm protecting my family and, whether you appreciate it or not, I'm giving you a chance to save yourselves."

"Dylan isn't the only one with an ego problem," Mitch said.

"He's going to wake up soon. I'd handle him before he attacks again. Who knows what else he has hidden around here that could kill you."

Ruthie took a step toward Cassie. "When we get off this island, I'm going to hurt you."

Cassie leaned in. "*If* you get off."

CHAPTER FIFTY-EIGHT

ALEX

He'd lost all control of the situation. Screw the headache and dizziness, the pain in his shoulder and slow shutdown of his muscles. Alex knew he needed to rein Cassie in. He'd tried many times over the years and failed, but he had to succeed this time. She'd become untethered in her need to keep the crumbling façade in place.

He waited until they left their friends, and she had a chance to take a few deep breaths away from the stench of death. "You know we can't do this. That was tough talk back there, but that's all it was."

She picked up the pace as she walked them around the house, scanning the landscape for a small inflatable or whatever Dylan used to get to the island while he parked his larger boat somewhere else. "We don't have a choice."

"Of course we do." When she didn't stop, he grabbed her arm and yanked her to a halt.

"We will lose everything, including our daughter." Her wild eyes matched her rapid speech. The practical veneer she wore collapsed as her armor fell. "What were you thinking back there, admitting to being on the bridge when Brendan died?"

"I was there." It felt oddly comforting to admit it out loud. "Going to Brendan's place was *my* idea. I'm the one who suggested we threaten him, beat him up if we had to, to get a confession. Me, not Will. He took the fall for me, and Dylan killed him for it."

The reality of dead friends and wasted lives crushed him, but he pressed on. He deserved the physical pain he was in and the emotional blow to come.

Will's confession acted like a slamming door in Alex's mind. No more pretending or bumping along. Cassie operated on fear. She pushed forward to outrun her panic about being dragged backward into the kind of upbringing she viewed as a death sentence. He'd played along for so long, blaming her and avoiding his own responsibility, cowed by the implied threat that she'd protected him and would ruin him if he talked. It had to end.

"If you would have told me that your genius plan to avenge Emily was to attack Brendan, I would have stopped you back then. I let my guard down for a few hours and you almost ruined everything," she said.

"Ruined your plans, you mean."

"Your future!" She shook her head. "Without me . . . do you . . . We wouldn't be in this mess more than a decade later if you hadn't gone off on your own."

"Well, before marriage I still thought for myself."

"And look how that worked out." She zoned in on what she clearly saw as his betrayal. "Your sudden show of honesty back there could destroy our family. So, once again, I have to clean up your mess. You should have kept your mouth shut."

"Dylan will wake up and kill them." He pointed it out because he didn't want to believe that was her twisted plan.

She headed for the dock next to the sunken causeway. "I warned them."

The breath squeezed out of his aching lungs. No denial. No softening of the possible outcome. She'd taken Dylan's gun and unloaded Ruthie's, leaving them all potentially defenseless against Dylan's rage. It was as if she welcomed the violence to come. "You want Dylan to attack them. You want us to be the sole survivors of this weekend."

"It's the only way for us to get through this with minimal damage."

Whatever line had kept them from becoming someone like Dylan blurred into nonexistence. She'd jumped over it, smashed it. Pretended she didn't see it. Knowing she could divorce her humanity from the pursuit of her lifetime goals didn't shake him as much as it should have because he knew. He'd lived it for years.

"You said Will killed Emily." It was tough to force the words out, but Alex did it, hoping she would rush to explain she'd gotten lost in the moment or something equally benign.

"That is the story we'll tell, yes. That is the story from now on."

He stopped walking. Stopped following her around in a daze like a lost puppy. "And the promise about contacting the police?"

She glanced at him over her shoulder. "I never promised that."

He'd devoted his life to a woman who claimed to love him and promised to support him. She'd been so strong back then. So in charge when his mind had turned to mush and fear had overtaken his reason. Now he wondered if she felt anything. "Do you hear yourself?"

She finally stopped moving. "The only other choice was to

kill all three of them, wipe out the witnesses, and I couldn't. I thought about it . . ."

Kill them. "Cassie, what's going on in your head? You sound as sick as Dylan."

"Don't you dare judge me." She waved the gun around, unhinged and uncharacteristically out of control as she stalked back up the slight incline to him. "I've been the one to hold us together. I kept you out of prison all those years ago by giving you an alibi the night Emily died and another one for the night you killed Brendan. You owe me."

She'd lied for him. Now she'd lie to preserve everything she'd built even if it meant sacrificing him. "The guilt will eat you alive."

She snorted. "It hasn't so far."

"It will kill me."

"Would you rather go to prison and never see Zara again? Because I will make that happen. I'll say you threatened me to keep your secret and then beg the court to take your parental rights away."

There it was. Her final card. He sensed she'd play it but hearing the words sounded so stark. Like an ending.

He hated her. He really fucking hated her. "How long have you been waiting to issue that threat?"

She used the gun to point at the canoe tied to the dock and bobbing in the water before pointing it at him. "Get in, Alex. As with every other part of our lives, I'm taking charge. Be grateful and move."

CHAPTER FIFTY-NINE

SIERRA

*N*umb. That was the word that floated into Sierra's clouded mind. She'd naïvely believed Cassie's love and years of affection for Mitch would protect him, but when the time came she'd picked her lifestyle over his life.

"Your friends suck." The words lacked punch, but Sierra wanted to make her position clear. If they got off this island, if they caught up with his wayward friends, she wouldn't hesitate to dismantle the comfortable world they'd created. Sierra's only hesitation was Zara, their daughter. She needed them . . . or someone.

Mitch blew out a long breath. "Agree."

"She's really hoping for a *Lord of the Flies* moment and that she comes back to find us dead and Dylan on the run." Despite everything and all her investigations into this group of people, Ruthie sounded stunned by the idea.

"We're not giving her that satisfaction." Sierra looked up and watched the gray clouds roll over each other. The light rain had turned to a fine mist but darker skies lurked in the distance. They needed to move. "Rope."

Ruthie frowned. "Excuse me?"

"We need to tie him up." And soon. She'd hit Dylan hard, but he could wake up any moment or, worse, he could be pretending and spring up for another round.

"The zip ties are in his pocket." Mitch crouched down and checked Dylan's neck.

"Pulse?" Sierra asked.

"Unfortunately."

Ruthie reached into Dylan's pocket and pulled out two zip ties. She didn't look up as she used the ties to bind Dylan's hands together, then his feet. When she stood up, she stepped back as if expecting Dylan to rise up and attack like a twice-killed villain in a bad horror movie. "Is that good enough?"

"He's not superhuman."

Sierra hoped Mitch was right about that.

Ruthie didn't look convinced. "Okay, now what?"

Other than burning down the rest of the house and hoping someone would see the fire, Sierra could only think of one option. One that would subject them to a whole new set of dangers. "The old rowboat."

Mitch stopped looking around, scouting for trouble, and faced her. "What?"

"The boat in the shed. The one I couldn't lift earlier." *The shed.* It hurt to even reference the place. The memories kept pounding at the back of her brain, begging for attention. The idea of inviting them in then creating new ones with a second visit to that horrible space made her queasy. She fought to keep all of that uncertainty and worry out of her voice. "We get it and join your former friends back at the car . . . and I punch Cassie."

Mitch's eyes narrowed. "Sounds good but even if we can make your plan work they'll be long gone."

"Will had the keys to our car. I think they're back in our room at the house." Ruthie visibly swallowed. "So that won't help us."

Yeah, about that. Sierra reached into her pocket and pulled out the key ring she'd snagged off the floor what felt like days ago but was likely more like an hour or so. "What about these keys?"

Ruthie shook her head. "I don't understand."

"I saw them on the floor and took them just in case we got away." Sierra shrugged. "The ones Alex and Cassie have are the property keys. That should slow them down."

"They could hot-wire the car," Ruthie said.

Mitch scoffed. "Do either of them look like they could hot-wire a car? They pay people to do everything for them."

Sierra was counting on that. "Let's not give them time to figure out a new skill."

Mitch and Sierra headed for the shed, but Ruthie's voice called them back. "What about him?"

Dylan still hadn't moved. Sierra didn't trust him, and there was no way she was dragging him along on this unwanted adventure. "Leave him. We'll send the police back for him."

They should run but Sierra slowed her steps before turning her back on the smoldering house and getting to work. Her throat closed as they approached the shed. An itchy sensation crawled up her throat. She fought the urge to scratch and claw for breath.

Mitch put his hand on her back, gently steering her the last few steps toward the shed. "It's okay."

It was like volunteering to venture back down to hell. So, no, it wasn't close to okay, but Sierra appreciated him trying to pretend it was. She'd underestimated him. She'd been so sure he would shut down when he heard the truth. So much of the stability he'd fought for turned sideways. Instead of retreating into his head, he stayed with them. Fought through it.

"I'll go." He walked in front of them and propped the door open with a rock.

A throat-punching smell floated out to greet them. A sickening mix of mold and rotting garbage. The tarp no longer trapped the worst of it. The dampness intensified the odor and had them all covering their noses.

Sierra tried not to look at the body or the head on the ground. She focused on the end of the rowboat, but the walls closed in on her before she even stepped inside. She opened her mouth and forced her body not to inhale. Ruthie switched between coughing and gagging, which didn't help Sierra. The sound grated until she could almost feel it vibrating inside her.

Without a word, Mitch walked to the back of the shed. Only a few inches separated the side of his sneaker and Jake's head. Mitch didn't look down or get lost while he tucked the oars inside the craft. He put his hand on one end of the rowboat and gestured for them to take the other.

He pushed. They pulled. The boat wouldn't move. It tipped to one side then it found a groove. It thunked against the shed's floor as they shoved it outside. The cool air pressed against Sierra's back, making the trek even harder. A few tugs and the boat hit the grass. Fresh air flooded Sierra's system a second later.

Mitch shut the shed door, hiding the horrors inside. "I didn't need to see that a second time."

Sierra wanted to say something, but what? There weren't any words to make this nightmare better.

Ruthie didn't even try. She looked at Mitch and Sierra with a new sense of urgency. "Let's move."

The pulling was a bit easier on the grass, but not much. They'd gotten a few inches when Sierra glanced inside the rowboat and froze. "Damn."

She'd never reached the point of relief, but she'd had hope. That died and tears of frustration took its place.

"What's wrong?" Mitch sounded out of breath.

"Remember the shot we heard when Dylan was out here, pretending to be a policeman? He shot the boat."

"I thought fiberglass stopped bullets," Ruthie said.

Sierra looked at the very distinct hole. "We're not that lucky."

CHAPTER SIXTY

ALEX

Alex's attention faded. He forced his eyes to stay open, to keep aware, but the battle wounds pulled him toward a sweet oblivion. His head pounded above his eyes, making it difficult to concentrate. His shoulder thumped. Every part of him, inside and out, from his muscles to his heart, crushed under the weight of his injuries and the reality of what was about to happen.

He wouldn't get in the car. She'd have to kill him, and he believed she would. The truth threatened her plan. Leaving their friends alive destroyed any hope she had for keeping the secrets buried. All common sense, all the loving and feeling parts of her, would step aside so her rabid determination not to live a life other than one she'd planned for and ruthlessly created could survive.

He heaved over the side as she steered them toward the shore. Cold air radiated off the water, stinging his face. She hadn't said a word since issuing her warning. He didn't bother either. His pleas couldn't penetrate the shell she'd built around herself. The only way in was to take her down. He hoped he could muster the energy and the will to do it.

The rhythmic clicking of the paddles. The swoosh in and out

of the water. The lurching of the canoe. The motion lulled him. Just as he started to drift off the bottom of the boat scraped against something.

He opened his eyes. They were still more than twenty feet from the fog-shrouded shoreline. He couldn't see the car, but he knew it was there . . . well, he hoped it was. He touched his pocket to reassure himself he still had the keys. In a flash of fear, he thought Dylan had stolen them, but he could feel the outline through the fabric.

"Shit. I think we hit bottom or got stuck on a ledge." She shifted in her seat, making the boat rock just shy of tipping over.

He grabbed the sides as his stomach rolled. "Stop."

"I can't get it loose." She stared at him as if she expected him to fix it.

"We could wait for low tide and walk the rest of the way." A smart-ass answer but he didn't care if he offended or annoyed her.

"We'll swim the rest."

In the freezing water. That was the part she didn't say.

He watched the choppy waves lap against the canoe. "I don't think I can."

"You will."

"Is your hope that I'll die out here, too?" The thought hit him and wouldn't leave his head.

"I'm trying to save you. Believe it or not, I love you." She wiggled and shook the sides of the canoe.

"You've been saying that for years."

She stopped moving. "You owe me."

"And you've spent our entire marriage reminding me of that."

Before she could respond, the canoe broke free. She rushed to grab the paddle before it slipped away from her. Using it now, she furiously stroked through the water, propelling them to land. Their in-house gym and all that expensive equipment had paid off. Her shoulders bunched and her jaw tensed. All of her effort went in to getting them off the water as quickly as possible.

Nausea rolled through him. He closed his eyes and when that didn't work he opened them again. Cassie, stark and sweating, disheveled and shaking, sat in front of him. She didn't lift her head until the bottom of the canoe crunched against the causeway, right near the boat launch.

"Finally." She didn't wait. She stepped out of the boat and jogged up the ramp until she stood on solid ground.

Now what. The words played over and over in his head. He hadn't been this lost, this unsure, since that night on the bridge all those years ago.

His legs barely held him as he crawled out of the canoe. The feel of hard ground under his feet should have soothed him but his heart raced. Anxiety intensified inside him until his breathing turned shallow and harsh.

She took out her cell phone and lifted it in the air, likely in search of a signal. When she let out a relieved sigh he knew the phone jammer no longer interfered with her call.

She tapped on the buttons. He wanted to believe she'd changed her mind and was calling for help, but he knew better. "If you call Zara you'll mess up your timing."

"What?"

"The call and the time will be traceable, and your plan to wait until . . ." His knees gave out as the last of his strength left his body. He teetered then fell, landing on his side. Whatever help he thought she might offer didn't happen.

She stared at him but didn't reach out.

"How are you going to explain leaving your dead husband in a boat parking lot?"

"We need to get you to a doctor." In a few steps she was at his side, lifting him up to balance his body against hers. He outweighed her and almost dragged her down.

They struggled over to the rental car. She balanced him against the driver's side door and held out a hand in front of him. "Keys."

It took a second for the word to compute. When it did, he didn't fight her. Going against her out here, in this wrecked condition, amounted to a death sentence. No, if he wanted to make a move he'd have to do it at the hospital or clinic . . . and beat her to it. He had no doubt she'd turn him in to save her own ass. She absolutely expected him to make that sacrifice and if he balked he would lose.

"Here." He dragged the keys out of his pocket and handed them to her.

She stood there, looking at the chain then at him. "Is this a joke?"

"This has been the least amusing day of my life."

She held up the keys. "There's no key fob on here."

His eyes finally focused. He saw the tag with the house address. The set to the car had the fob and two other keys he put on. One Will sent and it opened the chain for the golf cart. The other was an extra key to their house, which he carried just in case.

This set consisted of three keys, likely to the various buildings on the island. The wrong keys. How had he missed that? The injuries and the panic, maybe? He'd been moving faster than his brain for what felt like hours now, and that was saying something since his pace barely qualified as a crawl.

Sonofabitch. His world tilted until it flipped over.

"You idiot!" She yelled the words.

Good. This was better. He'd stopped her plan by accident, but the result would be the same. "We're stuck here."

Some of the anger cleared from her eyes as she glanced over his shoulder. "Maybe not."

He followed her gaze to the lone golf cart still chained to the security pole. They'd removed the lock earlier and left it off. "That's not going to get us very far."

"For your sake, I hope you're wrong."

CHAPTER SIXTY-ONE

RUTHIE

Dylan shot the boat. Well, of course he did. The action fit with every other annoying, dangerous, calculated thing he'd done over the last few months. He used her. She used him back. She then used Will, which she couldn't dwell on now. When the race for survival ended she would mourn, but she doubted that would wash off the stink of her complicity in this horror.

"Grab the tarp or whatever material is in there." Ruthie couldn't bring herself to walk back into the shed to get it. She passed the job off to Mitch, which wasn't fair but nothing about the guy's life had been fair.

He frowned at her. "For what?"

Sierra stared unfocused into the distance. The hole in the boat seemed to be the final shot that knocked them both off-balance. Neither functioned with any efficiency. They'd gone into some sort of fugue state. Blank and unhelpful. Ruthie needed them to snap out of it.

"We'll stuff it into the hole." She said the words nice and slow, hoping a sign of life would spark within them.

"Will that work?" Mitch asked, still sounding groggy and a bit lost.

"Yeah." *Sure . . . right?*

Sierra nodded as she snapped back into the woman who had helped lead them through hours of terror. "It can be temporary. We only need to get far enough across that we can make the last bit by swimming. Everyone can swim, right?"

Ruthie realized she shouldn't have picked an island for this adventure. "Life jackets?"

Mitch shook his head. "Not that I can see, and I really don't want to dig deeper in there."

"I guess I'm going to learn to swim the hard way." Ruthie really hoped that was possible.

The door creaked as Mitch disappeared into the shed. The sound of disembodied footsteps echoed around them. When he popped out again his face looked drawn and pale. He stopped in front of them with a greasy towel hanging from his clenched fist.

"What about the tarp?" Sierra asked.

"There's . . ." He cleared his throat. "There's blood all over it."

The driving need to survive should outweigh the horror of staring at Jake's blood as they struggled to row across the water. On an intellectual level, a biological level, that made sense, but their senses had been blown apart and boundaries shattered. Mitch drew a line and Ruthie didn't blame him. "Good choice."

"Let's go before Cassie figures out a way to sink the island with us on it." Sierra grabbed the rowboat again and tugged. Ruthie and Mitch didn't argue as they joined her.

They walked past the smoldering house to the closest dock, the less stable, floating one on this side of the island. Ruthie knew almost nothing about boats and rowing. She hoped that sort of thing proved instinctive because she refused to give Cassie the satisfaction of dying today.

The hill dropped off to a rocky coastline. After a few seconds of wandering around, looking for a place to put the boat in, they gave up and dragged it up the two steps to the dock. Ruthie winced as the rowboat's bottom slammed against each riser.

Standing there, looking through the planks to the peek of water below, she now understood what *floating dock* meant. The old wood balanced on containers that floated and rocked beneath her feet. Waves sent the dock bobbing as icy water splashed up around them.

She couldn't do this. She looked at the small seats and the oars and her mind rebelled. "I don't think—"

"This should do it," Sierra said as she stuffed the ratty towel into the bullet hole. "I don't think it will last for long."

"We'll row fast," Mitch said.

Ruthie hated this conversation. "What if—"

"Don't borrow trouble." Sierra took a deep breath and gestured to Ruthie to do the same. "Assume this will work."

Easy for her to say. "I'm not really built that way."

"Neither is Sierra." Mitch tested the towel then lowered the rowboat to the water. Strain showed on his face, but he didn't ask for help.

Ruthie appreciated the hero move because she couldn't remember how to make a fist at the moment. The initial surge of adrenaline had burnt out, leaving behind a mushy mess of nothing. Exhaustion swept through her as her brain begged for a few minutes of rest.

She was the only one not moving. Sierra put the oars in

position. Mitch placed a foot in the boat in what looked like a test of the boat's buoyancy. Ruthie breathed in and out and tried not to throw up.

The noises of the island swirled around her. Her damp hair fell over her ears and muffled some of the sound, but the rush of wind and rustle of the trees played in a steady cadence. She closed her eyes and let the lull overtake her. Calm her.

Crack.

The subtle sound barely rose above the rest, but it didn't fit. Probably a snapping twig. She opened her eyes and stared back toward the house.

Dylan, his hair caked with blood, stood at the point where the dock met the land with that damn poker in his bloodied hands. He'd snuck up on them and waited only a few feet away with the distance closing. He stalked them, staring them down.

"Guys." Ruthie took a step back and ran right into Sierra.

"What are . . ." Sierra's voice sputtered out as her gaze followed Ruthie's.

"How did he get free?" Mitch whispered the question.

Dylan answered with slurred words. "Can't you guess?"

"I'm not really in the mood for more games," Mitch said.

Dylan's sick smile appeared. "Ruthie didn't really tie me up. Did you, hon?"

CHAPTER SIXTY-TWO

RUTHIE

With a few words, Dylan sucked her back into his demented world, condemning her with lies. Ruthie could see the doubt move into Sierra's expression. "Don't listen to him."

Dylan stepped onto the deck. Made a dramatic show of doing it. He stood between them and land. A deadly barrier to surviving.

He swung the poker back and forth at his side. "You can stop pretending we're not working together."

Mitch shifted until he stood between Ruthie and Sierra. He would kill her if it meant saving Sierra. Ruthie knew and tried not to push him to that point.

"We set this up. All those long nights together. We laughed about how fun it would be." Dylan nodded in Ruthie's direction. "Her getting close to Will pissed me off, but it was necessary."

"Shut up." The words screamed inside Ruthie but came out in a harsh whisper.

Dylan looked around Ruthie to Mitch. "Here's a general hint . . . not that you're going to live long enough to use it, but she should've tied my hands in the back, not the front. There are a million videos online that teach people how to break zip ties and they all start with *hope your attacker isn't very smart and ties your hands in front so you can easily get free.*"

"You used the poker," Sierra said in a shaky voice. "You freed yourself."

"Maybe I did. Maybe Ruthie left it for me." Dylan twirled the makeshift weapon as he spoke. "Either way, I'm going to beat you to death with it while Mitch watches. So, if you want to finally tell the poor bastard that you're in love with him, now would be the time."

Words jumbled in Ruthie's throat. She rushed to get them out before he followed through with his threat. "Cassie called the police. She and Alex are on the way to get help right now."

Dylan laughed. "That bitch would crawl over all of your dead bodies to save her reputation. She's not calling anyone."

A flash of movement made Ruthie duck. Mitch's body flew past her and knocked into Dylan, whose smug look vanished as their bodies crunched together. Off-balance, they tipped off the edge of the dock and plunged into the water. Gravity pulled them under. Waves splashed up around them. Arms and legs rose above the water then disappeared.

After a flurry of whitecaps and bubbles, Mitch broke through the water again. He drew in a deep breath right before Dylan sprang up and punched him in the head. A crescendo of grunts and groans welcomed the fog-covered sunrise then the men dunked under again.

Sierra dropped to her knees on the edge of the dock. The thrashing and hitting sent ripples through the water, which made the dock buck. The creaking increased as the men rolled in the water. A foot appeared then both heads. The gasping died out as the bodies vanished into the dark water again.

"The gun." Ruthie meant to think the words, but she said them out loud.

Sierra's gaze shot to her. "Do you still have bullets?"

"Two." Ruthie reached into her pocket and pulled out the ones she'd grabbed as a precaution if she needed to reload, never expecting Cassie would steal the others.

Sierra pointed at the water. "Stop stalling and shoot him."

The rowboat banged against the opposite side of the dock. The shifting pulled the rope holding it in place taut.

Ruthie looked for Dylan, but his head didn't break through the dark water. She could make out shadows and pushing. A leg peeked out of the ripples in the water. One of them kicked, but she couldn't tell which. Then she saw Mitch's face underwater but near the surface. He grimaced as Dylan barrel-rolled him.

"What are you waiting for? He's choking Mitch."

The trembling of Sierra's voice made Ruthie move faster. She couldn't debate and find excuses as she fumbled with the bullets in her skirt pocket. One bounced out of her hand and pinged against the dock. She didn't bother to look for it because she had the other one.

Bubbles streamed up from the water's depths. The dock bobbed and weaved as Sierra grabbed the edge and looked into the churning waves.

Ruthie loaded and aimed. But where? Which one of them wore jeans . . . ? Both? The rain kicked up to a light drizzle. Drops pelted her face as she tried to focus. The water would change the bullet's trajectory. She thought she'd read that once, but maybe not. She couldn't be sure because every thought blurred together.

"Ruthie, now!" Sierra reached into the water, trying to grab for the bodies as they shifted and swam.

"I can't see . . . I can't . . ." Ruthie shook her head. She needed to concentrate to keep from hitting Mitch. Then she saw the poker.

Dylan must have dropped it when he lunged for Mitch. It had fallen between the slats on the deck. Ruthie crouched down. She stuck her fingers into the opening and wood moved, pinching her fingers inside.

"What the hell are you doing?"

"What if I miss?" But Ruthie couldn't argue now. She poured all of her energy into grabbing the poker. Her finger touched it then lost it. The deck rocked again as the water grew choppier from all the kicking and struggling.

Ruthie tried to remember the last time either man had risen to the surface to take a breath. They continued to scramble and thrash but they had to be running out of air.

She'd take the chance and use the gun. Just as she moved her hand out of the opening, her fingers touched metal. She grabbed and pulled the poker out.

The men pushed to the surface. The air filled with labored breathing and panicked huffing. Dylan had Mitch in a choke hold. Mitch tore and clawed at Dylan's arm but the determined, teeth-clenched expression on Dylan's face promised death.

Ruthie remembered how Sierra had wielded the poker and mimicked her. Winding up, Ruthie swung and brought the poker down in a swift arc. Dylan saw and shifted in time, sending the poker smashing into his shoulder. He cried out in what sounded like a mix of rage and pain, and his hold on Mitch loosened.

Before Dylan could grab Mitch's neck again, Mitch switched places. He squeezed Dylan's shoulder and dunked his head underwater. Arms flailed and water kicked up around them, but Mitch didn't let go. He held Dylan's face under. Used all of his weight and momentum, got hit and doused with water but didn't give up. Eyes bulging and muscles straining, Mitch held on. He panted through the frenzy of fighting and drowning until all the splashing stopped.

The motion of the water ratcheted down and dissolved into the usual foamy waves. Mitch still didn't let go. He held Dylan under as the minutes ticked by and Dylan's arms floated along the water's surface.

"Check his pulse." Sierra reached over to do it for Mitch but fell short.

Since Dylan had already bounced back from a hit and broken his way out of zip ties, Ruthie understood Sierra's call for caution. Dylan played games and this could be another one. Ruthie held the gun and the poker ready just in case.

Mitch followed Sierra's directions and shook his head. "Nothing. He's not breathing."

Dead. Ruthie silently repeated the word until she believed it.

The relief she expected never came. Watching Dylan's humanity unravel until only an empty shell remained had changed her. The idea that one tragic weekend so many years ago had claimed so many victims and created so many villains chipped away at her belief in justice. The role she'd played in the recent collateral damage made her question who she really was and what she was willing to do to get what she wanted.

Mitch held on to Dylan's unmoving body for an almost comical amount of time. No one could survive underwater that long without at least fighting for air. When Mitch pushed back, Dylan's body floated face down, moved around by the current.

His lifeless body made Ruthie think about Emily's last moments. Life snuffed out in a pool of nothingness. Ruthie never
wanted to be near water again.

"We need to get in the boat." Mitch's voice dragged as Sierra
pulled him closer to the dock.

More water. But he was right. Cassie and Alex's joint destruc-
tive force still loomed.

It took Ruthie and Sierra stretching and tugging to lift Mitch's
exhausted body onto the wobbling dock. He dragged himself
onto the firm surface and rolled to his back. The chill on his skin
scared Ruthie. He'd been in the water too long. Long enough for
his lips to turn blue. She feared sitting in the dampness as they
rowed to land would endanger him further.

Before she could mention any of that, he slid again. This
time boneless into the boat, nearly tipping it over. He couldn't
manipulate his cold fingers and every twist and turn made him
grimace.

Sierra wrapped her body around his. She rubbed her hands
over him, clearly trying to warm him. "My hero."

His teeth made a clicking noise. "Hold that thought until we
see if the boat works."

Love. Ruthie could see it arc between Sierra and Mitch. Bone-
deep respect mixed with attraction and affection. Mitch had to
see it . . . right?

Sierra looked at Ruthie then nodded in the direction of the
oars. "You're up."

"I was never his partner in this." Ruthie could hear the desperation in her voice. She'd spent her whole life being underestimated and pretending not to care. She needed them to believe
her this time.

Sierra's expression didn't give anything away. "A skeptic would say you hit him with the poker to keep him from talking."

The anxiety that had been churning inside Ruthie nearly choked her. "I didn't—"

"Lucky for you I'm not the skeptical type." Sierra stared at the oars again. "Row. We have assholes to hunt down."

CHAPTER SIXTY-THREE

SIERRA

Sierra held Mitch with her front to his back and her legs and arms wrapped around him to share their body heat. She bounced around as the boat moved across the water in jerky fits. Ruthie would row then lose her hold on an oar, sending the boat careening sideways until she corrected and got them moving again.

The choppy ride made Sierra's stomach lurch and her body crash into Mitch's over and over, but they made progress. Sluggish and uneven, but the boat moved through the lifting fog.

The distance they needed to travel gave her too much time to think. She tried not to dwell on how close Mitch had come to dying. How close they all had come and how Cassie had depended on them to lose.

With Dylan dead most of the threats had been neutralized, but not all. Cassie and her persuasive lawyer talk waited out there, promising to bite them. Sierra vowed not to let Cassie off the hook. No matter what it took.

"Go faster," Sierra mumbled under her breath.

Ruthie's jaw tightened as she fumbled to pull back on the oars. "I'm trying."

The tremble running through Mitch increased. He needed to get dry. Sierra took off the oversized shirt she wore over her T-shirt. The second she shrugged out of it the chill lifting off the water enveloped her. Her body temperature went into free fall. Coldness pricked her skin but she bit down hard, pretending the crappy weather didn't bother her.

"Take off your shirt." She hated the way her voice shook.

"What are you doing?" Mitch sounded groggy.

She didn't know much about hypothermia. It wasn't a topic that came up while she tilled dirt and laid garden pavers, but she feared they were testing the limits of what Mitch's body could handle. Rather than take the time to answer him, she stripped his wet top off and let it land with a smack on the bottom of the boat. She wrapped her dry shirt around him. It pulled tight across his shoulders, but she mentally declared it good enough. Better than the alternative.

Icy cold water gurgled up and around the material they'd stuffed into the hole. The boat continued to chug along, but her feet were now soaked. Lifting them up wasn't an option because shifting her weight could knock them off-balance. Her feet also provided a bit of a buffer for Mitch because he sat on them, keeping his body off the soaking bottom of the boat and on her.

The landscape, so beautiful and teeming with life during the previous day, took on a shadowed and gloomy tint in the aftermath of the wild storm. She didn't see a person or a building as the world passed by. She breathed in and closed her eyes, trying to find a moment to think as their fitful progress continued.

A scraping noise broke her silence. The front of the boat stopped moving and Ruthie dropped the oars. The back of the boat floated sideways in the current.

Sierra's eyes popped open. "What's happening?"

Ruthie looked over the side. "I think we hit a higher part of the causeway."

She'd eaten up most of the distance between the island and the shore. They were ten feet from firm ground. She could see the canoe Alex and Cassie used for their escape.

Sierra had spent the whole ride worrying and playing nurse. Now, she scanned the parking lot. Two cars, but no Cassie and Alex. "Where are they?"

Ruthie shook her head. "Hiding like the rats they are."

"Don't blame innocent rats." Mitch let out a pained groan as he pushed up to his feet, his body shaking.

"Whoa." Ruthie grabbed on to the sides of the boat as it rocked.

Sierra debated between holding on and reaching for him. "What are you doing?"

Mitch gestured toward shore. "They took the extra golf cart."

Sierra had missed that. Now she saw the empty pole and abandoned chain.

"How fast can one of them go?" Ruthie asked.

Mitch smiled for the first time in what felt like days. "It can't outrun a car."

They took turns stepping out of the boat. One would balance it, while the other jumped into the calf-high water. They didn't have time to secure the craft, so they let it drift and headed for the rental car Alex drove there.

Ruthie stopped at the back of the car. "Who's in charge?"

Mitch nodded at Sierra. "She drives as if she's a breath away from a heart attack and needs a hospital. That's true on a highway or in a drive-through."

"Good." Ruthie nodded. "Sierra wins."

Sierra didn't waste time. She put the heater on blast as she maneuvered the SUV down the long path, not bothering to slow down for the crumbling road or bent branches dipping into the path. At one point Ruthie made a squeaking noise. Mitch held on to the handle over the passenger side window but didn't balk at the careening ride.

About ten minutes later, after a few turns, the golf cart came into view. Cassie was driving and they hadn't gotten far. Unchaining the thing and getting it running probably had burned through time. Now Sierra had the advantage.

"What's the plan?" Ruthie yelled the question from the back seat.

"I'm going to run them down."

Mitch glanced at her but remained silent.

If Ruthie disagreed she kept it to herself. Sierra appreciated that because she didn't see another alternative. The narrow road and towering trees lining each side didn't allow for intricate maneuvering. That left them with two options. Cassie voluntarily stopping, which wouldn't happen, or a crash. Not a bad one, of course. Just a little tap on that empty seat at the back of the cart to let them know they needed to hit the brakes.

Alex and Cassie took turns looking over their shoulders at them. Cassie shook her head. Sierra ignored her. She vowed to give them a minute to do the right thing and slow down. She counted out the time and got to twenty before giving up.

"Screw it." She tapped the gas and brought the car right to

the back end of the golf cart, threatening and promising at the same time.

Alex started yelling but they couldn't hear what he said. It didn't really matter to Sierra. Alex and Cassie asked for this.

Sierra gunned it again, hoping the roar of the engine would make her position clear. When the golf cart kept chugging along, Sierra moved in one last time. This time, she tapped the cart's back seat. The rental car absorbed the bump but sent the cart spinning.

The back end swooped to the right side and Cassie's arms went wild. Alex slammed from one side of the bench seat to the other. Cassie's screaming outpaced Alex's swearing. The golf cart bobbled before coming to a landing a foot away from a tree, facing the car.

Sierra, Mitch, and Ruthie got out but didn't venture into the few feet of open space between the vehicles. They all hid behind the relative safety of open car doors used as shields.

"Explain yourself. What the hell was that?" Cassie's voice rose with each word.

Sierra didn't see a reason to lie. "Payback."

Cassie's red-faced anger didn't abate. "You could have killed us."

The tree pinned Alex in the vehicle. He looked shaky as he put his hand on the dash.

"Get out of the cart." Mitch took a step forward. "Now."

CHAPTER SIXTY-FOUR

ALEX

This, right now, qualified as the ultimate *I told you so* moment, but Alex let it pass because they had much bigger issues to deal with. The relief at seeing the three of them alive, banged up but fine, overwhelmed everything else.

Tossed and turned around in a moment of extreme danger back on that island, Cassie had made an unforgivable choice. She'd probably come up with a reasonable explanation that absolved her of guilt but, for him, it was an act that severed his last tenuous ties to their marriage. She could threaten but he was done.

They'd reached the point of mutually assured destruction. If either of them leaked their secrets the other would be destroyed. The fear of losing custody of Zara didn't fade. It was his nightmare, but their shared past consisted of several stark choices that could ruin them both, and that should spoil her perceived custodial advantage.

Confessing to his role in Brendan's death eased some of the pressure that had been building in his brain ever since that awful night. He'd tried to buy his soul back in a bunch of ways over the years. Volunteering. Donating. None of it worked. Redemption was a process, and if he was honest, he'd yet to take the first step, which required publicly owning his sins.

"I'm happy you're all okay." He meant that. Not liking Ruthie didn't mean he wanted her dead. He cared about Sierra because she loved Mitch. And Mitch. Hell, Alex had spent his entire adult life watching out for Mitch.

"Yeah, Cassie seems thrilled to see us." Mitch moved out into the open, almost daring Cassie to do something she couldn't take back.

"Be careful." Sierra didn't bother to whisper. She likely thought they'd moved far past the need for subtlety.

"I don't know what you're thinking we did, but—"

"Save it." Ruthie cut right into Cassie's comment. "We don't have amnesia. We all heard the threat. You wanted Dylan to kill us. You failed."

"That's ridiculous. We were going to get the police." Cassie slipped out of the cart and tucked the gun into the back of her pants at the same time. "Our plan was to save all of you."

Sierra held on to the open car door as she walked around it. She didn't stand next to Mitch, but she wasn't hiding either. "Call them now."

"I'm sure she already did since *she took all the cell phones*," Mitch said in a tone loaded with sarcasm.

Alex tried to think of a way to blunt the impact of Cassie's bizarre behavior, but nothing came to him. Every word they said about her plan was right. She did bet her move with the boat and golf cart would result in few, if any, survivors. He'd been too weak to stop her . . . and not only physically. He'd acquiesced so much of his power and his life to her. He relied on her to make the difficult decisions then blamed her for stepping up to act.

She'd been protecting a future back then and every moment since. He didn't know if that made him as culpable as she was for the choice to leave their friends behind, but it probably didn't matter. His decision to go after Brendan set the course. Her actions steered them for twelve years. They'd both failed as friends and humans.

It was time to admit that. "Cas, we need to—"

"Where's Dylan?" she asked.

Ruthie and Sierra joined Mitch in the clearing now. They stood on the lane that led to the water at one end and what should have been to a future on the other . . . but it didn't. This weekend had changed everything. Alex hadn't wanted to come and would regret for the rest of his life not insisting they skip it. That was the theme of his life—weakness in the face of Cassie's stronger will.

Ruthie tucked her hands in the pocket of her full skirt. "We killed him."

"Okay." Cassie blew out a long breath. "Good."

"Nope." Mitch shook his head. "You can't talk your way out of this."

He sounded resigned and exhausted. Whatever had happened in those last moments on the island changed them. Alex could see it in their expressions, in the way they stood alert as if being attacked had become their default presumption.

"Alex needs a hospital." Cassie stepped out to meet them in the clearing.

Seeing the weapon at her back scattered his thoughts. He feared what else she might have planned. He shifted on the seat, moving closer to Cassie's side and hoping his body would let him crawl out of the cart with some dignity and get to that gun.

"Mitch needs a jacket because he's soaking wet but that will wait," Sierra said in a flat voice. "Call the police."

Alex hadn't noticed Mitch's hair and pants, the odd-fitting shirt he wore unbuttoned and hanging in front of him, before now. "Why are you wet?"

"It doesn't matter."

"Help me out of this thing." Alex reached his hand out and Cassie grabbed it. She eased him across the bench and shouldered most of his weight as he stepped on the gravel and stood. His balance wavered and the world blurred in front of him for a second. The pain thumping in his head and radiating through his body made every muscle scream for relief.

Mitch watched every move. When Alex felt a sting of some new ache, Mitch winced. They'd been like that since they met. In sync. Loyal. Alex tried to hold on to that loyalty now.

Ruthie waited until they all stood together on that path that some called a road, only feet apart. "Who really killed Emily?"

"Come on." Cassie's shoulders fell. "We've been through this. Brendan."

But Alex sensed that automatic answer wouldn't be good enough this time. They'd walked into a showdown and neither side appeared ready to blink.

Mitch shook his head. "We need to hear the truth this time."

Alex had to fight that one. "Are you serious?"

Cassie grabbed his arm. "Alex, don't."

"No, Alex. *Do.*" Mitch's taunting voice issued a challenge. "What is it you want to say?"

Alex came close. All the pain and confusion, the threats and the frustration, balled up in him. He wanted to launch into a screed that would shut them all up, but he held on. "This isn't the time."

"You two want us all to match our stories." Ruthie threw her arms wide in a dramatic gesture that didn't help anything. "Tell us the truth and we might."

Cassie's hands clenched at her sides. "I don't believe a thing you say."

Ruthie laughed. "I don't care."

Enough. Alex had enough baiting and bullshit. He was ten minutes from falling over and they still hadn't settled anything. "Mitch, stop this."

"Why? I want the answer, too."

All the tamped-down, bottled-up anger inside Alex blew. "How exactly do you think this will end?"

Sierra's eyes narrowed. "So cryptic."

More poking. Alex was done with that. He pointed at Mitch. "I'm *saving* him."

Mitch just stood there.

His confused expression ticked Alex off. Years of restraint and practice backed up on him. "Maybe a little less bullying from you. Be fucking grateful."

"Exactly. We've all been through so much." Cassie used her mediator tone. Clear and concerned. Trying to sum up and fix things. "We're not thinking straight. This is the time when people say things they don't mean. I've been guilty of it, too. Back on the island you may have thought you heard—"

Mitch cut her off before she could spew more bullshit. "Honestly, just shut up."

That comment had the potential to touch off a Mitch-Cassie

fight that Alex didn't have the energy to stop. He needed to convince Mitch of that. "You have something to lose here, too."

Alex saw their expressions. Mitch and Sierra looked cautious but ready to fight. Ruthie edged away from them as if she wasn't sure who she could trust in this verbal battle.

"Everything . . ." The words punched their way out of Alex. "Everything we've done has been to protect you. So drop the act, say thank you, and let's figure out how to get through this with as little damage as possible."

"Say the words." Mitch held his hands palms up, as if inviting what was to come. "Say it."

"Fine!" Alex stared at Sierra. "Mitch killed Emily."

CHAPTER SIXTY-FIVE

SIERRA

Sierra hated roller coasters. She despised that sensation when her stomach turned weightless and life moved in slow motion as a steel contraption flipped her sideways and upside down.

Control. She thrived on it. Demanded it. Searched for it.

With Alex's words something inside her splintered. Competing shouts of *not possible* and *how could he* filled her head. She'd invested so much of her life in Mitch. They worked together, ate together, went to the movies, generally hung out with each other. People who knew them joked they were inseparable.

He owed her the truth. Not the save-your-ass kind of truth this group excelled at. Rough, knuckle-bleeding honesty, even if it hurt.

"Explain." She didn't break eye contact with Alex. "Right now."

"Sierra, you can't—"

She held up her hand to Mitch, silencing him. "Alex clearly wants to tell us a tale. You've got our attention. Speak."

Ruthie moved closer to Sierra. "I'm with her."

It killed her to do it, but Sierra blocked out the distress pulsing off Mitch. She pretended not to see Cassie or Ruthie. As far as Sierra was concerned, Alex needed to tell her his story without interruptions. No verbal gymnastics. Whisper it, if that made him feel better, but get it out.

Alex's red-faced anger gave way to a sheepishness that didn't fit with his usual big lawyer energy. He glanced at Mitch as if waiting for him to jump in, but he didn't.

"It was an accident." Alex gulped in a deep breath. "We'd all been drinking."

Another accident? Sierra forced herself not to push back. To let Alex continue.

"We were out there by the water for hours that day. The alcohol flowed. We brought some. Friends dropped by with more." Alex exhaled. "We made a run back to campus at one point. Maybe for beer? Earlier when Mitch talked about dropping everyone off he was telling the truth. That did happen but it was a temporary thing. We met up again at the labyrinth, this place in the woods near hiking trails and a community garden. It's not far from campus. I was out of it, so I'm not sure who decided we should go there. Too much alcohol. No common sense."

"You were drunk. I get it." Sierra couldn't figure out if he focused on the booze to paint a picture or to set up an excuse for the inexcusable. "Get to what happened to Emily."

Alex closed his eyes. When he opened them again the stress was right there. He looked haunted, and aching for a way to back out of the conversation he'd slammed down between them.

Cassie put an arm around Alex. "We need to stop. Nothing good can come from more information."

"Cassie? For once in your life don't try to manipulate the situation. Let Alex finish." Mitch's voice didn't reveal an ounce of emotion.

Sierra didn't know what to make of that comment but for some reason it eased the tension pressing in on her from all sides. If Cassie was determined to save Mitch, he was equally as determined that she didn't.

A secret this big demanded a joint effort to wrestle it into submission and lock it down. Alex had kicked the door open, and Sierra dreaded what would crawl out, but Mitch didn't even appear rattled.

"Emily had flirted with Mitch on and off for years. He never noticed, but the rest of us did. She had a thing for him but never acted on it because of their friendship and not wanting to unbalance the group's harmony." Alex looked at Cassie. "Right?"

She stared at a spot on the ground. "I don't want anything to do with this conversation."

Sierra's patience expired. "Get there, Alex."

"We were dancing and . . . honestly, I blacked out at some point." He rubbed his forehead. "I remember the laughter then some yelling. Then quiet. Hell, Mitch knows. Let him tell you."

Mitch didn't move. "This is your big moment. Say whatever you've been holding in for all these years."

Sierra remembered the gun Ruthie held. Cassie had one as well. As the tension spiraled and dark energy swirled around them with suffocating precision, all Sierra could think about was Mitch. Mitch hurting a woman. Mitch losing control. None of that fit what she knew about him.

"It's exactly what you expect. Mitch made a pass and it backfired. He tried something with Emily. She was into it, but then . . . I don't know, I guess she decided it was a mistake? She shoved him and things escalated." Alex talked faster now. Words tumbled out of him as if they needed to escape. "Mitch clearly thought he had a green light."

Sierra could count the holes in that story. "What exactly are you saying happened?"

"Mitch . . . he . . . pawed at her clothes. She hit him. He threw her down and she must have hit her head." Alex's uneven breathing buried some of his words. "Cassie tried to help."

"I did what I always do." Cassie put her hands on her hips, clearly pissed off that her name had got dragged into this. "I fixed the mess. Mitch lost control and went too far. I got there and saw the blood . . . I had to step in. We weren't the only ones in the area. Other students were drunk and walking through the woods. You could hear them singing. We didn't have much time."

Not an admission but not a denial.

The pieces came together in Sierra's head. She thought about who Cassie was and how far she'd come from the kind of life she despised and escaped, and what she'd had to do to make that jump. "You did all of this to save your future, right? Because if you were there when Emily died, or if Alex was implicated, your plan for the future imploded."

"Do not blame this on me." Cassie glared at Alex with a look that said *fix this.*

"I tried not to . . ." Alex shook his head. "I would have gone to my grave not saying a word."

Mitch stared at him. "Why?"

"*Why?* Because you didn't deserve more pain and police questioning. It was so awful . . . I mean, poor Emily. But you didn't mean to do it. It was the alcohol. That wasn't you. It was an accident, but I knew no one would see it that way."

Mitch made a strange humming sound. "The killer's son turned killer."

"Yeah." Alex shrugged. "I guess."

Sierra nearly screamed in frustration. Mitch needed to be definitive. To deny. His instinct was to hide from conversations he didn't like or that invaded his personal space. He'd play word games. Be sarcastic. Not answer. This time she needed him to respond and be clear. Not toy with people to evade a hard issue.

Mitch finally spoke up again. "There's one problem with your theory, Alex."

Sierra braced for the worst.

Mitch's blank expression didn't change. "I never went to the labyrinth that night. It wasn't me."

CHAPTER SIXTY-SIX

RUTHIE

Mitch denied the accusation without any drama or hint of hedging. He forced Alex to tell all, to spell it all out, and then refuted every word with a simple *It wasn't me.*

Ruthie let out the breath she was holding not because this mess was finally over, but because she suspected Mitch was telling the truth. His no and the way he delivered it affirmed her view of him. He could be a psychopath and utterly without remorse or emotion, but she didn't think so. She'd watched him with Sierra. Saw him in the private moments when he looked at her with a love and a yearning he didn't recognize and was powerless to control.

Ruthie couldn't imagine that guy, one who had seen the damaging impact of murder on such a fundamental level, would kill a woman over a rejected pass. Ruthie guessed she wasn't alone in her relief when Sierra's body relaxed. Her shoulders fell and the tight line of her jaw eased.

"You didn't," Sierra said.

Mitch gave her a quick side glance. "Of course I didn't kill Emily. She didn't come onto me. She joked about doing it to freak all of them out, but that was earlier in the evening. Whatever happened later that night I can't say because I wasn't there. My night ended with the group when I dropped them off on campus, as I said hours ago."

Alex sighed. "Look, I supported you for years but—"

"Listen to me. We've been friends for more than a decade. You know me. What you're describing didn't happen." Then Mitch's focus shifted. "Did it, Cassie?"

"I told you. I'm not getting sucked into this."

"But you are in it." Ruthie didn't doubt that for a second. "This disaster has your manicured fingers all over it."

"You were there that night," Sierra said. "You talked about saving them."

"I hate to break this to you but simply denying something doesn't make it true." Cassie shifted her arms behind her. "You need to be realistic. I know you don't want to hear that because you love Mitch. I love him, too."

Sierra scoffed. "Yeah, clearly."

The way Sierra believed Mitch made Ruthie dig in. She'd watched horror and disbelief morph into wariness then switch to certainty on Sierra's face. Ruthie didn't trust much about this crowd, but she trusted Sierra and her judgment.

Mitch shifted his weight but didn't move any closer to his college friends. "You were the one who planted this story and made Alex believe it."

"It's not a story," Cassie insisted.

An uncomfortable silence stretched between them. Mitch stood there, almost daring Cassie to come up with another accusation. Ruthie wanted to jump in and say what she knew and tear down their allegations one by one, but she needed to act, as much as possible, as an objective observer. If they all survived this—and she wasn't convinced the violence was over—someone had to stay clearheaded enough to tell the unbelievable story, including every nuance and every twist.

Mitch made a noise that sounded like resignation before he started talking. "I was perfectly lucid that night because I didn't drink in college. I don't drink now."

This sounded like an unnecessary overreach. Even Ruthie didn't buy it. Mitch risked destroying his credibility by insisting on a fact the people closest to him would know was false.

Cassie snorted. "What a lie."

"That's ridiculous," Alex said. "We were there. We drank with you."

"After years of being a fucking mess, I made a promise to my uncle before I went to college. Sobriety. No more hiding at the bottom of a bottle. No more lying about what I had been doing all night as I got lost in a haze of nothingness. I owed him and I wanted *him,* a recovering alcoholic, to stay sober, so we pledged to support each other and never take a drink again."

Alex shook his head then winced in what looked like pain. "Then you broke your promise because you drank with us all the time in college. You acted as designated driver a lot, sure, but—"

"No, *you* drank. I pretended. Sometimes I got the drink and poured it out. Sometimes I switched your almost empty beer bottles with my full one. I always knew how many I'd had because I didn't have any, and I always volunteered to drive so I'd have an excuse not to drink."

They all stared at him. Ruthie couldn't help it. She wondered if anyone could pull off that ruse for so many years . . . maybe?

"I had spent too much of my life as an outsider. People whispered about me, made judgments because of my mother. Accused me of things I didn't do," Mitch said in a softer tone. "I didn't tell you the truth about my no-drinking pledge because for the first time in so long I had friends who accepted me *despite* who my mother was. I didn't divulge the truth about my sobriety because, honestly, I was immature and embarrassed. I was desperate to be part of a group. I didn't want to come off as a loser, but mostly, I didn't want to give you all a reason to do things without me and shut me out, so I adapted."

Cassie shook her head. "That's not possible."

"We would have known." Alex didn't sound convinced.

"The pact is real," Sierra said. "His uncle told me about it the first time I met him. Mitch told me, too. This isn't a new thing he's saying as a cover. He doesn't drink. I've known him for years and know he doesn't drink. And I've seen him do the fake drinking thing at business meetings. After so much practice, he's damn convincing."

"*Now*. He doesn't drink now because of what he did to Emily." Cassie's gaze swept over the group. Every word carried her desperate need to convince them. "This proves nothing."

"You underestimate how skilled I became at a young age at pretending to be someone I wasn't," Mitch said.

Cassie didn't show any signs of letting go of the lie she'd carried and repeated for so long. Even with Mitch confronting her and breaking down her story, she refused to pivot. She fell back on that lawyer skill of being able to argue at full blast. "Like you're pretending now?"

"Here are the facts, counselor." Sierra returned to full Sierra mode. Protecting and not backing down. "His uncle was so proud of how Mitch had turned his life around and stopped drinking that he agreed to cosign a business loan for us to get started in landscaping. So believe me when I say Mitch's sobriety is very real."

"We were all out at the water that night. Alex was right about that, but he got the timing wrong. We had a cookout and partied with a bunch of other people. It got dark and you all were still drinking, but Emily worried about disappointing her parents by missing that brunch."

"This doesn't prove—"

Mitch didn't let Cassie take over the conversation. "I drove us all back to campus then Jake and I went to get something to eat. Used the drive-through."

Cassie shrugged. "Convenient."

"Not for you." Ruthie expected denial but the tenacity with which Cassie held on to the fiction was quite a sight.

"You all met up again. Jake and I didn't. The dancing and drinking you saw wasn't me." Mitch confronted Cassie head-on. "Right? You know because you weren't so out of it that night. You were pissed at Alex about all the drinking. I remember you yelling at him."

"I'm not your alibi."

"No, you're Alex's alibi." Whatever doubts Sierra toyed with, even for a second, disappeared and she came out firing. "That's what you told the police. You were home with Alex that night, which was a lie."

"I was trying to save Mitch. I didn't want to incriminate Mitch by talking about how he was acting around Emily and how he lost control." Cassie sighed. "I wish I'd been there every second at that damn labyrinth because I would have stopped Mitch. Emily would be alive."

Mitch's eyebrow lifted. "That's quite a statement. It's also a lie."

Ruthie gave Mitch credit for staying calm. His old friends probably thought he'd back down or keep the arguments private. They weren't counting on him maturing and tackling his trauma without flinching.

"Jake and I went back to the apartment. My uncle was there and ate with us. I told that to the police. Jake told the police. My uncle told the police."

"No . . . no, wait. He was covering for you. There was that news conference where the police spokesperson talked about not being able to confirm your whereabouts," Alex said.

"I found the ripped-up food receipt in my trash can once I left police questioning. I produced it. Maybe I never specifically told you that I found it, but I never thought I had to prove my alibi to you. It never dawned on me that you actually believed I killed our friend."

Some of the confusion cleared from Alex's expression. "It's why the police stopped looking at you and Jake as suspects."

Mitch let out a sigh before nodding.

Ruthie thought about all she knew and the evidence, and Mitch's explanation fit. Of course, he could *make* it fit . . . but she really wanted to believe him. "Emily must have dropped her purse and keys while she was on campus and before going to the labyrinth . . . or someone dropped them off there after she was dead. Trying to throw the police off, maybe?"

"I guess you're an expert at hiding things. Don't think we forgot your role in what happened to Will and the terror you brought into our lives," Cassie said.

Ruthie found Cassie exhausting. Her spouting a rabid defense while her story unraveled called every word she uttered into question.

"I take responsibility for bringing you here this weekend." But every time Ruthie said the words her regret lessened. Cassie deserved whatever she got. "That's it."

"Wait. You said it was Mitch." Alex didn't stammer that time. His voice regained its usual strength as he confronted his wife. "All these years. You blamed Mitch."

Ruthie could see the realization pumping through him, fueling him. She decided to give him another verbal push. "You were her ticket, and she couldn't let you get in trouble and ruin her future plans."

Cassie snapped. "Shut up."

But Alex didn't let go. "You blamed Mitch. You lied to me. How could you do that?"

Cassie's mouth hung open for a few seconds as if she'd realized she lost the support of her strongest defender. "Don't—"

"You selfish bitch." Alex fully turned on Cassie. Physically, emotionally, he separated from her. It was as if the truth had welled up in him and the bitter memories flooded his brain. "You let me think Mitch killed Emily. You blamed me for being too drunk to stop him and forced me to shoulder that guilt, and it wasn't real."

Instead of fighting back or defending herself, Cassie pulled out the gun. She didn't wave it around or hesitate. She aimed it at Ruthie. "This is your fault."

The sight of the weapon trapped Ruthie in slow motion. Thoughts of running or dropping bombarded her brain. They stood ten feet apart. A bullet would tear through her. The horrible realization hit her as she heard the bang.

A weight rammed into her side. Her body fell and gray swirled around her. Her breath hitched then turned into a labored gasp as she slammed against the ground. The force of the bullet surprised her, not giving her a second to brace.

The weight grew heavier, cutting off her remaining air. She lifted her hands and hit an arm. Alex? She laid in a sprawl with Alex pinning her down. Did he tackle her?

Then she saw the blood and heard the yelling. Cassie's voice. "No!"

CHAPTER SIXTY-SEVEN

ALEX

She shot me.

The thought broke through Alex's muddled mind as he tried to move. He felt softness below him and a sharp chill against his back. His muscles ignored every order from his brain and his eyes begged to close.

"Alex, no."

He could hear Mitch and a skidding sound like shoes running across pebbles. Alex's hand slipped into a pool of wetness. The rain . . . a puddle, probably. He felt banging against his chest and tugging on his useless arms. He wanted the punching to stop but he didn't know how to make that happen.

"I'm sorry. Please don't . . . I'm so sorry." Cassie's voice. Breathless. She kept repeating the words with a panicky edge that sounded off.

What was he doing before he blacked out . . . did he black out? He remembered pressure filling his head until it felt like his skull caved in. A giant collapse that sucked in and swallowed his memories and buried them in a pile of rubble. Words. Pieces and fragments Alex couldn't fit together.

Cassie's soft hair brushed his cheek. She seemed to be bend-ing over him, whispering to him. Touching him.

"Ease him on his back."

"You could injure him."

"We need to stop the bleeding."

"We need an ambulance. Give me a phone."

So many voices. Alex could pick out Cassie's comment about an injury. It sounded higher, more desperate than usual.

His body shifted and a shout of rage filled his ears. Jesus, it was so loud and shrieking that it overwhelmed everything else. Cold air hit his face but the rest of him felt numb. No pain, just a vast nothingness. Did that make sense?

Protect Cassie.

The voice sounded raw. He opened his eyes to see who made the comment . . . if anyone did. Maybe he dreamed the words after so many years of living them. A sea of gray greeted him. Above him. Around him. He wondered if he'd somehow landed in the water but then faces appeared, floating in front of his. They moved in and out of his vision on a low rumble of conversa-tion he couldn't ferret out.

Why was he wet? He tried to lift his hand to touch his shirt and Cassie grabbed it. No, not Cassie. She'd vanished. A woman's voice but not his wife's.

"Stay with me."

That was Mitch. Alex recognized the low tone. What Alex really wanted was to hear a joke or that touch of amusement that moved through Mitch's voice.

Wait . . . Mitch. Emily and Mitch.

Oh, shit.

Reality crashed in on Alex. He forced his eyes to stay open. He needed to apologize. Plead for forgiveness. He tried to say *sorry* but couldn't hear over the loud banging in his ears. What the hell was that sound? He mouthed the words, hoping they got through.

"No." Mitch crowded closer. "Look at me, Alex. You can't leave me now."

Were his eyes closed? Then Mitch was shouting. Alex didn't want shouting. He craved quiet. Sleep.

One thought slipped into his mind before he drifted off and he tried to say it. He hoped he got the thought out because it was all that mattered. All his sins, every awful thing he'd said and the mountain of words he forced himself not to say. Years of pretending. So much lying.

"I'm sorry."

CHAPTER SIXTY-EIGHT

SIERRA

Sierra sat helpless on the wet ground as the dampness soaked into her pants and chilled her bare skin underneath. Activity buzzed around her. Mitch, frantic as he pumped his arms up and down, administered CPR. Cassie pressed her hands over Alex's wound. Blood seeped through her fingers. She said her husband's name over and over as if lost in a chant. Mitch counted through Cassie's mix of crying, begging, and ordering Alex to wake up.

Cassie shot Alex.

Alex saved Ruthie.

The ultimate sacrifice.

Mitch leaned down with his ear just above Alex's mouth. "I think he's breathing, but it's faint."

Cassie rocked back and forth on her knees. "Keep going."

"Where are the phones?" Ruthie tugged on Cassie's shoulder when she didn't get an answer. "I need to call for an ambulance."

"We can't . . . we have to agree—"

"What the hell is wrong with you? Your husband is dying." Sierra could barely get the words out over her shock.

This bitch didn't stop. Cassie wanting the secrets of the island to stay on the island was bad enough. This disregard for Alex's well-being plunged her into a realm of evil that might be differ-ent from Dylan's, but it ended in the same place.

"I'm trying to save Alex," Cassie insisted.

Mitch sat back on his haunches. "You claim to do a lot of saving."

"I know you're angry with me."

Mitch shook his head. "That word doesn't touch how I feel about you right now."

"Well, I'm done." Ruthie aimed her gun at Cassie. "You have ten seconds to tell us the truth about that night twelve years ago."

"I already have." This time Cassie's gaze didn't meet Mitch's.

"Not even close," he said. "And we need that ambulance right now."

Cassie didn't say anything for a few seconds. She studied the gun in Ruthie's hand. "I took your bullets."

"All of them? Are you willing to bet your life on that?"

One bullet. Sierra swam through the anxiety swamping her. Forced her mind to focus and think back to the dock. Ruthie had exactly one shot, but she *did* have that one shot.

"And before you answer, I saw her reload the gun with the bullets she smuggled out that Dylan didn't know about. Remem-ber, Dylan is dead." That came close enough to the truth. Sierra didn't think Cassie deserved explanations anyway. Giving her a sentence only allowed her to dissect it, and they were done with that.

"Don't make me shoot you," Ruthie said.

Cassie's gaze shot to the gun she'd dropped after she shot Alex. It had landed right near Alex's head. She lunged but Mitch got there first.

He put his hand on the weapon and slid it closer to him, out of Cassie's reach. "You're not going to win this time."

"When do I ever win?"

Sierra could not take this woman one more second. "Give it to me. I grew up with hunters. Have been around guns my whole life." She walked over to Alex's motionless body for the handoff from Mitch, so he could go back to watching Alex for any further decline. "Don't test me, Cassie."

Ruthie held out her free hand to Cassie. "While you're at it, a phone."

Cassie looked around like a hunted animal. Small and ready to spring. Scanning and looking for a break to run. "On the floor of the golf cart."

Ruthie took off before Cassie finished the sentence. Sierra could hear Ruthie rummaging around in the smashed-up cart, but her attention stayed on Cassie. "Now, talk."

"Save Alex first."

"I'll take care of him. You talk." Mitch kneeled at Alex's side, rotating between checking his pulse and keeping pressure on his chest wound.

Sierra prepared herself for the very real possibility Cassie would make a move and lunge. Sierra stepped back, just in case. She heard Ruthie talking on the call. She was trying to explain where they were. Ruthie had studied the island and would come the closest to describing this place, so Sierra let Ruthie handle that task.

"Please don't make me count down. Answer the question about Emily." Sierra had enough drama for one day . . . had it even been a day? She hadn't slept or eaten and was running purely on adrenaline. When the energy drop came it would hit with the force of a bulldozer.

"They were laughing when I left. Alex started to doze off, which is what he does when he's had too much alcohol." Lawyer Cassie gave way to subdued Cassie. "Then I heard shouting. Emily was yelling and I started back to our group and could see Will grab her."

Sierra didn't trust the pauses or her flat affect. Cassie didn't give up. This was a scheme more than a decade in the making and she would not willingly let it unravel.

"He held on to her arms and shook. She looked like rag doll and when Will let go, she fell."

Too abbreviated. Sierra didn't buy it. "That's it?"

"She jumped back up and hit him. Hard. She was screaming about *ruining* him and how he didn't have the right to touch her." Cassie sat on the ground with her legs folded and her hand wrapped around Alex's. "I'm not sure how it all started. Will came back to the labyrinth without Mitch and was joking about how Emily had tried every other guy on campus but him, and it should be his turn soon."

Disgusting. Sierra could never really pin Will down, but now she did—misogynist asshole. "That sounds like hatred, not joking."

Cassie nodded. "That's how Emily took it. She was pissed but he was so drunk. All this bottled-up stuff spilled out. It's like he'd been holding it in, so controlled, all while silently pissed off that she didn't want to be with him. He mentioned how similar their backgrounds were and how they fit. They would make a great team if she'd stop playing games."

Ruthie put her hand over the phone and walked back to the group. It was clear she'd been listening to one group and talking to another. "They were yelling at each other and you left them alone?"

"Alex was right there, and I thought . . ." Cassie fidgeted while she played with Alex's hand. "I mean, Will wasn't exactly wrong about Emily and her playing around. She'd flirt with Alex then go find some computer nerd. It was weird."

Flirt with Alex. That didn't pop up by accident. Cassie had stored it. Stewed about it. Sierra would bet on that. "Emily dated. Big deal. That doesn't mean it was okay for Will to kill her."

"I didn't mean that." Cassie's jaw clenched before she started again. "It really was an accident. She kept hitting Will and he threw her off him. Like, slammed her to the ground. Fueled by alcohol, I guess. I pulled him off her."

Mitch frowned. "Off her?"

"She hit her head on these rocks in the labyrinth that are set up like chairs. She was bleeding and Will started screaming." Cassie dropped her head. "She died before I could call for help and then I had to calm Will down and wake Alex but . . ." She lifted her head again and looked at each one of them, almost pleading with them to understand. "No one would believe us. I did the only thing I could."

Sierra stayed on alert. She refused to be sucked in by an uncharacteristic show of emotion. Not from this woman. Not ever. "You could have called for help."

"Don't be so naïve."

Sierra tried again. "You cleaned up the blood. You hid the crime scene."

"Will did. He erased any sign that we'd been there." She glanced over at Alex, and her eyes filled with tears. "I had Will wrangle Alex and get him into the car while I moved Emily out of the clearing. She was in the open and . . . there were other people nearby earlier and I didn't know where they were. I couldn't take the chance of being seen."

"Sounds like you and Will were pretty coherent, not that drunk," Mitch mumbled as he continued to work on Alex.

"Little did I know Alex would form a vigilante party and go after Brendan." Cassie traced her fingers over Alex's still hand. "Once he did, I told him Mitch had killed Emily and Brendan had been innocent."

"You did that to hurt him, make him feel even worse. You ensured you were all complicit and no one would talk." Sierra didn't wait for Cassie to agree. "But why blame Mitch?"

"Alex would protect Mitch. He'd do anything for him. He would have turned on Will, and that was too risky for all of us." Cassie's hand moved to Alex's leg, as if she had to keep a connection to him despite all she'd done to him. "That's all of it. Will killed Emily. Only Will and I knew the truth. Alex knew what I told him. Jake spiraled because of the guilt over killing Brendan on that bridge. That's how our college years ended."

"And you kept the truth from me," Mitch said.

Cassie shot him a sad smile. "You're welcome."

A siren blared in the distance.

Help. Finally. Mitch had taken off the shirt Sierra gave him and tucked it around Alex's shoulders. His body was so still. Sierra watched to see if his chest rose and fell. Only Mitch, sitting next to him, checking on him every few seconds, really knew.

Red lights flashed through the trees. The ambulance was almost there. So close.

"You made it look like Emily was attacked. You're the one who put Emily in the water." Not questions. Ruthie spoke the words as if she didn't need verification.

Cassie gave it to her anyway. "Yes."

CHAPTER SIXTY-NINE

RUTHIE

When Ruthie left the hospital waiting room Alex had been in surgery and Cassie had been silently pleading for her freedom. She delivered a thunderous closing argument about how long it had been since Emily died, how traumatic the weekend had been for all of them, and how Zara needed at least one parent because Alex was likely to go to jail if he even survived.

Cassie wept, sounding genuine and contrite. She spoke of loving her family and fearing for her daughter because she'd be left alone. Cassie viewed her sister as beneath her and incapable of taking over. Losing Zara was her nightmare.

She gave the performance of her life.

Ruthie saved her support for Emily, who never got a chance to find a partner and have a family or live past graduation weekend. She was the victim. Brendan, an innocent bystander who sent one lousy text about a senior project, was a victim. Sierra and Mitch were victims. The collateral damage blew far and wide, and would likely consume Zara, too.

The police were back on the island. The whisper campaign through the hospital talked about the FBI being called in. There was so much focus on Dylan and the killings now, but the past would begin to unspool. Some secrets thrashed and screamed their way out. This pile-on of lies had burned over time until the fire roared and ran rampant.

Ruthie took a deep breath before walking back into the waiting room. She sat down next to Sierra on a hard plastic chair and handed her a cup of stale-tasting coffee. "You okay?"

Sierra winced over the rim of the cup. "No. You?"

"No." Ruthie wasn't sure she'd ever be okay again. Her entire life was about to change. It had to after all of this. "Alex?"

The bullet had damaged his lung, spleen, and ribs. There were whispers about potential damage to his heart. He'd stopped breathing in the ambulance, but the crew revived him.

"We won't know for a while." Sierra took a sip of the coffee then put the cup down. "I'm surprised the police aren't here."

"They're outside." Ruthie nodded toward Cassie and Mitch, who were locked in an intense private conversation. "I don't like whatever is happening there."

"You're not alone." Sierra tightened her hold on the blanket wrapped around her shoulders.

They'd been checked by the medical staff and their clothes had been bagged for the police. The staff had provided clean scrubs. Ruthie also borrowed a baseball hat and tucked her hair up into it, did everything to blend in and not be memorable.

Mitch finally broke away from Cassie, leaving her alone with her body slumped in the uncomfortable chair, and walked over to Sierra. He sat down without saying a word.

The symbolism of Mitch dropping the past and moving into the future wasn't lost on Ruthie. She couldn't imagine the pain rushing through him. The memory of him shouting *don't leave me* to Alex as he was loaded into the ambulance played in her head. Mitch whispered about forgiving his old friend as the vehicle drove away. She knew Alex had more to answer for than what he'd done to Mitch, but she understood the desire to grant absolution. Mitch's life had been shaped by grief. He knew the damage it could do.

Two police officers stepped into view through the waiting room windows. A nurse joined them in the hallway. She listened and nodded. She called over another nurse and after some discussion, both peeked into the waiting room.

Ruthie glanced at Cassie then nodded in the direction of the window. "They're here for you."

Cassie looked then did a double take. She bolted to her feet and joined them on the other side of the room. "What did you do?"

"When you admitted to putting Emily in the water, you accidentally admitted to killing her." Ruthie expected to feel triumph or at least some sense of relief. Only a gnawing emptiness hit her. Winning should feel better but all she could focus on was the damage . . . the continuing damage.

"I already explained. Will killed her."

The wariness in Sierra's eyes made Ruthie push through. She couldn't even look at Mitch. "Emily's brother gave me all the records the family had, and they included a piece of information that was never released to the public. Emily had water in her lungs. That means she was alive when she went into the water. Alive after Will did whatever he did to her. You finished the job. I don't know if you meant to, though I think you did, but the result is the same. You killed Emily."

"No . . . no." Cassie's eyes darted as panic overtook her. "That's not—"

"Did you really think she was dead? I'm asking because Emily had broken fingernails and scratches on her arms. A ripped shirt. No DNA thanks to her time in the water, which makes me wonder if you got lucky or if you knew that would happen and that's why you dumped her there."

Cassie shook her head. "You're wrong."

"Am I?" Ruthie delivered the final blow. "See, I think she came to and fought back. You thought you didn't have a choice. At that point it wasn't about saving Will or Alex. You were saving yourself. Emily would have destroyed you for dumping her in the water instead of getting help for her."

The police stepped into the room before Cassie could respond. "Cassie Greene?"

The next few minutes could only be described as chaos. The other family stuck in the room with them looked like they wanted to jump out a window. Cassie refused to say anything. It took two security guards and the police to remove her from the waiting room. Ruthie wasn't sure where they were going next, but she knew Cassie would be questioned and then she'd either invoke her right to an attorney and stay silent or talk and blame everyone else.

Once the noise died down and the nurses left again, Mitch turned to Ruthie. "Was all of that about the water and the injuries true? I don't remember those details."

"Some weren't released to the public. You probably tried to forget the rest," Ruthie said. "I told the police all of those details from back then and what happened with Alex now because I wanted to save you from being the person who got Cassie arrested. You don't need to take that on."

He hesitated for a few seconds before nodding. "She kept talking about Zara, and I worry about what will happen to her, too, but I would have told the truth."

Not a surprise. Ruthie had expected both Sierra and Mitch to collaborate about every horrifying second of that island vacation. That's who they were. "Now when you do talk it will be to verify what I've said. You won't be the one lowering the boom."

Ruthie saw how close together Mitch and Sierra sat. They were almost on top of each other. She hoped they'd figure it out. Lecturing them about their feelings now while they waited to see if Alex survived sounded wrong. So, Ruthie stood up. "I need to make some calls. I'll be back to check on Alex."

Ruthie almost made it to the doorway before Sierra spoke up. "Even if you're telling the truth and you didn't plan the weekend with Dylan, you never fired that gun at him. You could have taken Dylan out and ended the bloodshed as soon as he stepped into the house. Refused to put on that zip tie."

Ruthie didn't have an excuse. She didn't try to offer one. Those decisions, the hesitation, didn't make sense even to her.

Sierra continued. "You knew Dylan was dangerous and that he planned to target Emily's friends, or you at least suspected it. Why did you risk holding the party on the island? Why didn't you warn them?"

Leave it to Sierra to pinpoint a weakness and drag it into the light. Ruthie knew the answer to this question. She admired Sierra so she didn't sugarcoat the answer. "Because I didn't think they deserved to be saved."

CHAPTER SEVENTY

SIERRA

Three Weeks Later

Sierra looked at the temporary grave marker. They'd stayed in the trees, out of sight, for the duration of the private ceremony. A few people she didn't know stood around as the casket was lowered into the ground. No one from Bowdoin. No Cassie. One identity she could guess was the adorable little girl at the front with a woman dressed all in black.

Zara, holding the hand of the sister Cassie repeatedly dismissed as unworthy. The sisters looked alike. Pretty. Tall with a certain presence that had nothing to do with wealth. A sister who showed compassion and stood up for Zara when her parents couldn't. In Sierra's view, a woman who didn't deserve scorn and harsh judgment for her lack of money or the choices she made when she didn't have many options.

The small crowd dispersed a half hour ago, but Sierra and Mitch remained until everyone left and they no longer needed their hiding place. Between all the interviews with law enforcement and time spent fielding and ignoring press calls over the last few weeks, they'd been busy. Mitch also craved the grounding of home, so she didn't push. When he commented on visiting to pay his respects this weekend, she agreed because how could she not.

"This is the wrong place to say this, but I truly hate your college friends." She whispered the comment, but it still felt disrespectful.

"Me, too. Mostly." Mitch stared at the marker. "But despite everything, and what happened with Brendan was awful, I loved Alex. He was the first friend I trusted after Tyler. His support never wavered."

"It's okay to love the good memories and reject the rest. To celebrate what he meant to you." She repeated what the psychologist had told her during their recent consult. Sierra went because she wanted to help Mitch through this. More trauma. More death. More disbelief. Yes, he was a grown-up and all that, but he'd buried three friends and saw another one taken to jail after their weekend away. A person could only take so much.

She also went for some help for herself because she needed to talk to someone objective. All those years trying to get a handle on Mitch's grief and now she had her own. When she figured out how to sleep without a hammer under her pillow again she might stop going to the doc. But, for now, she had a follow-up appointment.

"It's amazing to think my entire college experience would have been different if it had ended two days earlier." He zipped up his jacket against the cold whipping through this part of Rhode Island. "I remember we joked about skipping graduation and heading to this place Emily's family used to rent when she was growing up. I wish we'd done it."

The forecast promised snow and Sierra could feel it in her

bones. But she stood there. Let him talk as she leaned into him to block the wind.

"Other than with Alex, I'm not sure we would have stayed friends. Probably enough for a text now and then or a yearly meeting. We were bound to splinter and not be as close as we once were. We all wanted different things, including to live in different states." He exhaled. "But at least they'd be alive."

"I'm sorry."

"I can't believe he's gone." Mitch shook his head.

Alex never came out of surgery. He died on the operating table from a gunshot wound inflicted by his wife. Cassie's wail of despair when the doctor informed her had echoed throughout the hospital. She dropped to the ground, inconsolable, as nurses rushed to help.

Standing in that waiting room was the first time Sierra had seen Mitch cry. She'd held him as the haunting sound washed through her.

In the end, Sierra and Mitch didn't mention Cassie's plan to leave them on an island with a killer. She had enough legal trouble ahead. Alex's family waited until she was arrested to hold this service. She'd be out on bail soon enough, but for now she was cut off from everything, including Zara.

Mitch broke the comfortable silence. "We need a vacation."

"No water. I hate the water." That wasn't an exaggeration. Lakes, the ocean, a bath—all made her insides jump in panic now.

"The mountains?"

He had to be kidding. "I'm going to skip any trip that puts me in an isolated place, but thanks."

"Fair enough."

"All I want is to curl up on my couch for a month, watching

movies and eating junk food." That wasn't *all* but the combination did sound good.

"Want company?"

She always wanted him nearby. "Sure."

"I'm going to try seeing a therapist to untangle some of the messiness in my life, so I might be good company . . . eventually." He exhaled. "It's hard to imagine right now. There's been so much death. So many people I cared about—"

"None of that was your fault."

"I'm sorry I dragged you into this." He stopped her before she could wave his worries away. "I don't understand why you—who are amazing—would want to be with me. You really shouldn't bet on me. You absolutely should run . . ."

He sounded so unsure. "Mitch?"

He smiled. "But I hope you don't."

She just stared at him because . . . *what?*

He wrapped an arm around her shoulder. "I'm not as clueless as everyone thinks. I know what I want and hope you'll let me earn the right to be with you."

Oh . . . "Really?"

He winked at her. "Really."

Before she could decide if she should grab him for their first real kiss ever, a man in a dark suit approached them. "Excuse me. I didn't mean to interrupt."

Sierra stiffened when she recognized the visitor as one of the detectives working on the twisty mess of cases the engagement weekend had dumped on them all. Before she could rush to Mitch's defense—for what, she didn't know, but she was programmed to react as far as he was concerned—the detective started talking again.

"I was hoping the two of you could tell me what you know about Ruthie Simmons. Do you have a contact number or any photos? I have descriptions from the officers and others who were at the hospital and saw her, but she managed to avoid the hospital cameras and took off before she could be questioned at the hospital."

"Almost nothing. We don't know her." Sierra had never said a more truthful statement in her life. "She was best friends with Emily growing up, so someone in Emily's family or in her hometown might know."

"Yeah, that's the thing. She wasn't Emily's friend. No one there has ever heard of her. The Ruthie Simmons name, no variation of it, appears in any school yearbook with Emily. No one remembers this Ruthie person. And I've talked with Emily's best friend from back then. She's a professor at Amherst. Her name is Leesa, not Ruthie."

"But . . ." Sierra couldn't think of anything else to say. None of that made sense.

The detective shrugged. "Related to that, what do you know about Dylan Richter?"

Mitch dropped his arm from around her shoulders and held her hand instead. "He's dead."

That was right . . . *right*? Panic raced through Sierra. *That guy . . . alive?* "Didn't you find his body?"

"We fished a man out of the water. That wasn't Dylan Richter. Dylan Richter is a woman."

CHAPTER SEVENTY-ONE

BOOK NOTES: THE PAINFUL TRUTH

This project started as a way to clarify what happened that night twelve years ago. When Emily's life intersected with Brendan's, his loss got added to the pile. The public dragged him into the center of the messy aftermath and labeled him as a young man to fear.

As the truth spills out and the real story blows wide, slipping into new podcasts, documentaries, and true crime shows, a clear vision will emerge. One of innocence, lies, and deadly mistakes. One of a tragedy that claimed lives over decades. A killing on a college campus that ended on an island in ways no one could have foreseen.

These book notes. Stray thoughts on slips of paper. Notebooks filled with thoughts for a possible future book. Ideas never meant to be seen and now they wouldn't be because the book can't be written, at least not in this form or with this author. The story won't end with a triumphant public reveal. All those plans died when a man dressed as a police officer showed up uninvited to a party on an island and pretended to be Dylan Richter.

His real name was Vince. A smart and at one time well-intentioned guy deep in grief for the sister killed by a boyfriend at college years ago. One of thousands of individuals out there broken by grief and looking for a way to feel whole again.

His sister's murder sharpened his focus and gave him a purpose. It changed the course of his life. A computer genius who morphed into a guy who spent years on forums, searching down clues, and desperate to solve cold cases and help people because he hadn't been able to help his sister. His initial goal was to give answers to family members like him who were reeling from loss . . . but that changed.

An inheritance gave him financial freedom. All those hours stoking his anger stole his life.

His computer skills and experience made him invaluable, but his dedication made him easy to manipulate. All those hours together spent spinning tales of revenge. With every interview and medical record review and all those long talks about theories over dinner, his obsession, guilt, and fury coalesced into a driving need to inflict damage. He became a warrior for justice. His form of justice.

The real Dylan Richter used him. Worse, she'd accidentally weaponized him. She'd taken his skills and his determination and bent both to serve her ends.

I know because "she" is me.

The problem with obsession is it can backfire. Vince became uncontrollable. Dangerous. Cutting him off had been a risk. It fueled a sort of demented anger that couldn't be suppressed. He acted before all the answers had been collected. He'd been snooping and never disclosed that. He wasn't supposed to know about the planned island weekend for fear he'd attack, and that fear turned out to be valid.

Killing Tyler? A total surprise and unrelated to any plan. In some ways, a red herring.

By the time he showed up on the island, Vince *was* Dylan . . . or acted as if he thought he was. He merged the details of his life and his pain with what he knew about Dylan's. He played the role to perfection, adopting Dylan's life, skills, accomplishments, fortune, and anger over Brendan's death and the failure to be heard.

Dylan wasn't supposed to be on the island. The goal was to gather intel and write an exposé. Finally unveil Brendan's killer and see the killer or killers locked up then step into the spotlight and say *I told you so,* like I'd been wanting to do ever since I gave a statement to the police all those years ago.

Vince, by pretending to be Dylan, ruined that. There could only be one Dylan—the real one. But admitting who I really am now, after pretending to be Ruthie, would shine a different kind of spotlight on me. Thanks to Vince, I lacked credibility. I couldn't argue that I didn't know what Vince had planned. I watched Vince play the role of Dylan and said nothing. I let the Bowdoin group assume Brendan's gamer friend and cousin was a boy, which meant I now had to be someone else. I had to let someone else tell Brendan's story.

The only solace? I'd been desperate to avenge Brendan. Over time, the need for justice shifted to a palpable need to punish those who deserved to be punished. And now they have been.

ACKNOWLEDGMENTS

This book grew out of my love for locked-room thrillers. Blame Agatha Christie's *And Then There Were None* and the hundreds of amazing books by other talented authors since. I also wanted to write about how an interest in true crime and a genuine desire to help can go very wrong. I'm not judging. I've watched *Dateline* so often that I feel as if I know some of the prosecutors who frequently appear. But crime victims can get lost, and this book is my fictional version of how that can happen. If you also sense some horror film vibes as you read, well, that's on purpose.

So many people have a hand in publishing a book. I'm grateful to everyone at HarperCollins and William Morrow for their work in making it happen for me. And a special shout-out to HarperCollins Canada for being so supportive of my books. From the production and distribution people, to PR and marketing, to sales, to editing, to the art department, to the departments who work on the book that I don't even know about—you all take something that starts as my idea and my dream and make it a beautiful reality. Thank you.

A special thank-you to my fabulous editor, May Chen. We've worked together through good times and bad, through personal mess and personal triumphs, through good sales numbers and not-so-good sales numbers. I adore you. My respect and appreciation for you grows with each book. I'm happy we found each other.

Thank you to my supportive husband. You're the best and absolutely nothing like the killers and creeps I sometimes write about. And to Laura Bradford, my hardworking agent, who makes the book contracts happen and listens to my whining. She also found my TV/film agent, Katrina Escudero at Sugar23, who has made impossible dreams possible three times (and counting) now. I'm grateful to both of you.

Dear bookstagrammers, librarians, and reviewers: I love you. Seeing my covers, reading reviews, all the promo you give to my releases—your work makes a difference and I thank you. I'm also grateful to my fellow thriller authors who have welcomed me and made me feel like I'm part of this amazing community.

My biggest and heartfelt thank-you is reserved for my readers. If it wasn't weird I'd come to your houses and hug each one of you. This writing career—these books—only happens because of you. Thank you.

ABOUT THE AUTHOR

DARBY KANE is a former divorce lawyer with a dual writing personality. Her debut thriller, *Pretty Little Wife*, was a Book of the Month pick, #1 international bestseller, and has been optioned by Amazon for a television series starring Gabrielle Union. You can find out more about Darby and her books at darbykane.com.

ALSO BY DARBY KANE

THE LAST INVITATION

Darby Kane, the author of the critically acclaimed and #1 International Bestseller *Pretty Little Wife* , has crafted another gripping and twisty suspense about an invitation to an exclusive club that comes with deadly consequences.

THE REPLACEMENT WIFE

The #1 internationally bestselling author of *Pretty Little Wife* returns with another thrilling domestic suspense novel that asks, how many wives and girlfriends need to disappear before your family notices?

PRETTY LITTLE WIFE

#1 internationally bestselling author Darby Kane thrills with this twisty domestic suspense novel that asks one central question: shouldn't a dead husband stay dead?